WHISKERS,
WREATHS &
MURDER

A Dickens & Christie Mystery
Book III

Kathy Manos Penn

Also by Kathy Manos Penn

Dickens & Christie Series

Bells, Tails & Murder

Pumpkins, Paws & Murder

Whiskers, Wreaths & Murder

Collectors, Cats & Murder

Castles, Catnip & Murder

Bicycles, Barking & Murder (2022)

https://www.amazon.com/gp/product/B085FSHQYW

Would you like to know when the next book is on the way?
Click here to sign up for my newsletter. https://bit.ly/3bEjsfi

*Long before Amazon took over the world,
my mother and I shared the joy of
haunting used bookstores and
discovering yet another good mystery.*

*These books are for you,
Mom.*

Sooner or later, everyone sits down to a banquet of consequences.

— -ROBERT LOUIS STEVENSON

CONTENTS

Cast of Characters

WHISKERS, WREATHS & MURDER
CAST OF CHARACTERS
The Americans

Aleta "Leta" Petkas Parker—A retired American banker, Leta lives in the village of Astonbury in the Cotswolds with Dickens the dog and Christie the cat.

Henry Parker—Handsome blue-eyed Henry was Leta's husband.

Dickens—Leta's white dog, a dwarf Great Pyrenees, is a tad sensitive about his size.

Christie—Leta's black cat Christie is sassy, opinionated, and uppity.

Anna Metaxas—Leta's youngest sister lives in Atlanta with her husband Andrew, five cats, and a Great Dane.

Sophia Smyth—Leta's younger sister is married to Jeremy and lives in New Orleans.

Bev Hunter— Bev is Leta's Atlanta friend who fosters dogs.

Dave Prentiss—A journalist from the States, he and Leta hit it off when he stayed at the inn.

The Brits

Martha and Dylan—The donkeys in a nearby pasture look forward to carrots from Leta.

Libby and Gavin Taylor—The Taylors are the owners of The Olde Mill Inn.

Gemma Taylor—A Detective Sergeant at the Stow-on-the-Wold station, she's the daughter of Libby and Gavin and lives in the guest cottage behind the inn.

Paddington—Libby and Gavin's Burmese cat is fond of Leta.

Beatrix Scott—Owner of the Book Nook, she hosts the monthly book club meeting.

Trixie Maxwell—Beatrix's niece works in the bookshop.

Wendy Davies—The retired English teacher from North Carolina returned to Astonbury to look after her mum and has become good friends with Leta.

Peter Davies—Wendy's twin and owner of the local garage, Peter is a cyclist and cricket player.

Belle Davies—Mother to Wendy and Peter, Belle lives at Sunshine Cottage with Wendy.

Tigger—Belle and Wendy's cat is a recent addition to Sunshine Cottage.

Rhiannon Smith—Rhiannon owns the Let It Be yoga studio where Leta and Wendy take classes.

Jill and Jenny Walker—Jill works at the Olde Mill Inn, and her sister Jenny is a barista at Toby's Tearoom.

Toby White—Owner of Toby's Tearoom, he gave up his

London advertising job to pursue his dream of owning a small business.

George Evans—George is the owner of Cotswolds Tours.

Constable James—Constable Jonas James works with Gemma.

The Watsons—John and Deborah live next door to Leta with their little boy Timmy.

The Morgans—The couple lives across Schoolhouse Lane from Leta's cottage.

Barb Peters—Barb is a barmaid at the Ploughman Pub.

Caroline—Caroline is the cook at the Manor house.

The Coates Family

Nigel, Earl of Stow—Recently deceased, Nigel was an RAF pilot in WWII and owner of Astonbury Manor.

Reginald Coates—Reginald predeceased Nigel and was his oldest son.

Ellie, the Dowager Countess—Ellie is Nigel's widow and is active in village affairs.

Matthew and Sarah Coates—Ellie's son and daughter-in-law live on the Estate in a large cottage close to the Manor house.

Harry Coates—Harry is the eldest son of Matthew and Sarah and lives on the estate.

Sam Coates—The youngest son of Matthew and Sarah, Sam attends Cambridge.

Nicholas Coates—Nicholas, Reginald's son, has inherited the Earldom and the estate.

Julia Coates—Julia is Nicholas's wife and is now Lady Stow.

PETER'S
GARAGE

SUNSHINE
COTTAGE

PLOUGHMAN
PUB

THE OLDE MILL
INN

DONKEYS

M

SC

RIVER ELFE

To
CHELTENHAM
←

ST. AND

ST. AND

VILLAGE I

VILLAGE

ASTONBURY

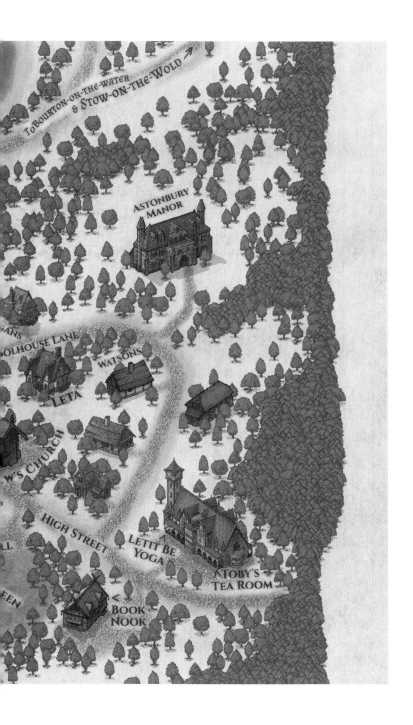

Chapter One

Early December

"Aargh," I groaned as I groped for the buzzing alarm clock. *Yes*, I reminded myself, *I do want to cycle this morning.* Still, 6:30 was awfully early. I'd been out late Saturday night, and all I wanted to do was burrow deeper beneath my down comforter. It was an eight-pound black furball landing on my chest and meowing in my face that finally got me up. No matter when my alarm went off, Christie took it to mean it was time for milk.

"Hold on," I grumbled as I pulled on my red fleece robe and slid my feet into my wool slippers. *What was I thinking when I promised Peter I'd meet him at eight?*

A black tail swished back and forth in front of me as I trekked downstairs. I hit the ON button for the coffee, opened the back door to let Dickens out, and pulled the milk from the fridge. "Here you go, little girl."

As I poured my first cup of coffee, I glanced at the thermometer outside the kitchen window. It read

-1°C, which I calculated to be about 30°F. Not too cold for a bicycle ride when dressed properly. The chill in the air meant Dickens wouldn't want to come in any time soon. His thick white fur was made for this kind of weather. Henry, my late husband, used to call him "the little boy in the fuzzy suit."

Hurrying upstairs, I changed into heavy cycling leggings, a fleece turtleneck top, and a quilted parka. I smiled as I pulled on the red fleece headband my sister Anna had given me as an early Christmas present. She'd had it embroidered with my initials, APP for Aleta Petkas Parker.

Downstairs, I grabbed a banana and glanced out the window to see what Dickens was up to. He was sniffing along the stone wall that bordered the garden and occasionally turning his nose to the sky. He would have been content to stay out there for hours or to take a morning walk, but today it was not to be.

He came bounding in when I called his name. "Are we going for a walk?" he barked. "Do you have the carrots for Martha and Dylan?"

"Sorry, boy, not this morning. I'm cycling with Peter, but I'll take you out this afternoon."

Christie strolled over to add her two cents. "Don't be gone too long. Today's a good day for snuggling in front of the fireplace, don't you think?"

I chuckled at my four-legged companions. Having animals I could converse with meant I was never lonely. I'd been able to "talk to the animals" since I'd been a child but had figured out pretty quickly I was the lone ranger in that regard—and I'd do well to keep my strange talent to myself. Neither my family nor my closest friends knew my secret.

"All right, you two. Maybe we can do both. An afternoon

walk to see the donkeys and then a nap in front of the fire. I'll be ready for a rest after cycling *and* walking."

As the sun began to rise, I texted Peter I'd see him in twenty minutes and took off. My route was lined with stone walls in the rich honey-color the Cotswolds were known for, and the sun rising over the walls was a beautiful sight. The bright rays of sunshine reflected off the frost on the grass and the hedgerows, making them sparkle. Thankfully, I warmed up as I rode past the donkeys, the Olde Mill Inn, and the pub on my way to Peter's garage. He lived in a flat above his business and was outside pumping up his tires when I arrived.

"I didn't see a soul on the way over here," I called. "I hope that means we have the road to ourselves all the way to Stow-on-the-Wold."

That was our destination this Sunday morning. We'd eat a hearty breakfast at Huffkins and then make the return trip. Depending on how we felt, Peter might accompany me back to my cottage and on to the village of Astonbury so we could get in a few more miles.

"Okay, almost ready to go. Goodness, I'm glad you suggested this outing. I'm having trouble getting back into shape after nursing my shoulder these past several months. How is it I could ride almost daily for years, and be so out of shape after only a few months off?"

I chuckled at my tall, athletic friend. After injuring his shoulder in a cycling accident, he'd had to forgo his daily ride for close to three months. "You're preaching to the choir. Remember I'm the gal who hadn't been on a bicycle in ages until you encouraged me to get back on? It didn't matter that I walked and took yoga. Working up to being able to ride fifteen to twenty miles again has been a bear."

Almost two years had passed since my husband Henry had

died in a cycling accident in Atlanta. *Life can change in a heartbeat*, I thought. One minute we'd been cycling our final uphill leg to lunch, and the next he'd been struck by a car. As usual, Henry was ahead of me on the hill, so I didn't see the accident, but I heard the crash—a sound I'd never forget.

It was a tragedy that changed my life, a tragedy that propelled me to pursue a lifelong dream. But not before I did all the things a freshly minted widow was expected to do. I grieved nonstop. I gave away Henry's clothes, his tools, and his bicycles. I tended to our finances. I downsized from our five-bedroom house to a two-bedroom condo. I resumed my banking career and threw myself back into sixty-hour workweeks.

Finally, after a year, I did what my financial planner had told me I could do—I retired. Even though she'd been encouraging me to step back and think about taking early retirement, I'm sure she never envisioned me moving to the Cotswolds. But heck, isn't that what's meant by *carpe diem*? I seized the day and did something I'd only dreamed of.

And here I was, living in a storybook cottage with Dickens and Christie, making new friends, and making my way. I was a work in progress.

Peter patted me on the back, and we set off. As Henry had, Peter liked for me to take the lead, so he could keep an eye on me—until we hit the hills. I was a slowpoke on the steep ones, so Henry and now Peter would power past me and wait at the top. This morning's route was filled with *gently rolling* hills, so I was able to maintain a consistent pace.

We passed the turnoff to Sunshine Cottage where Peter's twin sister Wendy lived with their mother, Belle. Wendy and I were about the same age and had lots in common. She'd taught high school English in the States and only recently retired and come home to live with her mum. I too had taught English, but for only four years to her thirty. She was divorced. I was widowed. We were both avid readers and enjoyed yoga. We'd hit it off right away.

Peter spoke as he pedaled up to ride alongside me. "Can't believe we haven't seen a car. Maybe we *will* make it to Stow without any traffic."

"Maybe there, but not back," I replied. "Oh, look at the sun shining on the river. What a gorgeous morning."

Crossing one of the several narrow stone bridges over the River Elfe, I marveled at the water glistening in the sunlight before shifting my gaze back to the road. "Oh look!" I exclaimed as I pointed and slowed. "What's that, Peter? Skidmarks?"

Peter sped past me and stopped just before the curve. "What the . . . ? Looks like a car's gone off the road here."

We pulled our bicycles onto the verge and looked into the woods. I saw a glint of either metal or glass and tire tracks going down the embankment to the river. A feeling of dread came over me, and I had a flashback to Henry's accident. Tears sprang to my eyes as I looked at Peter.

"Leta, you're white as a sheet." It must have hit Peter what my problem was. "Crikey, I'm sorry. You're thinking of Henry. Stay here, and I'll check it out."

He'd only taken a step or two before he exclaimed, "I know that car." Pointing to the trees lining the river, he said, "I take care of that silver Bentley for the Earl of Stow—well, I mean Nicholas."

I felt numb and shuddered before responding. "Right, well, Nicholas is the Earl now that his grandfather Nigel's passed away. Can we get down there? "

We worked our way down the short steep hill, trying not to

slip in the frozen undergrowth. The car was slightly canted on its side, driver side up, two wheels in the air. Peter made it to the driver's door and looked inside.

"It's Nicholas alright. Let me see if I can get the door open." He muttered as he pulled first on the front and then the back door. "Just can't think of Nicholas as the Earl. I know Nigel was in his nineties, but I still find it hard to think of him as gone—and to think of his grandson as taking his place."

I was behind him when he exclaimed, "Bloody hell. I hate these automatic locks. I'll have to break a window."

He removed his jacket and glanced around. Grabbing a rock, he wrapped his jacket around his hand, slammed the rock against the rear passenger window, and reached through. He unlocked the driver's door and pulled it open. Only then could he get to Nicholas to feel for a pulse.

"He's alive. . . barely," he called. "Weak pulse and lots of blood. Can't tell more than that. And we can't chance pulling him out in case he has a neck or spinal injury. I'm calling 999."

Once he'd given our location and explained the situation, he tucked his jacket around Nicholas. I handed him mine to use too. *How long has Nicholas been out here in the freezing temperatures? When did he go off the road?*

I looked at Peter. "Are you thinking what I am?"

"That we saw Nicholas last night at the birthday party at Astonbury Manor? And he's staying there, so what's he doing out here?"

"Exactly. It was eleven when I got home, and the Manor house is back beyond my cottage. What's he doing miles up the road? There's nothing open in Astonbury or any of the neighboring villages after eleven. And, he's wearing his tux, so he must have gone out last night, not this morning. Based on the direction of the skid marks, doesn't it look as though he was on the way back?"

Peter looked at Nicholas, a worried expression on his face. "Yes, I think you're right about the direction of the skid marks. I wonder how long he's been out in this cold. Let's hope he's warming up. He's in bad enough shape without hypothermia."

"How long before the ambulance gets here, do you think?"

Peter pulled the jackets higher around Nicholas's neck. "From the hospital in Cheltenham? Maybe fifteen minutes at the most."

As I waited helplessly, my brain swirled with questions. "I wonder, did he fly off the road all on his own or could someone have run him off deliberately? Can you tell that from the skid marks?"

"Leta! There you go, imagining the worst. You watch too many crime shows. All you need are my mum and Wendy to egg you on, and before you know it, you'll decide this *accident* needs investigating."

"Not on your life. Even though your mum has dubbed us the Little Old Ladies' Detective Agency, I'm not getting involved. I'm just curious. That's all."

I told myself it was happenstance that had caused Wendy, Belle, and me to get caught up in two murder investigations. I had no intention of making amateur sleuthing a habit. I could just imagine Gemma's reaction if she thought I was sticking my nose into her world yet again.

A Detective Sergeant at the Stow-on-the-Wold police station, Gemma Taylor lived in the guest cottage behind the Olde Mill Inn in Astonbury, and she would likely be the officer to show up at this accident. I was friends with her parents, Libby and Gavin, who owned the inn. I guess I was friends with Gemma too, but sometimes we seemed more like adversaries. Was it my fault I was naturally curious and observant? Was it my fault folks tended to confide in me?

Wendy thought it was something about my corporate work in conflict resolution, something about my ability to listen, that made people comfortable sharing information with me. Often, it was information they hadn't shared with anyone else.

Peter was right to be concerned about the three of us, but that didn't stop him from climbing back to the road and examining the skid marks. I could see him walking back and forth and kneeling in spots.

He returned to the car where I was watching over Nicholas. "Leta, there's only one set of skid marks, so the answer to your question is this was a single-car accident. No one ran him off the road. So put that out of your head. Could he have fallen asleep? Sure, and like the rest of us, he'd probably had plenty to drink."

I wondered aloud. "Could it have been something mechanical?"

"Couldn't have been. It's my job to keep this car in tip-top shape, and I tuned it up in anticipation of Nicholas's arrival. The Bentley hasn't been driven much these last few months, what with his grandfather being bedridden since the spring and passing away in September.

"I can't pop the hood with the nose of the car at this angle, but now that you mention it, it looks like the back tire may have blown out. I checked the tires too, so that shouldn't have happened unless Nicholas damaged it somehow this week, maybe picked up a nail somewhere."

Peter knelt by the back wheel and poked and prodded. It wasn't long before he sat back on his haunches. "I can't believe what I'm seeing."

"What? Is it a nail?"

"No. It's a small horizontal cut on the tire wall. I was looking for something in the tread, something he could have run over. But, this isn't a puncture. It's a slash in the side of the tire—about two centimeters wide."

"What's that in the inches, Peter? So I can picture it?" I asked.

"About three-quarters of an inch. It had to have been deliberate."

He stood up and dusted the knees of his cycling tights. We looked at each other, speechless at the implications of what he'd found.

My voice quavered. "Guess I *wasn't* imagining the worst. The worst *happened.* I know he rubbed some folks the wrong way, what with his talk of turning Astonbury Manor into a resort, but . . .

Our conversation was interrupted by the arrival of Gemma and an ambulance. I was still a bit shaken about being at the scene of an auto accident and was counting on Peter to tell Gemma what he'd observed. She carefully came down the embankment, trying not to trample the tire tracks. Peter and I hadn't thought of preserving them. We'd been focused on getting to the car.

There were no smart remarks from Gemma this morning. "Guess this wasn't what you two had in mind when you set out for a morning ride, was it?" she said.

I stood by as Peter explained what we'd seen as we approached and what we'd done to try to help Nicholas. Peter started to tell her about the tire, but she cut him off.

She motioned the EMTs to come to the car and cautioned them to be careful not to disturb any evidence. "Let's get him out of the car and on the way to the hospital, and then we can talk more."

"Good job with the coats," said one of the EMTs. "His body temperature isn't too terribly low, and we should be able to bring it up quick enough with the heated blankets we have. But his pulse is awfully weak."

Gemma, Peter, and I preceded them up the embankment. At the top, Gemma stood with her arms crossed, studying the skid marks. "You're right, Peter. It was a single-car accident. Since you're the mechanic for the vehicles at Astonbury Manor, I'm guessing the family would want the car towed to your garage. Can you take care of that?"

"I could, but I've more to tell you that may change your mind," he said. "Here, let me show you."

We three headed down the embankment, and Gemma rested on her heels by the rear tire as Peter showed her the slash. "Bloody hell," she exclaimed. "So, this wasn't just an acci-dental blowout. Let me think a minute . . . You're right, Peter. The slashed tire changes things. It will be best for the Scene of Crime Officers to tow the car to Quedgeley. That way, they can not only examine the tire, but they can also dust for prints and ensure the proper chain of evidence. I can picture someone putting their hand on the fender while they lean in to slash the tire, can't you? If we're lucky, they'll have left prints. And the SOCOs should be able to tell me what was used to slash it—I'm guessing a knife."

I was trying to wrap my brain around someone sabotaging the Earl's car when a random thought popped into my head. "Gemma, has anyone from the Manor house called the station to say Nicholas is missing? I mean, I know the place is huge, but . . . could it be they've slept in and haven't missed him yet?"

"Great minds *must* think alike because I'm wondering the same thing. To answer your question, we've not received any calls about him. Surely his wife has noticed his absence by now."

I frowned. "You would think so, but maybe they slept in separate rooms."

"Seriously? I thought only old married couples did that. And why's he dressed in a tux? Oh right, Ellie's birthday party was last night—I always have a hard time referring to her as Lady Stow or the Countess."

Thinking about the party and titles was a welcome distraction. "If you can believe it, I've been corrected about her title a few times in the last week. Since her husband died and the grandson inherited the title, Ellie is now the Dowager Countess. If that isn't a mouthful.

"And yes, the party was last night and was quite an event. Ellie invited business owners from the village, book club members, and those who worked the hardest on the Astonbury Tree Lighting—in addition to the family."

"So a long evening of cocktails and dinner? What time did it break up?"

I nodded yes to the first question and explained I'd arrived home around eleven. I was fairly sure most of us had collected our coats and moved to the gravel courtyard around the same time. Peter confirmed my memory of the general timing and added that a few diehards had stayed behind.

As an afterthought, I added, "Despite some tension in the air, I think Ellie enjoyed her celebration, though I'm not sure her son Matthew did. And his son Harry was in the same camp. They're both frustrated over Nicholas's plans. And your dad is too."

Gemma rolled her eyes. "Yes, Dad's been like a broken

record about how Nicholas is going to destroy Astonbury's charm, disturb the wildlife, and increase the traffic. I think he's right on all counts, but I'm tired of hearing about it morning, noon, and night."

Peter nodded. "It's been the hot topic at the pub most of the week. The village is divided as to whether the resort's a good or a bad idea. Some shop owners are hopeful it will bring in more business. Others worry about the traffic and congestion on High Street. Then there are folks like George Evans, who can't make up their minds what to think. For George, it could mean more business for Cotswolds Tours, but it could also mean he'll no longer be able to take customers to tour the Manor house."

Gemma shook her head. "Can this situation get any worse? Not only do we have a serious accident, but it also appears someone engineered it. Factor in the drama over Nicholas's plans, and we've got a right mess."

She looked at me. "I'll talk to Mum for a refresher course on the Earl of Stow and the family. She's been friends with Ellie for ages, and I know she'll have the inside scoop. All that rigamarole about how someone comes to inherit a title is beyond me. Like how is it Nicholas, a *grandson* from the States, came to be the new Earl instead of Matthew, a *son* who lives here in Astonbury? Don't know that it has a bearing on what happened here, but I guess I need to understand it."

Now was not the time to tell Gemma I knew a bit about that "rigamarole," as she put it. An offhand remark would do instead. "Puts me in mind of Downton Abbey, though Astonbury Manor isn't quite as grand."

I returned to the road as Peter and Gemma stood by the car talking. Watching the EMTS settle Nicholas in the ambulance and hook him up to goodness knows what, I hoped they'd be able to stabilize him quickly. And then it happened. Equipment started beeping. One EMT started CPR. The other grabbed the defibrillator. It was over in a flash. All to no avail.

The one who'd complimented us on the coats looked around, and his mouth dropped open when he saw me standing there. He leaped out of the ambulance and got to me just as my knees began to buckle.

"Whoa, let's sit you down. Sorry you had to see that, miss. Are you okay?"

His words barely registered. This was déjà vu of the worst kind. Thankfully, Peter and Gemma ran up at just that moment. Taking in the scene, Peter looked aghast.

Before I knew it, someone draped my jacket around my shoulders, followed by a heated blanket. Gemma offered me a sip of water. I wiped the tears from eyes and tried to breathe deeply. *Focus on the here and now*, I thought. *Don't you* dare *think about Henry*.

I stared at the skid marks to avoid the scene inside the ambulance. I tried to think of something else—anything else— as I took deep breaths.

Peter had begun pacing and blowing on his hands. "If that's it for now, it's probably time Leta and I left you to it. These cycling clothes are fine when you're moving and your blood is pumping, but not for standing around. I'm freezing, and I bet Leta is too."

He was right. Even with the benefit of a blanket, I was chilled to the bone. We climbed on our bikes and cycled to his place.

Why would someone slash the Earl's tire? I thought as I left Peter and cycled toward my cottage. Since I'd returned from my Thanksgiving trip to the States, I'd caught up on village gossip over lunch at the Ploughman and coffee at Toby's Tearoom and been intrigued by the buzz about the new Earl. It was all anyone had talked about last week, but . . . had there been harsher notes beneath the seemingly light chatter? *Did my jet lag cause me to miss signs of something sinister?*

Chapter Two

Sunday the Week Before

Boy, am I glad to be home, I thought. I opened the door to my cottage to a delighted dog and a cranky cat.

"Leta, I missed you. Are you ready for a walk? Can we visit the donkeys?"

Ah yes, I could count on Dickens to be chipper even though I'd left him and his feline sister behind when I went to the States. I'd been gone ten days and had missed them both, but I knew my friends had taken good care of them.

Peter had stopped by on his bicycle to walk Dickens and feed Christie. They both adored him, and I thought it had a lot to do with his resemblance to Henry. Both were tall, slim, and blonde with blue eyes. Little Timmy from next door had also visited daily. I was sure Dickens had gotten plenty of belly rubs and Christie had been well fed. The princess was quite particular about her puddles of milk and dabs of wet food, so I knew I'd hear complaints. Still, I was confident she hadn't starved.

"So, you decided to return?" meowed Christie. "Took your sweet time, didn't you?"

"Oh come on, you can't begrudge me a trip to see my sisters, can you?"

"Pffft. Don't think for a second you're fooling me. I know you made a side trip to New York City to see Dave. You'd have been home much sooner if not for him."

It was Dickens's cue to get involved. "Hey, I like Dave. He gives great belly rubs."

The two debated the merits of my overseas friend as I carried my luggage upstairs to the bedroom. I have a thing about unpacking before I do anything else. Once done, I made a detour to light the fire in the sitting room prior to returning to the kitchen.

My flight from New York had landed at Heathrow at breakfast time, but the airline had plied me with food all the way across the Atlantic, so I hadn't been hungry. Now, though, after driving my refurbished London taxi to my cottage, I was famished—famished and exhausted. Thankfully, the Sunday traffic hadn't been bad, so at least I wasn't stressed out to boot.

I handed Christie a new stuffed mouse and tossed Dickens one of several old racquetballs, compliments of Anna and Andrew in Atlanta. My sister and brother-in-law had several cats and a Great Dane, so they knew what would make my two companions happy. Andrew played racquetball weekly and saved the old balls for his dog and mine.

"A boy can never have too many balls," barked Dickens.

I chuckled at his excitement. "How well I know. You have balls of all sizes scattered around the house and the garden, and Christie is forever digging them out from under the furniture and chasing them around."

Christie was rolling on the floor with her mouse between

her paws, tossing it in the air and rubbing it with her nose. When I sat down at the kitchen table with a cup of tea, she brought the mouse over to drop at my feet.

She looked at me and tilted her head. "Love the mouse, but aren't you forgetting something?"

"Yes, dear," I said as I went to the pantry. "You need a dab of wet food, don't you?"

As she twined around my ankles, she said, "Gee, I was worried you'd been gone so long you'd forgotten. Heaven forbid."

I was settling onto the couch with a second cup of tea when the phone rang. It was Libby from the inn. "Hi, checking to be sure you made it home in one piece, and of course, I want to hear all about the trip."

"Oh, it was fantastic. I stayed a few nights with my friend Bev and then shifted to Anna's house. I felt right at home with Bev's latest foster dog, Spunky Monkey, and all of my sister's animals. Her kittens Crunch and Munch are a mess. I ate lunch out every day with different girlfriends, indulged in a bit of retail therapy, and even rode bikes with my brother-in-law on the Silver Comet Trail."

"And did you get your traditional Thanksgiving dinner?" asked Libby.

"You bet. My sister Sophia and her husband Jeremy flew in from New Orleans, and Anna cooked an amazing Thanksgiving feast, complete with the desserts she's famous for—pecan pie, pound cake, and brownies. I was definitely 'over-served,' as Henry used to say."

"I can only imagine," said Libby. "I want to hear all about the New York visit with Dave, but I see a few of our Sunday guests are leaving and I need to see them off. Promise you'll fill me in later, okay?"

As I sipped my tea, I reflected on my trip home. From the moment Bev greeted me outside the Atlanta airport until Dave hugged me goodbye at New York's JFK, my days and nights had been jam-packed. It had been a whirlwind trip. I'd anticipated I would miss Henry and have tearful moments as I visited with friends and family, but time had softened the sorrow. Laughing with them while we recalled things Henry had said and done kept the good times alive, and I was able to keep the nightmare memory of his accident at bay.

When Andrew delivered me to the Atlanta airport for my flight to NYC, I was in a good place—thankful for the life I'd shared with Henry and excited about spending time with Dave. I was also very nearly in a turkey coma and had texted Dave I didn't want to see food until the next morning. The phone rang again, and this time it was Wendy. "How's the world traveler? Weary, I expect."

"Oh yes. You know how it is after making all those transatlantic flights when you lived in North Carolina. I'm trying to stay awake until my regular bedtime when all I want to do is crawl beneath my down comforter right this minute and call it a day."

Wendy sighed. "I know the feeling, and I'm glad those days are behind me. I enjoyed my time teaching in Charlotte, but I'm happy to be home with Mum and Peter. Now, tell me about everything. I'm dying to hear all about Atlanta and New York—well, especially New York."

I shared the Atlanta portion again and took a deep breath. I hadn't yet processed my visit with Dave. "Wendy, don't read too much into this, but the best way to describe it is that it felt like an experience out of a Hallmark movie."

"Oh my gosh. Are you serious? I was afraid he was too good to be true."

I had to admit I'd wondered the same thing about Dave Prentiss after meeting him in September at one of Libby's cocktail parties. He was based in New York City but was in England researching an article about Arthur Conan Doyle for Strand Magazine. We'd gone out a few times and hit it off. Our mutual interest in books, especially by British authors, and the fact that we were both writers had fueled the attraction—though I considered his literary articles *real* writing as compared to my weekly columns for small-town papers in the States.

"I've had similar thoughts," I said. "And, of course, I keep telling myself I'm on the rebound and the time isn't right for a man in my life."

Christie was all ears and felt a need to express her opinion. "I keep telling you, Leta, a long-distance relationship is just the thing. No strings. You can still play the field over here."

"What's Christie going on about? Oh wait, she's offering relationship advice, right?"

If only Wendy knew how accurate she was. "Oh yes, she has a perspective on everything. You know she didn't take to Dave right away, though she slowly warmed to him. Dickens, on the other hand, thinks he's grand."

"Well, I like Dave *and* Peter," offered Dickens. "I think Peter has the cycling thing going for him."

Wendy shouted above the animals. "Can you hear me over that racket? Those two are awfully vocal all of a sudden. Anyway, back to Dave. There's no rule about when it's the right time for a new relationship. It's about you being happy, Leta. And, if Dave makes you happy, then why not let things take their course?"

"I know, I know. You're probably right. And there's no danger of things moving too quickly with us living on separate continents. Being able to visit a boyfriend in NYC isn't all bad either. Gee, it sounds strange to use that word—*boyfriend*."

"See," said Wendy. "You're getting there. Now, give me some details. You know, it's been so long since I've had a date, much less a relationship, I have to live vicariously."

And so, I regaled her with stories of seeing the Christmas windows at Macy's and Saks, of dinner out, of making our way to the Top of the Rock with its view of the city lights, of wandering Central Park hand in hand, and more.

"Oh my. You're right. Hallmark movie material for sure. So, when will you see him again?"

I sighed in contentment. "I can hardly believe it, but he's taking a flight the day after Christmas and will be here through New Year's. We're thinking of spending a few days in London."

Wendy laughed. "Another location for the Hallmark movie. I'm so happy for you. Now, for more mundane matters, let's take Rhiannon's ten a.m. yoga class Monday morning. That way, you can sleep in a bit."

Rhiannon stuck her head out the door of the Let It Be Yoga studio as I climbed the stairs. "You look a bit weary. Did you have a marvelous time back home?"

I smiled. "Yes, I did. It was everything I could have hoped for. My sisters and I didn't even have any disagreements, unusual for us."

"Do you often disagree?"

"It happens. We're all pretty different, and I was expecting them to start in again with the 'Why did you have to move to England?' questions. Thankfully, they refrained."

Rhiannon chuckled. "And Dave, how is he?"

I couldn't help myself. I broke out in a huge smile. "That was the best part. He's fine, and we had a ball touring New York City decked out in its Christmas finery. I couldn't have asked for a better host."

Rhiannon stepped away to greet more clients as we prepared for class. I waved at Wendy as she came in, spread her yoga mat, and gathered two blocks and a bolster. Stretching and shifting to a cross-legged position, I picked up on a pattern in the pre-class buzz. It was all about the goings-on at Astonbury Manor—the arrival of the new Earl and his wife and rumors of his plans for the Estate. That meant this morning's visit to Toby's Tearoom would be gossip-filled.

I was thankful the class focused on standing poses rather than headstands, which were always difficult for me. Wendy and I waited as Rhiannon answered questions and locked the studio, and then we three walked up High Street to the Tearoom. It was filled with locals and tourists on this crisp Monday morning.

Toby called to me as we were grabbing a table. "Leta, welcome back. We're still offering pumpkin lattes if you want one."

I gave him a thumbs up. I wasn't sure which I enjoyed more, pumpkin or gingerbread, but either was perfect for a chilly morning. It was good to see the shop filled to overflowing, as I knew business would slow down after the holidays.

"Okay," I said to my friends after my first sip of coffee. "What's all this about the new Earl?"

Wendy frowned. "There are all kinds of rumors flying around, and it's hard to separate fact from fiction."

"Right," said Rhiannon. "The one thing that doesn't seem

to be in question is he wants to turn Astonbury Manor into a resort."

"What? Can he do that?" I asked. "I mean, isn't it Lady Stow's—or Ellie's—home? Goodness, I get tangled up when I refer to her."

Wendy shook her head. "It's complicated. Time for your lesson on the aristocracy. Reggie, the Earl's eldest son, would have inherited the Earldom, but he died a few months before his father did. That means Reggie's son Nicholas inherited the title. The property is also entailed, as in it goes to the male who inherits the title."

Rhiannon picked up the explanation. "So, it's not like Downton Abbey, where the whole kit and caboodle might have been lost because there wasn't a male heir. In this case, the title Earl of Stow goes to Nicholas along with the physical property—the manor house and adjoining acreage—but the money is divided equally among Nicholas, Ellie, and her son Matthew. I doubt Matthew had any expectation of getting the title given he's the second son, but his nose may be a bit out of joint seeing his American nephew waltz in here to become the Earl. The good news for Matthew and his family is we hear there's a substantial amount of money, so no worries on that front."

I frowned as I struggled to digest the details. "Okay, Nicholas is the new Earl because his father Reggie was the elder son. But, but, what about Ellie? She'll still live in the manor house, right?"

Wendy shook her head and continued the story. "She can if she so chooses because the will gives her the right to live there as long as she likes—the rest of her life, if she'd like. If Nicholas were happy to have the title, own the property, and be on his merry way back to New York, there wouldn't be a problem. I think the family expected he'd be too busy with his investment banking business to take any interest in the running of the estate—that he'd let things continue as they are with Lady Stow in her home and Matthew running things.

"But that's not happening. One of the rumors is he wants to shift Ellie to a few rooms in the Manor House to make his plan work. Can you imagine living in the home you shared with your husband for close to fifty years, and it's become a resort filled with strangers? It's your home, but it's not?"

Rhiannon added, "We hear talk of a pool, tennis courts, a heliport, and goodness knows what else. That's where the rumors get murky."

"I can't imagine Matthew is happy about disturbing his mother," I said. "She's only just lost her husband, and Nicholas wants to move her from the family home? And what about Matthew? Doesn't he live in a cottage on the property and act as Estate Manager? I seem to recall his son Harry's made a going concern of the sheep too. Surely Nicholas wouldn't disturb his grandmother and kick out the rest of the family, would he?"

Wendy sipped her coffee. "That's why I said it's complicated. First, Lady Stow isn't Nicholas's grandmother. His father, Reggie, was the old Earl's son by his second wife. Ellie is the third wife. Not that the relationship was ever a problem, according to what we've heard. It's such a tragic story. Nigel Coates, the Earl, lost his first wife during the War. He was an RAF pilot, and she died in the bombing of Coventry. He waited a good while before marrying the second time, and that wife died when Reggie was only a boy. Nigel didn't marry Ellie until years later when Reggie was in his teens. Matthew came along a few years after they married."

I was having a difficult time keeping up with the story.

"Good grief, you weren't kidding when you said it was complicated. I need a family tree so I don't get lost. So, how does all this impact Matthew and his family?"

Rhiannon's frown deepened as she spoke up. "If the rumors are true, Nicholas is still working out the details for the resort. We here in the village don't know what the plans are for Matthew, his wife Sarah, and their sons Harry and Sam. Nicholas *could* ask Matthew and his family to leave, as they have no claim to their cottage and the rest of the property. Or maybe he'll want Matthew to stay on as Estate Manager or in some other role. No one knows."

"Is there any upside to having a new Earl?" I asked.

Wendy nodded enthusiastically. "Yes, he's already made a sizable donation to St. Andrews Church, some of it designated to repair the roof and more to purchase new robes for the choir. It's not that Ellie and Nigel didn't support the church, but Nicholas's infusion of cash comes on top of their annual donation. He's also donated a large sum to the Village Hall so they can run more programs, and he's quite enthusiastic about his role at the tree lighting this Friday."

"Well then, maybe he plans to be more involved in the community. Could be his relative youth will be a bonus for the village," I said as I stood. "Who's up for another cup of coffee? And I hear a scone calling my name. Anyone else?"

My jet lag was taking over, and I was ready for an early nap but needed to make a Sainsbury's run to replenish my empty larder. I'd just parked my car at the store when Dave called.

"Hey there. I know from your text that you made it home

safely, but I want to hear about the reception you got from the menagerie."

"Ha! I bet you know without me telling you. Who do you think was ecstatic to see me? Who was grumpy?"

"Dickens and Christie, in that order?"

"You got it."

He chuckled. "Thought so. And are you recovering from your jet lag? Taking it easy today?"

"Still jet-lagged, but I managed to make a mid-morning yoga class and coffee with Wendy and Rhiannon. Now I'm going shopping at Sainsbury's. Christie made it known this morning that I'd best not return without fresh milk."

"Oh, I can picture her standing by her dish giving you that look. Well, have you gotten your tree lighting assignment yet? Isn't that this weekend?"

"Oh fiddle, I'd completely forgotten about that. I should have had an email by now detailing my duties. Maybe it's there and I overlooked it. I *did* have an engraved invitation to Lady Stow's birthday dinner, though, in the pile of mail Deborah left on the kitchen table." Deborah was my next-door neighbor and Timmy's mum.

"Oh, dinner at the Manor House. Sounds pretty posh."

I laughed at his expression. "Trust me, the attire may be formal, but Lady Stow's fairly egalitarian. There will be plenty of villagers there—business owners and community leaders, members of the book club from the Book Nook, and some of the folks who are helping with the tree lighting."

"Speaking of the book club, did you finish reading *Mr. Dickens and His Carol* on the flight home?"

I yawned. "Not quite, but I'll be done by Thursday night's meeting. I'm enjoying the author's writing and don't want to rush through it. Do you think I need to read parts aloud to Dickens?"

"You do that," Dave replied. "And let me know what he thinks of the great man's writing. Okay, I heard that yawn. I'll let you do your shopping and get home for your nap. Rest up, and I'll call you tomorrow."

I had a silly grin plastered on my face as I walked into the grocery store. *Enjoy it*, I thought, as I filled my basket with salad fixings, eggs, milk, and a few containers of fresh-made soup.

I needed to watch what I ate this week before the pounds I'd gained over Thanksgiving settled in for good. Watch my intake, take Dickens for walks, and see if I could get Peter to do a long bicycle ride soon. I could go on my own, but riding with a companion was much more enjoyable.

Dickens greeted me when I opened the door. "Can we take a walk, pretty please? I want to see Martha and Dylan, and I bet Christie would like to go too. She didn't get to ride in her backpack the whole time you were gone."

I grumbled as I put the groceries away. "The last thing I want to do right now is take a walk, but maybe we can go later, okay?"

My happy-go-lucky dog was fine with going later in the day, and I could tell Christie's ears had perked up at the mention of her backpack. I was behind on my emails and my writing and felt I had to take care of a few things before I could think about a walk. Maybe after all that I could get in a late afternoon nap.

I pulled a bowl from the cabinet and tossed together tomatoes, feta cheese, Kalamata olives, olive oil, and a dash of red wine vinegar. That would be my lunch after I did some work in the office.

Christie sprinted ahead of me and leaped to the desktop, knocking my notepad and pen to the floor. I was amazed the desk had stayed neat while I was gone. Even when she didn't dislodge notebooks and heavier items, I could count on finding pens, pencils, and paper clips on the floor when I entered my office in the mornings. It was as though she had to stake her claim.

Dickens followed and went to his spot beneath the desk. He made a perfect footrest. *Email first*, I thought, *then a column.*

Christie meowed, "Aren't you forgetting something? The file drawer, if you please."

She was right. I'd neglected to pull the drawer open so she could curl up in it. Now, with everyone in place, I could get to work. I scrolled through my emails. I needed to respond to Bev, Anna, and Sophia, who'd all written to say they wanted the scoop on my NYC trip. They'd seen the photos I'd posted on Facebook but wanted the details. If I started with a column about my New York trip, I could use those highlights as the basis for an in-depth personal email.

I enjoyed writing and felt fortunate my editors and readers were happy with any topic I chose. My "Parker's Pen" column was about whatever struck my fancy, and my fancy was mostly positive and humorous. Diatribes about politics or any topic that would elicit rage were not for me.

Describing the colorful Christmas windows made me smile, as did the memory of standing outside on the roof of Top of the Rock and seeing the Empire State Building decked out in red and green lights. I'd visited New York often on business trips and always managed to squeeze in a trip during the holiday season. In my book, nothing compared to the city's Christmas lights, and I never tired of seeing them. Maybe that was because Christmas was my favorite holiday.

Dave and I had taken in the Rockettes Christmas show at Radio City Music Hall too. I could never decide which was more spectacular—the March of the Toy Soldiers or the live nativity scene at the end. Dave marveled at my childlike delight in everything we saw, and I had to remind myself he was new to my Christmas spirit.

Henry had grown used to my Christmas fervor. I'd decorated our Atlanta home to the hilt each year, while he sat in his recliner. Sure, he helped put up the tree and the lights and hang a few ornaments, but mostly it was me bustling around arranging cuddly animals, candles, and decorative plates. No matter how many decorations I had, I always found room for one more. After I'd inherited my mother's ornaments, though, I could hardly fit everything on one tree. I treasured Mother's collection, many still in their original Woolworths boxes, and they came with me when I moved to Astonbury.

I bet how I decorate my new home for Christmas would make another good column. With that thought, I put the finishing touches on the New York column and decided it was time for lunch.

My four-legged companions followed me to the kitchen, and I let Dickens out to the garden. This was his kind of weather.

Christie stared at me as I pulled my bowl from the fridge. "I can see you need to be retrained," she meowed.

"Pardon me, did I forget to give you some wet food before I fed myself?"

I forked a small dab in her dish and sat in front of her. She sniffed it and sat back. "It needs to be stirred."

Sighing, I obliged and stuck the fork in it. Retraining, indeed. She was a persnickety cat, but the second stir did the trick. True to form, she licked it up and looked at me again. She didn't have to say anything. I knew to place another dab in the dish.

I opened the door and called Dickens. "Ready to come in, boy?"

"Not yet, I'm not done inspecting the garden. While you were gone, Peter took me on walks, and Timmy rubbed my belly, but I didn't get to spend much time on my corner-checking duties."

His serious tone made me laugh. He considered it his job to sniff along the walls made of the golden Cotswolds stone, checking for what, I didn't know. Intruders? Critters? I only knew that the corners required extra checking.

I turned back to the kitchen and spoke to Christie, who was reclining in a sunspot. "It's pretty chilly today. Do you want to go with Dickens and me on our walk or would you prefer to sleep in front of the fireplace?"

"How far?"

"Only the mile to see Martha and Dylan and the mile back. And I could put a small fleece blanket in the backpack for you to snuggle in if you'd like."

Christie studied me for a moment. "I've missed the donkeys, so I'll chance it. If I'm frozen, will you turn back early?"

"Of course I will, silly girl, but since we've waited until the afternoon, you should be okay."

I retrieved her backpack from the hook in the mudroom, tucked a blanket in it, and placed it on the kitchen floor.

Christie crawled inside and turned around and stuck her head out. Zipping my winter jacket, I stuck my hands in my gloves, snugged my black cloche on my head, and put my arms in the backpack. I grabbed Dickens's leash, and we stepped outside to get him.

"Ready, I'm ready," he barked. "Did you get the carrots?"

Gee, maybe Christie was right and I *did* need retraining. Carrots for the donkeys were a must. I'd forgotten to get fresh ones at the grocery, but there were a few shriveled ones in the basket on the counter.

"Thanks, Dickens. Now we're ready."

We walked our usual mile along the road to the stone fence. When Martha and Dylan spied us, they trotted over. What was it about rubbing donkey noses that was so special?

It was cold enough that the warm donkey breath formed small clouds. Christie stretched a tentative paw out to touch Martha's nose, and Martha lifted her head to make it easier for Christie to reach. Everything was fine until Martha snorted, causing Christie to dive into the backpack.

Dickens barked. "You need to get used to them, Christie. They won't hurt you."

"Easy for you to say," she meowed from deep in the pack. "How close have you gotten to those snouts?"

"Okay, you two, shall we go a bit further or head back?"

"To the inn, to the inn," said Dickens.

"No, it's too cold. I vote we turn around," meowed Christie.

I was chilly and ready for a nap, so I played the tiebreaker. Once in the cottage, I brewed a cup of tea and found my book. When I laid down on the couch with my book and a blanket tucked around my legs, Christie made herself comfortable on my chest. Between me and the book, of course. Dickens lay beside the couch.

I attempted to read without disturbing the princess who was purring contentedly. *Give it up*, I thought. *You can nap now and read later.*

The sound of a racquetball rolling around the flagstone floor followed by Christie chasing after it woke me. My first thought was that I hadn't emailed Bev and my sisters yet. That just wouldn't do. Instead of tea, I made a cup of hot chocolate to take to the office and settled in to copy bits from the column I'd drafted about New York and add more personal highlights of my time with Dave.

Dare I use the phrase Hallmark movie in this email? Bev would be ecstatic and supportive, but I wasn't sure I wanted to open myself up for unsolicited romance advice from my sisters. Maybe I should write two separate emails—one for my sisters and one for Bev.

Anna and especially Sophia, who was a foodie, would be happy to hear about the restaurants we visited, the wine we drank, and the sights we'd seen. I could wrap up with some general line about Dave and I continuing to enjoy each other's company and looking forward to seeing him after Christmas.

In Bev's email, I shared more about Dave seeming almost too good to be true and my concern that it was too soon for me to feel this way about another man—whatever *this way* was. *How would I describe it?* I thought. I was tempted to say I was *in love*. Having experienced that euphoria a few times before I met Henry, I knew it didn't necessarily lead to *loving* someone.

Sometimes, the giddy sensation passed and the relationship faded away—the phone calls, texts, and touching gestures dwindling until one day it was over. Or worse, it ended with one person falling out of love and leaving the other hurt and angry.

Typing my stream of consciousness email to Bev didn't help me clarify how I felt, but it moved me closer to deciding to go for it and enjoy the relationship while it lasted. *Seriously, you need to take it a day at a time and stop overthinking it. Carpe diem* would be my mantra through New Year's.

Chapter Three

Tuesday morning I was perkier. I was up early not because my body clock was off but because I was rested. I followed my usual routine of sipping coffee in front of the fireplace while I read the paper online and played Words with Friends. I was none too pleased to see Anna had played a 92-point word. She tried not to gloat over beating me more often than I beat her, but she *did* send messages like *cha-ching* when she played a high-scoring word.

Beatrix called while I was getting two eggs from the fridge. "Hey there, have I given you enough time to recover from your trip before we talk about the tree lighting?"

"Sure. Besides, I don't want to get behind, and I know there's plenty to do."

"Good, because you're right. Libby, Ellie, and I all need your help. We've declared you the Packaging Queen. You'll be preparing little drawstring voile bags with goodies inside. The Book Nook is giving out magnets and a 10% off coupon, and I need you to put one of each in red voile bags. I may also have you attach candy canes when you tie the satin ribbon. Trixie will hand them out at the tree lighting. Hopefully, that will bring people into the bookshop that evening or sometime over December. You know December is a make or break month for us."

"That's a great idea for getting people in. How late will you be open Friday night?"

"All the shops are staying open until 8 instead of our usual 6 p.m., so we're hoping for a big night."

"Okay, do I need to call Libby and Ellie about their packaging? Or are you in charge?"

"Oh no," Beatrix replied, "I'm not in charge, but I know Libby plans for you to put Christmas cookies in green voile bags. She had Jill bake and freeze cookies the whole month of November. Just ring her to find out when she needs you. I'm betting they'll pull them out of the freezer first thing Friday morning. My bags you can do any time, and you'll have to check with Ellie, I mean Lady Stow, about her bags."

"Okay. I'll get in touch with them both. By the way, I've been calling Lady Stow Ellie since I met her at your book club some months back. What *am* I supposed to call her?"

"She says we should call her Ellie, but for some reason when we start doing major events like the Astonbury Tree Lighting, I think of her as Lady Stow. Who knows why? But come to think of it, she's no longer Lady Stow."

"Huh? She doesn't have a title now?"

Beatrix clucked. "Oh, she has one alright. She's now the Dowager Countess, and I bet she hates that title. Dowager puts me in mind of a little old lady hobbling around, not someone energetic like Ellie."

I agreed with her on that count and told her I'd be by in the next day or so to fill her bags. Next, I called Ellie. She sounded flustered when she answered.

"Oh Leta, welcome back. I'm so glad you called. I could really use your help to get organized. Having Nicholas and Julia here is wreaking havoc with my plans."

"No worries, Ellie, I'm glad to help any way I can. Beatrix told me about packaging things in little bags, but I can do other things too. Shall I come by this morning?"

"Oh my goodness, you are a treasure. Yes, please do. You can help me think things through, and then we can get started. And please bring that adorable dog. My Blanche could use someone to play with."

The mention of Blanche made me laugh. "Ha! Dickens will be beside himself at the thought of seeing Blanche. I think he's quite smitten with your little corgi."

"Well, they sure hit it off when we had the planning lunch last month. Basil is too busy wandering the estate to spend much time with Blanche."

Basil was a Great Pyrenees like Dickens, except he was a full-size Pyr, and Dickens was a dwarf version. Basil spent his time with the flock of sheep who called Astonbury Manor their home and weighed 120 pounds compared to Blanche's twenty and Dickens's forty. The three of them together were a sight to behold.

It was about a half-mile up Schoolhouse Lane to the entrance to Astonbury Manor, with the driveway stretching a mile to the manor house. I was sure Dickens would happily forgo the usual walk to see the donkeys if it meant he'd get to see Blanche. Instead of scrambling eggs, I wolfed down a protein bar and hurried upstairs to change.

"Dickens, would you like to see your girlfriend Blanche?" I asked.

"Are you serious? You're not teasing me, are you?" he barked as he bounced up and down.

"No teasing, boy. Ellie needs us, so let's go."

No matter how often I knocked on the manor house door, I was in awe each time. Never in my wildest dreams could I have foreseen having a countess as a friend, much less one who lived in an English manor house. It was her son Matthew who pulled the large front door open with Blanche at his heels.

Blanche darted around Matthew to greet Dickens. "Hi, cutie pie. I've missed you." If a dog could blush, I was sure Dickens would have. Instead, he barked and pranced and followed Blanche inside.

I was almost as smitten with Blanche as Dickens was, as I'd always thought corgis were adorable. Blanche had fawn and white coloring, and, of course, those big ears. At one point, Henry and I had considered getting a corgi. Well, I had. Henry had never cared for smaller dogs and referred to them as "starter" dogs. It took seeing their temperament described as stubborn, willful, bossy, and feisty to help me decide not to get one.

Matthew glanced over his shoulder as the two took off and then turned to me. "Boy, I'm glad you're here. Mum is a bundle of nerves about Friday. She's usually so calm, but the last few days with my nephew Nicholas and his wife have been stressful for her . . . well, for all of us . . . and I know you'll calm her down and help her focus."

I took all this in as I stared at Matthew. Did he know about the rumors flying around the village? What should I say? I didn't have to worry about saying *anything* because he must have taken my silence as encouragement to continue.

"I mean, the holiday was bound to be difficult this year

after losing Dad in September, but Nicholas and his wild ideas have caught us all off guard. I can't believe he wants to shift Mum out of her bedroom, maybe even out of the house. Oi! And you're probably thinking 'too much information, Matthew'."

He turned around and waved at me to follow before I could come up with a response. Thank goodness I'd gotten an inkling of what was going on before I'd arrived. Interestingly, he hadn't mentioned what his situation might be.

I followed him to the massive kitchen, where we found Blanche and Dickens choosing toys from Blanche's toy basket and Ellie sitting with her chin in her hands. She was a petite silver-haired woman with a peaches and cream complexion. Despite being in her seventies, she could easily have passed for a woman ten years younger.

She greeted me effusively. "Leta, you're a sight for sore eyes. I hope you enjoyed your visit with your family. And Dickens, I think Blanche is happy to see you."

Dickens and Blanche pulled nearly all the toys from the basket and darted around the kitchen. With the room almost the size of the one at Downton Abbey, they had plenty of space. Matthew motioned towards the coffee pot and poured me a cup when I nodded yes. I sat at the table with Ellie and gave her a few highlights of my trip. I could tell she was eager to get down to business, so I kept it short.

Matthew brought two boxes to the long table and opened them. One held gold-colored voile bags and the other coasters and keychains with the Astonbury Brewery logo. "Harry and I thought the gold bags were a good choice for advertising our Stow Golden Ale. What do you think?" he asked.

"They're perfect," I cried. "I especially like the keychain. I can even read the tiny label on the miniature beer bottle."

Ellie looked relieved. "Good. That's the task, then, filling 500 voile bags with one keychain and one coaster each."

"I think the two of us can handle that. Good thing we don't need any help from Blanche and Dickens. They're too busy scattering toys all over the kitchen."

She laughed. "Isn't it amazing how we can carry on a conversation while they're playing? I love seeing them do downward dog at each other and then spring into action. Some might consider it unseemly to have dogs underfoot, but their antics make me happy."

"I know what you mean. One dog is enough for me, but I enjoy seeing Dickens play with his friends. Is Basil out with the sheep?"

"Yes, you know he keeps a close eye on them, though they don't really need protecting like the herds that roam the moors or those you find in the mountains of France."

I nodded. I'd read lots about the Great Pyrenees breed and was fascinated by their role with flocks of sheep and goats. The Pyrs didn't herd the animals as Border Collies did. Instead, they guarded them. Their deep bark was usually enough to ward off any predators.

While we chatted, Matthew brought several more boxes into the kitchen. "Mum, I'll be off then, unless you need anything else."

"Thank you, Matthew. I think I can manage now. Will you be back in time for tea?"

"Lots to do today, Mum. I'll ring you later to let you know. Bye, Leta. Thanks for helping out."

Dickens and Blanche trailed after Matthew but soon returned to the kitchen. I sipped my coffee, thinking I should ask Ellie what brand she used. "Ellie, what else can I help you with? Harry has everything organized about bringing the sheep over Friday afternoon, right? And Matthew will be setting up tables with kegs of beer?"

She smiled. "Oh yes. Harry enjoys showing off Basil and the sheep. He'll bring ten to fifteen of them and set up a pen on the Village Green. He gets a kick out of introducing Basil to the children and explaining about the Cotswolds Lions."

I'd learned about the Cotswolds Lions on my first trip to the area, and I had a sweater made from their wool. The sheep had a distinctive look I thought of as Raggedy Ann hair. In medieval times, the Cotswolds had been known for their wool trade, and this breed of sheep was renowned for its especially fine wool.

"Will Matthew be manning the kegs?"

"Yes, and Gavin will help him. We'll sell half pints and donate the proceeds to the Village Hall to help fund their projects."

"And soap? Will Sarah be selling her sheep's milk soap? Ever since I discovered hers, I can't live without it."

Ellie nodded. "Oh yes, Sarah will have a table set up. She always packages her wares in voile bags, so she's good to go. Astonbury Manor will be well represented."

Sarah was Matthew's wife. They and their son Harry were forever coming up with new ideas. Several years ago, she'd moved her soap-making venture into one of the small deserted cottages scattered around the estate, and now Astonbury Soap was carried in village shops all over the Cotswolds.

"It sounds as though you have everything under control. What am I missing?" I asked.

Before Ellie could answer, a tall, willowy brunette walked into the kitchen. She may have been dressed in flannel pajama bottoms and a teeshirt, with her hair in a messy ponytail, but she was still stunning. This had to be Nicholas's wife Julia. Per the buzz at yoga, she'd been a much-in-demand model in her heyday, and was now semi-retired. I understood she still did the occasional photoshoot, but since marrying Nicholas, she didn't appear in magazines as often as she had.

Ellie made the introductions, and Julia sat down with us. "An American?" she commented. "What brings you to the area?"

I gave the short version of retiring to the Cotswolds from Atlanta. She shared the story of how she'd been born and raised in England but had signed with the Ford modeling agency in her teens and moved to NYC.

She rubbed her eyes and yawned. "I'm going to Northampton today to spend a few days with my dad. I don't get back here as often as I'd like and don't want to miss an opportunity for a visit. I was hoping I could convince Nick to go with me, but he's still a bit under the weather, plus he can't tear himself away from business. It's okay, though. Dad and I have plenty to catch up on."

"You'll be back for the weekend happenings, right?" I asked. "I've never been here for the tree lighting, but I hear it's a real village affair. Plus there's the birthday party Saturday evening."

Julia had a beautiful smile. "Oh yes. I wouldn't want to miss either one, and this will be the first time Nick gets to throw the switch to light the tree, his first big role as the Earl of Stow —Oh heck, Ellie, I'm sorry. I know how you must miss Nigel. My mouth got ahead of my brain."

Ellie was gracious. "Please don't worry, Julia. We're all adjusting."

Ever intuitive, Dickens came to Ellie, put his front paws on her chair, and licked her hand.

Blanche nipped at his rump. "Hey, it's my job to take care of Ellie. Move over."

I chuckled at the two as they competed to comfort Ellie. *People who don't have pets don't know what they're missing*, I thought.

Taking an apple from the fruit bowl, Julia left to get ready for her trip. I watched as she sauntered out. "She's gorgeous," I said. "How long have she and Nicholas been married?"

"Two years now, I think. She's his third wife, so I admit I have a difficult time keeping track. Oooh, I expect that sounded catty."

I chuckled. "Well, no, just factual. How long was he married to the first two?"

Ellie looked amused. "About two to three years each, a timeframe which doesn't bode well for Julia. Watching the dynamics from afar, I'd say he's been trying out different models and can't settle on the brand that suits the image he's trying to project."

Whoa. This was juicy. "What do you mean, Ellie?"

"The first was a debutante from one of the New York banking families. Lovely girl, but just out of college and, in so many ways, childlike. Oh my, did I just say that? She knew which fork to use, but she wasn't up to conversing with his business partners and clients. What's the term they use these days? Arm candy?"

I couldn't help chuckling at that. "Oh! And wife number two?"

"I think he purposely went to the other extreme. She was a sociology professor at New York University and could certainly hold her own with the business crowd, but she was quiet and serious, not like Nicholas at all. She was a few years older than him, too. All of which led to Julia, I think."

I commented, "She must be about his age, and she *is* beautiful. I didn't speak with her long enough to assess her intelligence, though. Are you sensing a change in the air?"

Ellie sighed. "No, not at all. She's a lovely thing. Seems not to take any guff from him, but at the same time is very caring. The few days they've been here, she's fixed him rice and broth and plied him with toast and jam—trying to find something that doesn't upset his stomach. It's more his pattern that makes me wonder how long this marriage will last. Oh well, on to the task at hand."

Ellie and I arranged the bags, coasters, and keychains on the kitchen table and got started. We worked in companionable silence punctuated by the occasional exclamation over the antics of the dogs. One minute they'd be lying by the stove or at our feet. The next they'd bark, leap up, and run out of the room.

"You've got such a level head, Leta," said Ellie, "and Belle tells me you're a good listener. That's not a trait you find in many people these days. If only people put as much effort into listening as they do into arguing, we'd have much less conflict in this world."

I wondered where this was going. I'd been told before I was a good listener, and she was right about listening in general. When I worked in Human Resources, we were forever coaching folks to *hear and understand* what someone said *before* preparing a response—or, in many cases, a rebuttal. That advice worked well in business and personal relationships, though people found it difficult to follow.

"You know, Ellie, I like to think I was a decent listener early on in life, maybe because I'm an introvert. But I think it was my years as a leadership trainer that taught me how important that trait is. We used to quote Stephen Covey—

remember *The 7 Habits of Highly Effective People?* Wow! That's a blast from the past. That book came out in the late eighties, and people are still referring to it."

Ellie smiled. "Oh, I remember the book. I attended a seminar on it at the Village Hall. One of the habits was 'Seek first to understand, then to be understood.' Instead, most of us focus on our replies. And therein lies the problem. "

Okay, I thought, *I'm listening and I'm trying to understand. Is this only an intellectual conversation or is there something else going on here?*

"I don't lightly share family goings-on, but I could use an impartial sounding board, dear. May I talk some things through with you while we work?"

Oh! This was a surprise. I knew Ellie from book club and community gatherings, but not well. Maybe the downside to being a countess was being somewhat isolated and not having close friends to confide in, though I knew Libby and Belle considered her a good friend. Perhaps it was a matter of my being in the right place at the right time.

By now, I was dying of curiosity. "Sure, Ellie. I'm happy to listen."

"I'm sure the village is abuzz with talk of Nicholas's plans, and if the grapevine is true to form, it's filled with exaggerations and inaccuracies. The truth is distressing enough. Oh my, where to begin."

And Ellie *looked* distressed. If her hands hadn't been busy with bags and trinkets, I was sure she'd be wringing them. I didn't yet have the full story, and I was hurting for her.

"First, do you understand that the estate is entailed and what that means?" she asked.

"I think I do. Nicholas inherits both the title and the property, but not necessarily any separate investments, right?"

"Yes, dear. Before Nigel became the Earl of Stow, his father thought it important for him to make his own way in the world, and that he did. Did you know he was an RAF pilot in World War II? That background led him to start a small airline that flew routes from the UK to the continent. Richard Branson and others followed in his footsteps, but Nigel was one of the first to see the future and profit from the business.

"Thankfully, he left us all well provided for. I have more than enough to live on, as do Matthew and his family. We're fortunate in that regard. The sticking point is the Manor House and the property. Nigel made provisions in his will for me to live here until I die, and that's been my intent. I hope to go peacefully in my sleep in the home I've lived in for nearly fifty years."

I nodded. "And that's still the plan?"

Tears in her eyes, Ellie gripped the edge of the table. "Unless Nicholas makes it intolerable, and his plans seem designed to do just that."

Here it comes, I thought. *What exactly does the new Earl have in mind for his step-grandmother?*

"What does Nicholas want to do?" I asked.

"He intends to turn my home into a luxury resort, and he's offered me two options, neither of which I find acceptable. If I choose to live out my days in the Manor House, I must leave my bedroom and move my living quarters to an upper floor. He's suggested installing a small kitchenette, as if that would do the trick. Could he really think I'd be content to wither away far from the main level—no longer welcome in the kitchen, the library, the dining room—all the areas in which I've lived my life. Those rooms would be off-limits. Imagine! I could tell he thought he was being gracious when he suggested I could take advantage of room service."

"So, the rumors about the estate becoming a resort are true?"

"Yes, he seems determined to turn this peaceful property into a destination for the rich and famous. I'd probably do well to choose the second option he offered me—retiring to a cottage on the estate. A remodeled cottage, mind you, but a cottage nonetheless."

I had visions of the cottage Carson and Mrs. Hughes had moved to at Downton Abbey. Fine for someone like me, but for Ellie? She'd been Lady Stow, mistress of the manor, for too long for such a drastic shift. At least that's how I saw it.

"Oh Ellie, I can see why you're distressed. That's a lot to digest. If I may ask, what does it mean for Matthew, Sarah, Harry, and Sam?"

"That situation's not nearly as clear. It's not enough Matthew is concerned about me. He may or may not keep his job as Estate Manager, though Nicholas says he's welcome to continue living in the cottage.

"With Nicholas undecided about the sheep, the brewery, and the small cottages used by local artisans, everything is up in the air. Either he's not thought it all through, or he can't bring himself to tell his Uncle Matthew and his cousin Harry their livelihoods may disappear. At least Sam, Matthew's youngest, is off at Cambridge and blissfully unaware of what's going on here.

"And that's just the family. What will happen to the weaver, the spinner, and the others that let the cottages for a pittance? Where will they go if Nicholas's plans don't include them?"

I'm sure I looked shocked. "Oh my gosh, Ellie, I'd heard rumblings about this but hadn't fully grasped all the ramifications, and I hadn't thought of the artisans at all. Frankly, I didn't know what to believe. The rumors of a heliport and tennis courts and goodness know what else seemed bad enough for our bucolic village. Losing you would be unbearable. You, your family, and the Manor House are in many ways the heart and soul of Astonbury."

Ellie gave a shaky laugh. "Thank you, dear. Contemplating the unknown is enough to make one crazy, and I guess that's the state I'm in right now. It's difficult to settle my nerves and make decisions when I don't know what will transpire."

I wasn't sure whether Ellie wanted me simply to listen or also to help her problem-solve. "How can I help, Ellie?"

"You've already helped by letting me talk to you, someone who's not directly impacted. You know what I mean. You may be disturbed by the changes—the construction, the heliport, and goodness knows what else—but it's not personal."

"You're right. The changes to the village are minor compared to the anguish you're going through. I'd be like a deer in headlights if I were in your shoes."

She sighed. "I think that describes my state pretty well. I can't get beyond the uncertainty to consider my options—beyond what Nicholas has offered. I know how fortunate I am Nigel left me comfortably off. That means I could walk away. I could build or purchase another country estate. I could travel for a bit. For me, much depends on what happens with Matthew and the family."

As we'd talked, Blanche and Dickens had taken up position on either side of Ellie's chair. She smiled down at them and seemed talked out. I realized we'd stopped filling bags as she'd shared her story, so I picked one up and resumed work. Ellie followed suit, and we soon finished the task.

I was packing the little bags into boxes when a petite, blue-eyed, blonde came into the kitchen. She sported an Astonbury

Brewery ballcap. Ellie's face lit up. "Leta, have you met our new cook, Caroline? We're so lucky to have her."

At first glance, I took her to be right out of school, likely because of her height and the cap on her head. People always took me for the youngest of my sisters instead of the oldest, and I was sure it was because I was a mere 5'2". A closer look told me Caroline was in her thirties. "I don't think we've met," I said, "but I sampled your delicacies when I attended the last planning meeting. It was a tasty lunch."

The pert blonde smiled. "Thank you. I'd started the week before and was eager to show off a bit. The chicken pie is a recipe from the Chipping Camden Café, where I work several days a week. Now, Ellie, how many will there be for the evening meal?"

Ellie sighed. "That's a good question. Julia won't be here, and I'm not sure about Nicholas. He was up and out early this morning before I came down. And he's still got that stomach bug. If he does join us, he may only want broth. Let's plan on five—Matthew, Sarah, Harry, and me. You always make more than we need, so if Nicholas feels up to it, there will plenty for him."

If Nicholas *did* make it, I foresaw a strained family meal—one where you could cut the tension with a knife. It was hard to imagine them all sitting down together and not discussing the elephant in the room. *The herd of elephants*, I thought.

I declined Ellie's offer of lunch so Dickens and I could walk the estate. Dickens, of course, hoped we'd encounter Basil. I hoped to get a head start on working off the pounds I'd gained on my trip. We meandered in the direction of the River Elfe, which formed a natural boundary to one side of the estate.

Dickens spied the sheep before I did. "Look, Leta. Where there's sheep, there must be a guard dog. Basil never wanders too far from them."

Sure enough, it wasn't long before I heard a deep booming bark and Basil came bounding towards us. "Greetings, Lil' Bit, and you too, Leta. Haven't seen you two in a while."

"Hi there, Basil. How's the herd today?"

"Come see for yourself. I think they know they'll be on display Friday night 'cause they're humming with excitement—well, as much excitement as you can get from sheep."

They trotted toward the sheep in the distance. Dickens knew that one of Basil's littermates had been a dwarf Pyr like Dickens was. The way Dickens told the story, Basil had looked after his sister when their siblings played too hard with her. All the pups in the litter were given names by the breeder, but Basil called his sister Lil' Bit. And that's what he called Dickens the first time he saw him. Dickens had initially gotten huffy, but once he understood the nickname was a term of affection, he was honored—rather than insulted.

I continued toward the river, knowing Dickens would find me eventually. I could see the waterwheel in the distance and made my way in that direction. I was a frequent visitor to the Olde Mill Inn, and the waterwheel was one of its distinguishing features. I'd never viewed it from this side of the river.

The River Elfe wasn't very wide. In some spots it was deep, and in others shallow enough to wade across. The waterwheel still turned, though it no longer ground wheat as it had in the 1900s. To the right of the wheel splashing through the water was Gemma's cottage.

Libby and Gavin had restored the small building as a one-bedroom guest cottage when they'd purchased the property. They'd left the mill intact and transformed another small building into a garage and the largest structure into the inn proper. When Gemma transferred to the Stow-on-the-Wold police station from the Thames Valley force, her parents had happily installed her in the cottage.

I wondered what they thought of Nicholas's big plans for the land directly across the river from them. I was soon to find out.

Chapter Four

L ibby and Gavin didn't often take a break from their jobs as innkeepers, but Tuesdays and Wednesdays tended to be slow days for them. Guests who came for a long weekend departed on Monday and the bulk of the next weekend's crowd arrived Thursday or Friday.

This week they had only one couple staying Sunday through Saturday and wanted to take advantage of the midweek lull to have lunch at the Ploughman Pub on Wednesday. Along with the usual gang—Peter, Wendy, Belle, Rhiannon, Beatrix, and Toby—I'd received an email to that effect Monday evening. It was doubtful Beatrix and Toby would be able to leave their shops, but I expected the rest of us would show up.

Intent on getting in plenty of exercise, I informed Dickens we'd skip his morning walk in favor of a longer trek to the pub at lunch. He thought that was a grand plan. I dressed in my quilted black parka, my plaid scarf, and my red beret. I looked longingly at the pair of leather gloves my sister Sophia had brought me from her latest trip to Italy but decided against them. They were fashionable—black with each finger outlined in a different jewel tone—but they weren't lined, and I knew a long walk on a chilly day required warm gloves.

Dickens, unlike many of the dogs we encountered, didn't need a cute coat to keep him warm. His long white fur was coat enough, and he bounced up and down in excitement as I grabbed his leash.

"Oh boy, donkeys! Do you have the carrots, Leta?"

"Oh yes. My brain has finally recovered from my jet lag, and I've got 'em right here in my pocket."

At the stone fence bordering the donkeys' pasture, Dickens rose on his hind legs to get as close as possible to Martha and Dylan. The pair helped out by lowering their noses so he could lick them. I kept telling myself I had to get a photo of the three of them, but with a leash, carrots, and now gloves to juggle, it was an impossible task. Maybe when Dave came and we walked together, he could take one. I smiled at the thought of him arriving at the end of the month.

I spied Wendy and Belle seated near one of the fireplaces when we arrived at the Ploughman, and Dickens did too. I dropped his leash when he tugged, and he went straight to Belle. By the time I made my way to the table, she had removed his leash and he'd settled himself at her feet beneath the table.

I kissed Belle on the cheek as I took my seat. "Well, he didn't waste any time getting comfortable, did he?"

Belle laughed. "I do believe he considers me his grandmother. What do you think?" Close to ninety years old with a head of white hair, Belle looked the part.

Wendy added, "Then I guess that makes me and Peter his aunt and uncle. And, by the way, how's Christie—or Miss Priss, as I think of her?"

We chatted and laughed about our pets and their personalities as we waited for the rest of our crowd. Libby and Gavin were the next to arrive, and they confirmed what I'd surmised —Beatrix and Toby didn't feel they could sneak away this week —but they were expecting Rhiannon and Peter to make it.

Once the whole gang was there, we motioned Barb over to take our orders. It was hard for me to stick to soup and salad when most of my friends were ordering hearty sandwiches, but I managed. It helped that Rhiannon, our resident vegetarian, ordered a salad too. I did, however, indulge in a midday pint.

Libby sipped her Astonbury Pale Ale and sighed. "It's nice to have a break. Starting Thursday, we'll have a full house at the inn, and then we've got the tree lighting Friday evening." She raised her glass. "And here's to Jill. Thank goodness she's baking all the cookies for Friday."

As I toasted Jill, I asked, "And do I get to sample them when I come over to put them in bags?"

Gavin winked and stroked his greying goatee. "That goes without saying, but I think Libby's counting on you to keep it to only one or two. She's not letting me anywhere near the kitchen when the preparation starts because I can't resist sweets. Smelling those cookies baking every day for the past month has been almost more than I can bear."

The talk of Jill's cookies led to a discussion of the contributions from the village businesses. Rhiannon told us she was giving away string bracelets of green and red, and Toby had Jenny, Jill's sister, putting together voile bags containing a teabag and a coupon for the Tearoom. I shared what Beatrix was giving away and what I'd prepared with Ellie on Monday.

Peter spoke up. "Looks like the weather will be good too—crisp and cold. The nursery is delivering the tree this afternoon, and George and I will put the lights on it Thursday. We'll set out the boxes of ornaments Friday afternoon, and the local school children will have the tree decked out in time for the lighting at seven. Thank goodness Deborah Watson is supervising the decorating. Last year, I was in charge of that and keeping an eye on the kids. I can't say I was particularly good at it."

We all laughed at that, and Wendy recalled seeing her brother chase a pre-schooler who was intent on throwing one of the large woven ornaments for his dog to fetch. The little boy was convinced it was a dog toy.

The chatter died down as Barb delivered our orders. That was also the cue for Dickens to become more alert in anticipation of someone sneaking him a snack. I watched as first Peter and then Gavin tore off chunks of their burgers and reached under the table with them. I cleared my throat, and they both looked at me innocently.

Dickens barked, "Hey, Leta, don't spoil it for me. Just because you're trying to lose your Thanksgiving weight doesn't mean I should suffer."

What could I do but shake my head, especially when Peter said, "I think Dickens wants another bite."

"Of course, he does," I responded, "and when he becomes a little butterball, I'll know who to blame." Seeing Harry and Matthew walk in, I added, "Ask Harry. He'll tell you this breed doesn't require as much food as people think."

We all waved at the two. Though they waved back, they moved to a table in the far corner without coming over to say hello. Gavin leaned into the center of our table and spoke softly. "I'm sure they've plenty to discuss, what with Nicholas making their lives a misery."

Rhiannon studied Gavin a moment and said, "I know you

and Matthew are big friends. Do you know the truth behind the rumors?"

Fury flashed in Gavin's eyes. "I sure do, and it's not pleasant. If only Nigel had thought to change the entail on the property after Reggie died."

"What does that mean?" I asked.

It was Belle who explained. "The title had to pass to Nicholas as the male descendant of the oldest son, but Nigel could have altered the entail on the property so that Matthew and Harry inherited part or all of it.

"According to Ellie, he never saw a need to do that when Reggie was alive. Despite the differences in their ages and Reggie living in New York City, he and Matthew were close and were in agreement as to how to run the estate. Reggie planned to retire and play the country squire and wanted Matthew to continue living in his cottage and managing the estate as he always has. And Nigel felt it best to have one person own everything so there was no danger the property would be broken up."

I could see I wasn't the only one who had to process the details. Rhiannon asked, "But when Reggie died, why didn't the Earl do something? Why didn't he take care of things then?"

Belle sighed. "They say the hardest thing in the world is to lose a child. Nigel didn't foresee outliving his son. Though he was in his nineties, he was in decent health until Reggie died. Ellie says the grief took its toll, and he went downhill. Six months after Reggie's death, Nigel was gone too. Is it any wonder he didn't deal with the entail?"

I was dumbstruck. I hadn't known the details because Reggie'd died before I moved into my cottage. I'd met Ellie at a book club meeting early on, but she'd stopped coming when

Nigel's health took a turn for the worse. We'd reconnected at the November meeting and gotten to know each other better at several planning meetings for the tree lighting.

We all looked at Gavin as he started to interject, but Libby gave him one of those looks—one only a wife can give. "Never mind," he said.

It was at that moment the voices from the far corner grew loud. I couldn't make out what Matthew and Harry were saying to each other, but it only took a glance to see they were arguing. Harry started to rise, and Matthew put his hand on his son's arm as if to sit him down. Harry sat, but he slammed his fist on the table. Other customers were looking at them too. Matthew said something, and Harry put his face in his hands. They quieted down after that, and most of the clientele went back to their conversations. Our table was a little slower to recover.

Gavin said, "There's a reason they call him Hotspur Harry —boy's got a quick temper. He and Matthew arguing can't be good. If Harry's upset with Nicholas, that's to be expected, but I hope he's not angry with his dad too."

Wendy smiled. "I haven't heard the name Hotspur in ages. I seem to recall he died at the Battle of Shrewsbury in the 1400s."

Rhiannon blinked in surprise. "How on earth do you know that?"

Belle had a ready answer about her daughter's knowledge. "She knows because she taught English, and Hotspur Harry was a character in Shakespeare's Henry IV. He rebelled against the king. Let's hope our Harry isn't planning a rebellion of his own."

Dickens could hardly contain himself as I donned my coat, hat, and gloves for the walk home. "Hurry, hurry. I've got to fill you in," he barked.

I wondered what he thought he knew. There'd been lots of information shared at our table, but surely he understood I'd taken it all in. *Did the conversation remind him of something he'd heard from Blanche or Basil? Who knew?*

He was so excited, he pranced down the gravel drive. "Leta, have you forgotten my hearing is way sharper than yours? I bet you didn't hear what Matthew and Harry were saying, did you?"

I stopped for a moment and looked at him. "You did? I mean, I know you hear better than I do, but they were across the room."

"I heard every word. I may not be able to repeat it all, but I can tell you most of it. They were arguing about Nicholas. Harry's upset about the sheep, for starters. Seems Nicholas wants to reduce the herd and pen them up or get rid of them altogether. He thinks they're bad for the environment."

"What? How can sheep be bad?"

"That part was more than I could keep up with. The only small piece I understood was something about the sheep being hard on the pasture. Matthew's take is that Nicholas has read just enough on the internet to be dangerous. I don't understand that either—how does reading make you dangerous?"

I laughed and explained to Dickens the phrase didn't mean dangerous the way he and I thought about it. "I certainly don't know enough about the impact of sheep on the land to argue one way or the other."

Dickens went on. "I think I heard something about making it clean so the guests of the resort can wander without worrying about stepping in sheep 'you know what' all over the property."

"Oh for goodness' sake," I said. "We've wandered the pastures and managed to avoid sheep poop. What's wrong with Nicholas? Has he been a city boy too long? Has he forgotten the time he spent here as a child? From all accounts, he enjoyed his brief visits—sheep and all."

"Leta, it sounded like Nicholas's ideas don't sit well with either Harry or Matthew, but Matthew wants to wait him out. He thinks the more ideas they let Nicholas toss out, the sooner he'll abandon the ridiculous ones. He said something about scattershot I didn't quite catch."

I thought for a moment. "It sounds to me like Matthew advises being patient and letting Nicholas run in circles until he settles down. Maybe he knows Nicholas better than Harry does, but it doesn't surprise me Harry's upset. And now that I've heard his nickname, it surprises me even less."

"Well, Basil said Harry'd been sad and angry lately. Could this be why?"

Not much gets by our four-legged companions. Basil had sensed something was off with Harry, much as Blanche and Dickens had tuned into Ellie's distress. It struck me that Dickens had used the phrase "for starters" when he began sharing what he'd heard.

"Dickens, what's Harry upset about besides the sheep?"

"Something about Matthew and the brewery, but I was more interested in the sheep."

No wonder Harry was upset, I thought. *The sheep are his babies, so to speak.* Nicholas was trampling all over the one thing Harry considered his own, the enterprise he managed for Astonbury Manor. Matthew had overall responsibility for the estate and had gotten the brewery going, but Harry had put his heart and soul into the sheep. Together, father and son had made going concerns of both.

My curiosity was piqued, and I wondered how I could get more details. *Gavin would know,* I thought. *Time to invite myself over for a glass of wine with my friends. Time to get the scoop.*

Chapter Five

C hristie was nowhere to be seen when we arrived at the cottage, so I had time to light the fire and put the kettle on before she demanded a dab of wet food. A cup of tea in hand, I was studying the wine rack in the pantry when I heard her meow as she came yawning into the kitchen. "What are you doing in the pantry? Getting me a new can of food, I hope."

I watched as she stretched and flopped onto her side. Henry had referred to that move as her "flop and roll" technique. That position made anyone who saw it want to lean over and rub her fluffy belly, and I did just that. "Yes, dear, I'll get your food as soon as I decide on a bottle of wine to take to the inn. I'm about to call Libby and invite myself over for an after-dinner drink."

Christie righted herself and strolled to her dish while I opened a can of food and carefully forked a dab into the dish for inspection. The initial bit met with her approval, but she took only a taste or two before meowing loudly. "It's moved to the edge and needs to be centered and fluffed, please." She was quite particular and demanding. After several more rounds of fluffing, she indicated she'd had enough by strolling to my office. *How did she know I had work to do?* I thought.

Dickens followed us to my desk, I gave Christie a treat from the supply in the drawer, and the three of us had a peaceful afternoon. I, of course, was the only one working. Several more columns would be due in December, so I considered ideas for the next few weeks. I'd already sent off the one about my time in New York City. Another about the Astonbury Tree Lighting was a must. Maybe because I was already listening to Christmas CDs on my small CD player, I thought about writing a column on my favorite holiday tunes.

I'd missed my daily routine while I'd been in the States. The Christmas music column came together easily, and I'd tackle the tree lighting topic this weekend after the Friday night event. *'Tis the season*, I thought.

My call to the inn inviting myself for a visit was met with enthusiasm from Libby. She reminded me I hadn't yet shared the details of my visit to New York City, and that she'd be all ears. Since Dickens and Christie were snoozing in front of the fireplace, I decided to go solo to see my friends.

I broke into a huge grin when I pulled into the driveway to the inn. Gavin had put Christmas lights on the sign at the entrance and the rowan tree in the center of the courtyard. The sign also had a large wreath hanging on it. As I approached the front door, I realized that Raggedy Ann and Andy were also trimmed in lights and had some new accessories. The scarecrows had been auctioned off at the Fall Fête, and Libby had been bound and determined to win the whimsical pair.

She came out as I was admiring the handiwork. "What do you think of their scarves and mittens?" she asked. "I thought the candy cane stripe was the right touch."

"They're adorable. If they hold up, maybe you can do something else for Valentine's Day."

"I'm way ahead of you," she said. "I think as long as I replenish their straw stuffing from time to time, they'll last quite a while. I see bunny rabbits and a basket of colorful eggs at their feet for Easter, and who knows what after that." She looked down at the cat, who'd followed her out. "As long as I can convince Paddington they're not cat trees, that is. I've had to peel him off several times already."

Paddington glanced my way and grumbled. "Of course they're cat trees, especially with the knit scarves I can dig my claws into."

I chuckled about Paddington as we walked inside. Libby directed me to the sitting room and took the bottle of wine to the kitchen to uncork. I found Gavin in his favorite chair with his feet propped on the ottoman, a tray of cheese and crackers and three wine goblets already on the coffee table.

"Libby tells me we finally get to hear about your trip to New York—and, of course, your visit with Dave. I can't believe you've been home since Sunday, and she's lasted this long without hearing all about it."

Libby caught that line as she walked in with the wine. "Right. Like you're not just as interested as I am."

That was one of the things I enjoyed most about the couple—their comfortable banter. I'd become almost a member of the family when I stayed with them while I was househunting, and I'd never heard a cross word pass between them. They were also my only Astonbury friends who'd gotten to know Henry, as we'd stayed a week at the Olde Mill Inn when we'd visited the area a few years back.

I chattered away about my trip, and then we spoke of decorating and putting up our trees. Libby had begun her indoor decorating but wasn't quite done. The stockings were hung from the mantle and festive candles were scattered about, but she planned to put greenery on the mantel, down the stairway banister, and around the common areas.

Gavin sipped his wine and asked, "Do you need help getting your tree? I could probably find some time on Sunday if you do."

"Believe it or not, Peter's already offered, and we're going Saturday to get three trees—one for Wendy and Belle, one for Peter, and one for me. That's the beauty of having a friend with a pickup. I'm picturing my tree in the sitting room, maybe in front of the windows that look out on the garden. I have so many ornaments that I may get a second, smaller one for my office."

Our conversation drifted to the tree lighting and then took a natural turn to the fate of Astonbury Manor. *Phew*, I thought. *I didn't even have to ask.*

Gavin refilled our wine glasses. "I think the tree lighting will go off without a hitch, at least logistically. Astonbury will be decked out in its Christmas finery, and the tourists and locals alike will enjoy the festivities and the shopping. What concerns me is the tension between the new Earl and his family, not to mention the worry the situation's causing the rest of us.

"The good news for the majority of the villagers is they don't know what's at stake personally for Lady Stow, Matthew, Sarah, and the boys. So they're not worried by that uncertainty.

They are, however, distressed about the talk of the resort. Sure, it could mean a few jobs for the locals, but not enough to offset the disruption to our tranquil little world. It's the beauty and serenity of Astonbury that brings the tourists our way."

I nibbled a cracker and nodded as Libby spoke up. "I simply cannot fathom Nicholas suggesting Ellie move out of the bedroom she shared with Nigel all these years. He's taking the wording of the will quite literally—it states she can live out her days at Astonbury Manor, but of course it doesn't specify in which rooms, for goodness' sake."

I nodded. "Yes, Ellie explained that to me when I was there working on the bags for Friday night. It sounds rather heartless. As if that weren't enough, she's worried about Matthew, Harry, and Sam."

Gavin harrumphed. "As well she should be. Sam's been off at Cambridge reading history like his dad did before him, so he's not been exposed to the turmoil yet, but Harry? He's especially devoted to his Cotswolds Lions. Even before he attended the Royal Agriculture College, he was passionate about those sheep. They were a mainstay of the Cotswolds in the Middle Ages, and they all but died out in the latter part of the twentieth century. He started with around twenty and now has a herd of close to a hundred. He's focused on increasing the number and helping bring back the breed."

Libby chimed in. "And he's done it all himself. From that foundation, his mum Sarah has built a profitable soap business with the sheep's milk, and he's got spinners and weavers set up in the small cottages scattered across the estate. He's active in the Cotswolds Sheep Society, and he's known for having top-of-the-line sheep. Nicholas is threatening to throw a spanner in all that."

I had some idea of why Nicholas was bent on getting rid of

the sheep based on what Dickens had overheard, but surely there had to be more to it than his distaste for sheep poop. "What's Nicholas got against the sheep?"

"Aw hell," said Gavin, "he doesn't like the looks of the lambing shed and shearing barn, and he's full of talk about climate change, pollution, and the impact of Brexit. Frankly, I think he's barmy. "

"I agree," added Libby. "Ellie says he's also mentioned wanting to crisscross the estate with walking paths. She and Nigel had already put in a path around the boundaries. Why add more?"

I thought for a moment. "Not that I agree with that plan, but could it be so guests don't have to walk the entire way around—so they can take shorter walks?"

Libby shook her head. "Who knows? There are already paths to the various cottages and the brewery. And if he *does* go ahead with his ideas for tennis courts, a pool, and a helicopter pad, for goodness' sake, there'll be plenty of paths. Let's hope he's not considering paving anything. Ellie says he's tossed out so many ideas, it's difficult to keep up."

Gavin sat forward. "Hell, he's not even sure what he wants to do with the brewery."

"Why does he have to do something with it?" I asked. "Haven't Matthew and Harry only recently resurrected it and made a going concern of it? I think there's something special about ordering Astonbury Ale at the Ploughman. You'd think Nicholas would see it as good PR."

"Not exactly a going concern," murmured Gavin. "I mean, Matthew's invested heavily in getting it going. Brought in an experienced brewer early on, but now he mostly handles it himself. He tells me it will pay for itself probably in another year and then start to turn a profit. That's why

64

they've kept it small and supply only nearby pubs in the Cotswolds. They send out kegs in small vans, not large lorries."

"I should ask Matthew for a tour," I said. "I understand it's one of the few open-vat breweries still in existence."

"It's unique in that regard," said Gavin, "and it's one of only two log-fired breweries in the country. By all means, take a tour. It's an impressive operation, but if Nicholas should decide to enlarge the original structure, it could lose its charm. Seems our new Earl alternates between wanting to shut it down and wanting to bring in so-called experts to expand it."

Libby went to the kitchen to get another bottle of wine. When she returned, Gavin and I were glad to see she'd also brought a small plate of Christmas cookies. Sampling Jill's sugar cookies made me think of possibly baking some Greek cookies for the holidays. It was time I dug out my recipe for kourabiedes and stocked up on almonds and powdered sugar.

"So, Gavin," I asked, "setting aside the concern for Ellie and the family, how do you see this impacting the Olde Mill Inn with the estate being just across the river?"

Libby choked on her sip of wine. "Oh my, Leta, you don't want to get him started."

Gavin wasn't taking the hint. "For starters, can you imagine helicopters landing in the pasture when you're sitting in our garden or the conservatory? I have an image of them landing at all hours disturbing our guests, not to mention us. Libby and I left London for what we hoped would be the quiet countryside.

"And you should be concerned about the increased traffic on Schoolhouse Lane. The Manor house has twenty bedrooms. If Nicholas remodels it with plenty of bathrooms, there will be guests coming and going nonstop. And he's talking about turning the main level into a bar and restaurant. Think about it."

I *was* thinking about it. That last bit was news to me. "Oh! I certainly don't want traffic in front of my cottage. I enjoy my quiet walks to see the donkeys and you two. I wonder what the business owners on High Street think about the resort idea. There's no doubt it would bring in more business."

Gavin reached for the last cookie. "It's interesting. They have mixed feelings. On the one hand, more business can't hurt—if, in fact, that's the result."

"Why wouldn't it be?"

"Here's the thing. The resort would bring in new visitors, but it could very well drive others away. Already, tourists complain about the crowds in places like Bourton-on-the-Water, and Astonbury benefits from that. Plenty of people visit our village and a few others off the beaten path because they want to walk up and down High Street without being crushed in a crowd. They like being able to find a parking place and get into restaurants without reservations. If they wanted the crowds of London, they'd stay there."

I could tell Gavin had the pulse of the village. "So, what does the consensus seem to be among the businesses?"

"Most are against the resort idea. When they think it through, they see maintaining the ambiance of Astonbury as the best path long-term, even if it means forgoing some short-term increases in sales. If you listen carefully Friday night, you're bound to pick up on what they're thinking."

Libby sat back and gazed at the fire. "Time to change the subject, don't you think? Have you shown Leta your birthday present?"

I'd missed Gavin's late November birthday when I was in the States. He grinned and went to the bookshelves. The floor-to-ceiling shelves on either side of the fireplace were filled with a mix of books, porcelain figurines, and World War II memorabilia. Also displayed was Gavin's small collection of knives—ranging from some he'd had as a child to more recent acquisitions.

He brought me a folding knife, one that was unique in its design. "Have you ever seen such beautiful craftsmanship?" he asked. "I've long coveted those Nigel had displayed in his library—especially the one that belonged to his father and grandfather before him, and Libby searched until she found this one."

"Oh! It's lovely, Gavin. I recall you and Henry discussing your collection because he had one too. I gave it to my brother-in-law Andrew before I moved."

"You'll have to tell Andrew about this one, then. It's a Capuchadou, a knife carried by French shepherds who used it for everything from preparing their lunches to caring for their flocks of sheep. See the four-leaf clover with the reddish Cora-line gemstone in the center? It's for good luck."

I touched the carving as I turned it over in my hand. "Was Nigel's identical to this?"

"A bit. His is a Laguiole that's been in the family since the late 1800s. It was his grandfather's and was handcrafted in France. This is a Capuchadou also crafted in France, but this design preceded Nigel's Laguiole, so I'm mighty proud of it. I wish I could have shown it to him. Of course, I don't have a family story to go with it." He handed me a penny from the bookshelf. "Do you know the superstition about knives as gifts?" he asked.

I shook my head no and he regaled me with the story. "There's some disagreement as to when the superstition originated, but it's long been believed that giving a knife to someone will sever your relationship with that person. It's even worse to give knives as a wedding gift because it will sever the bonds of marriage. The antidote to that bad luck is to give a penny with the knife, so the recipient can turn around and give it back. So, in this case, Libby gave me a penny taped to the knife, and I gifted it back to her. Voila! Our relationship has not been cut!"

"Gee, I'm thinking someone gave Henry and me a set of knives in a butcher block as a wedding gift. Luckily for us, there were no ill effects."

Libby added. "As you can imagine, Gavin has been on the receiving end of quite a few pennies from Gemma and me. When all else fails, knives are our go-to gift for him, though I must admit, I had quite a time finding this particular one. Now, it's not just shepherds who want them for practical purposes. Collectors want them for the craftsmanship."

I laughed at the thought of Gavin's pennies as I handed him his knife. "You're not carrying it in your pocket?"

"Not a chance! This is a collector's item. My trusty Swiss Army knife is the only thing going in my pocket."

"Thanks for the history lesson, Gavin. It's fascinating, particularly the part about the shepherds. Because Dickens is a Great Pyrenees, I've always been intrigued by the stories of his ancestors guarding flocks of sheep through the centuries, and how the shepherds use the knives adds another aspect to the tale."

Libby cocked her head and said, "Heard a car. That must be Gemma, and she's early, for a change. Let me see if she'd like to join us."

Before Libby could get up, we heard Gemma holler hello. She popped her head in the sitting room and said, "Oooh. Is there enough left in that bottle for me? Let me make a sandwich, and I'll be right back."

When she returned, she set her plate down and shed her suit jacket. To me, Gemma always looked professional no matter how early or late it was. She favored dark suits and crisp white blouses and wore minimal makeup. The look suited her blonde hair and fair complexion.

"I see you're showing off your knife, Dad. I think it may be the best one yet."

Gavin smiled at his daughter. "You could be right, dear. When I showed it to Matthew, I think I saw a hint of jealousy. A rare thing for a man who owns a Laguiole."

"Gemma," I asked, "will you be able to attend the tree lighting and Ellie's birthday party this weekend, or are you on duty? I expect it's not easy to get two weekend nights off."

"You're right, so I've opted for Friday night. I'd much rather see the tree lighting and all that goes with it than attend a black-tie affair, and I'm especially looking forward to hearing the St. Andrews choir sing Christmas carols. To me, watching the children decorate the tree on the Village Green is the true start of the season."

"Well, my season kicked off with my trip to New York City. It was magical, and I've been listening to Christmas carols ever since. But Christmas in England? I see the tree lighting Friday and then getting my tree up on Saturday as the official start of my first Christmas here—in my very own Cotswolds cottage. That reminds me, I'm planning a Trim the Tree party for next Saturday. Any chance you'll be able to get another weekend night off?"

Gemma chuckled. "Not likely in the best of circumstances, but I was selected to attend a week-long leadership course at the College of Policing, and I leave on Monday. Hate to miss a party at your place, though, especially if you're making pastitsio again. That and your Greek salad are hands down the best I've ever had."

Receiving a compliment from Gemma was always good, as we were often at odds. Oh, we managed to get along and joke in social settings, but we'd locked horns over the past several months when she thought I was sticking my nose into her murder investigations. Truth be told, I *did* stick my nose in, but she finally admitted both times that my involvement was helpful. I got bent out of shape when she chastised me and rolled her eyes at me, but I could only laugh when she called me *Leta Nosy Parker*.

"Tell you what, I'll wrap up a portion and send it home with your mum. And I'll probably bake some Greek cookies too, and send a few of those. I try hard to give most of them away because if they're sitting in my house, I can't resist 'em. Now, tell me about this course. Is it a step towards becoming a Detective Inspector?"

At that question, an uneasy look appeared on Gemma's face. "Yes, and no. It's not a requirement for promotion, but it helps. The higher-ups are concerned we've had two murders in our area since September when we haven't had any for several years. That started talk of the Stow station needing a DCI— Detective Chief Inspector. I honestly think they might promote me to Detective Inspector as a preventative measure."

I had to think about that for a minute. Gemma was a Detective Sergeant, so the DI job would be a step up and one step away from becoming a DCI. "Not that having a new title would help you prevent murders, but it would *prevent* them from having to add another person to the staff? Something like that?"

"Pretty much. As a Detective Inspector, I'd take direction from an existing DCI in a larger Cotswolds station, and they wouldn't have to add one here in Stow. Sure, I want a promotion, but I would have preferred to get it another way—not because we've had two murders. Like you and I have discussed, we have a manpower issue. Promoting me keeps management from having to increase our station numbers."

Now it was my turn to roll my eyes, not at Gemma, but the management comment. "You know, it sounds much like the way it was when I worked in banking. It was all about the staffing numbers. You might get a promotion, and then almost immediately you'd be asked how you could do more with less. Must be the same all over." I grinned. "Words cannot express how very glad I am not to have to worry about those things any longer."

That seemed a good note to end the evening on. I drank my last sip of wine, thanked my hosts, and told Gavin I'd see him at book club Thursday night.

Chapter Six

Dickens and Christie were trying to convince me to take them to the Book Nook when Wendy pulled up in the driveway. "I want to see Tommy and Tuppence," meowed Christie, "and you promised you'd take me back to the Book Nook."

"Me too," barked Dickens. "And aren't you discussing my namesake tonight? All the more reason to take me." I'd taken them both for a visit in October, and ever since Christie had gotten her backpack, the pair pretty much expected to be taken everywhere.

"Not tonight," I said. "Three cats and a dog chasing each other around the book shop wouldn't go over well during our discussion." The barking and screeching I heard as I locked the door behind me left no doubt as to how they felt about being left behind. *You'd think I'd locked them in the cupboard instead of a nice warm house with plenty of food and water.*

As I climbed in Wendy's car, she exclaimed, "I can't wait to discuss this book. You know how I enjoy biographies, and I think this novel comes close to being one."

"My feelings exactly. I was up late googling Charles Dickens. It's amazing how much the book incorporates actual events and people. I never considered the literary giants who were gaining fame at the same time as he was. Who knew he socialized with the likes of William Makepeace Thackeray and Wilkie Collins?"

"I know what you mean. Have you read all of his books? I think people expect we English teachers have read everything the greats wrote, but I haven't read that many of his."

"That makes me feel better, especially since you taught high school English much longer than I did. I'm pretty sure I only read *David Copperfield, A Tale of Two Cities,* and *Great Expectations.* I saw *The Mystery of Edwin Drood* as a play. Does that count?"

Wendy chuckled. "Sure it does. I read the same plus *Oliver Twist.* And I've seen *The Christmas Carol* as a play a gazillion times. Bet you remember the Mister Magoo version too."

That made me hoot. Watching the cartoon version of Dickens's book had been a fixture of my childhood, and I was pretty sure I'd watched it the first time it ever came on. Wendy and I were both laughing as we parked in front of Beatrix's book shop.

We were arriving early so that we could package Beatrix's doodads for the Friday tree lighting. Wendy had generously offered to help, and we could make short work of the assignment with two of us working on it. That meant all I had left on my list of to-dos were the cookies for Libby.

Beatrix was busy behind the counter when her niece Trixie opened the front door to usher us in. Over a frilly white blouse, Trixie was wearing a green velvet vest, or waistcoat as the Brits called it, and a matching ribbon in her strawberry blonde hair. Beatrix was dressed in a matching outfit and had arranged the counter with tonight's book club selection plus several versions of *A Christmas Carol* and other works by Dickens. A few biographies were also displayed.

The front window featured Christmas books tucked beneath and around a six-foot tree. For children, I spied *The Polar Express* and *The Night Before Christmas* along with *How the Grinch Stole Christmas* and *The Snowman*. "Wendy, look," I said, "did you know Agatha Christie wrote a Christmas mystery? *Hercule Poirot's Christmas*? I've got to get it."

Wendy furrowed her brow. "Mum's such a Hercule Poirot fan, I bet she knows that, but I don't think she has the book. Odd that we didn't see it displayed when we visited Dame Agatha's summer house in October. The marketing staff at Greenway should have had it out."

We'd allowed an hour for filling the voile bags, and Beatrix had them set up in the backroom. The two of us quickly settled on a process—I inserted magnets and coupons and handed the bags to Wendy, and she attached a candy cane to each ribbon as she tied the bags shut.

We had them put together and neatly placed in a box with time to spare, and Wendy's eyes lit up as she surveyed our work. "Those bags are lovely, if I do say myself."

I high fived her and agreed. "I'd say we know a thing or two about getting things done. Now, let's enjoy the rest of the evening."

Our monthly book club meetings at the Book Nook were usually well attended, but there was so much going on this holiday season, I wasn't sure what the crowd would be like tonight. As we walked back to the front of the shop, Rhiannon hurried in, her long blonde hair flying. She always had to rush to make the meeting after her last class at Let It Be Yoga. She pointed to the left of the counter. "Look at that! Beatrix decorated her scarecrow for Christmas."

I turned in that direction. The librarian scarecrow Beatrix had gotten at the Fall Fête wore a Santa hat and a Christmas apron. Tucked in her arms and the big pocket of the apron were more Christmas books.

I put my purse and book in a chair and headed towards the refreshments. Gavin had poured two glasses of wine and was moving toward the row of chairs. "I saved you ladies seats with me and Ellie."

"Oh, that's right, Ellie's leading part of the discussion tonight. I'll be there as soon as I get my wine." I waved to Rhiannon and Wendy and pointed toward Ellie. They got the message and made their way to the seats Gavin had saved for us.

It was nice to have Ellie back at book club. She'd only been to one meeting in the spring when I'd first arrived in Astonbury. That was around the time the Earl's health had begun to decline, and she hadn't felt comfortable leaving him alone at night. For her return, she'd asked Beatrix if she could share a story from *Sketches by Boz* after Gavin led the discussion of tonight's novel. I'd never heard of that book until I found it on the internet the night before.

When Beatrix brought the meeting to order, I was surprised to see we had a full house. She introduced Gavin, and he led a fascinating discussion of the book. As I'd discovered in my research, *Martin Chuzzlewit*, the book Dickens had written before *A Christmas Carol*, hadn't been well-received, and his publishers wanted him to quickly write a book for the holidays. How fortunate for us that demand had resulted in the treasured Christmas classic.

"Did you realize Dickens had ten children?" asked Gavin. "Is it any wonder he worried about money despite his fame?"

One of our regulars piped up, "I'd worry too. It's hard enough to feed and clothe the three I have."

"Right," said Gavin. "Given those circumstances, it does make me wonder how he could also support a mistress." Our local innkeeper was doing a good job of keeping us entertained, and that tidbit raised a few eyebrows in the room. I'd seen mention of his mistress, Ellen Ternan, so I wasn't as surprised as the others when Gavin shared the story. Their relationship started in 1857 and supposedly lasted until Dickens's death in 1870. His reading public didn't know, and his biographers theorized it would have ruined him if they had.

"Can you imagine something like that being kept secret in this day and age?" asked Trixie, who had some experience with a cheating spouse. "It would be on the telly and in the papers in no time."

After a lively discussion of the perils of infidelity, Gavin wrapped up his portion and turned the talk over to Ellie. She was well-loved in the village, and the group clapped heartily as she rose from her chair. She held up a book and opened with, "Who's heard of *Sketches by Boz?*"

I was the only one to raise my hand. None of us had known Boz was Dickens's nickname until we read it in *Mr. Dickens and His Carol*. Ellie explained he'd started using that name when he was a reporter, and it had stuck. The book she was holding was a collector's item and was one of only a handful originally published in 1839 as *Sketches by Boz, Illustrative of Every-day Life and Every-day People*. The illustrations by George Cruikshank accompanied by Dickens's descriptions and short stories were published in newspapers over several years, and it was those stories that brought Dickens to the attention of publishers. He began using his real name with the publication of *The Pickwick Papers* 1836 to 1837.

The group had so many questions and comments, we were beginning to run over. We might have continued if Beatrix hadn't reminded us of the time. She had wisely ordered several copies of *Sketches by Boz*, and the group scooped those up along with many of Dickens's other classics. As Trixie showed us out and locked the door, I looked back to see that the countertop was empty. It had been a good night for Beatrix.

Got to get a move on, I thought as I rolled out of bed Friday morning. I'd considered making an early yoga class but thought better of it. Instead, I fixed breakfast for Christie, Dickens, and myself—in that order.

Christie had given me the silent treatment when I returned home the night before, and I knew that was her way of telling me I was not yet forgiven for leaving her behind. I'd learned not to make a big deal of her pouting. Ignoring her led to a resumption of our congenial relationship much sooner than asking questions. Sure enough, all was well this morning.

"The milk was yummy, and I'm ready for my food now." My, my, it was amazing how sweet she could be—on occasion.

Dickens, on the other hand, was perky most all the time. When I opened the door, he ran in from the garden and hit me with a series of rapid-fire questions. "Who are we visiting today? The donkeys? Basil and the sheep? Let's go, Leta."

I almost tripped over him as he darted around. "Hold your horses, boy. Soon enough, we're going to walk past the donkeys and on to the inn. I've got work to do there, packaging cookies for tonight."

I glanced sideways at Christie to see if she'd picked up on the bit about going to the inn. Her ears perked up and she sat back from her bowl. "The inn? I'm going too, right?"

I had created a monster when I got the backpack for her, and she'd been pestering me for a return visit to the inn for over a month. I regularly took her to see the donkeys, but we three hadn't been to the inn together since our initial visit. "Will you be nice to Paddington this time?"

She looked up. "I was polite last time, wasn't I? It was Paddington who was rude."

I rolled my eyes. "Right. He may have been the one making nervous cat sounds, but only because you taunted him. It's his home, remember?"

She stood and stretched and pranced out of the kitchen. Dickens looked at me, ran to Christie's dish, and cleaned it with one swipe of his tongue. "I love it when she leaves me a snack."

And so it went. Our usual morning routine. I bundled up, got the leash and the backpack—and of course, the carrots— and we were soon on our way. We didn't linger long with the donkeys. It was cold, and I was on a mission.

Paddington was outside eyeing Raggedy Ann and Andy when we arrived. He and Dickens had become pals, and he ran over to give my boy a head bump. In the daylight, I could see the wear and tear the Burmese cat had inflicted on the pair. Raggedy Ann's head of red yarn hair looked chewed, and her red and white striped stockings had a few holes. *Libby may have to make them entirely new outfits before long,* I thought.

I mentioned that to Libby when I found her in the kitchen. "I'm counting on them making it through Valentine's in those outfits," she said, "and Jill has offered to make them spring clothes, maybe something in green. That girl is all-around talented."

Jill smiled as she looked up from the trays of cookies she was arranging on the kitchen island. "Aw Libby, you know I love baking *and* sewing, and I'm happy to do it. I've even asked Belle for some ideas about their outfits. She's a pro with her ancient Singer sewing machine."

That comment led to a discussion of the outfits Belle had made Peter and Wendy for the Fall Fête we'd all attended. Peter had been a hit in his Cowardly Lion costume and his twin had looked the spitting image of Peter Pan. I always chuckled when I thought of the two being twins, given Peter was over a foot taller than Wendy. They had the same coloring, but there the similarities ended.

Dickens and Paddington took off together, and I set the backpack on the floor and let Christie out. She chose to stay in the kitchen with us, and after checking out a few chairs, selected a cushioned one for a nap.

Jill brought out the voile bags. "Here you go, Leta. I'm going to change the linens upstairs, but if you need me, just holler. I expect I'll find Paddington and Dickens up there at the top of stairs waiting for me."

Those two had a favorite pastime—diving in and out of the pile of dirty linens Jill accumulated upstairs as she worked. Only when she gathered the pile to take to the laundry room would the two party animals come downstairs in search of a new activity.

I worked on the bags, while Libby prepared a large pot of vegetable soup. "What's Gavin up to? Is he over at the brewery helping Matthew?"

Libby glanced over her shoulder. "Not yet. He's gone to the co-op for groceries for the weekend crowd arriving tonight. Jill wants to make that strawberry cheese ring you told her about as tonight's offering. She's really upped our game as far as hor d'ouevres. Then tomorrow morning, she'll make her usual scones while I prepare a quiche and fruit salad.

"As for helping Matthew, that's this afternoon. This morning, though, he's stopping by the Manor House after his co-op run to deliver some meds for Nicholas. Matthew's tied up with brewery stuff, and Harry's gone to pick up his brother at the train station. Seems Nicholas can't shake this stomach bug he's got, so Ellie asked her doctor to suggest some anti-nausea medicine and asked Gavin to pop into Boots to pick it up."

"Yes, she mentioned he was sick when I saw her Tuesday. Stomach trouble for several days sounds like more than some kind of virus. Wonder if it's the change of diet or something. Does he have a history of stomach ailments?"

Libby shook her head. "I don't know much about Nicholas, much less his health history. Ellie says he wasn't feeling well when he first arrived last Thursday, but he put it down to fatigue and something he ate on the plane. By Tuesday, he was beginning to feel better. Then the next day, he had the same symptoms all over again. Julia got back early afternoon yesterday, and she's been trying to nurse him with the usual assortment of broth, tea, and white rice."

"Hope he feels up to flipping the switch for the tree lighting and saying a few words. This is his big debut as the new Earl. Will his wife have a role too? Since I've never been, I don't know how the Earl and Lady Stow handled things."

"Oh, those two were low-key about most things. Nigel said a few words and flipped the switch. If Ellie had spearheaded some kind of fundraiser for the event that year, she might thank a few people, but mostly she just mingled like the rest of us. They were a bit more formal for her annual December birthday party, but even then the formality was more about attire than behavior. I wonder what it will be like this year. It's got to be sad for Ellie, all these firsts without Nigel—her birthday and Christmas."

I nodded in agreement. *I should plan to spend some time with her after Nicholas and Julia leave, since I know firsthand how she must be feeling. She'd probably be glad of the company.*

I held up two green bags, one in each hand. "That's all the bags, then. What do you think?"

"I think the idea of bags was brilliant, and the cookies with the red sprinkles show off nicely in our green ones. How did Beatrix's red bags turn out? Did you do the candy canes too?"

I grinned. "Oh yes, with Wendy's help, they all turned out fine. We two work well together. The same goes for Ellie. I was going to do it all on my own, but she sat with me, and we had a quiet hour or two getting everything ready. With the bags done, all I have to do is show up tonight and enjoy myself, maybe pitch in if anyone needs help. Can't wait."

Christie stirred and stretched as Jill, Dickens, and Paddington trooped through the kitchen to the laundry room. It was as though she sensed it was time to go home.

For some reason, I couldn't get the new Earl out of my mind as I walked home. Maybe because he kept coming up in conversation. Even at book club Thursday night, I'd picked up bits and pieces of "the new Earl this and the new Earl that." All of Astonbury was waiting to see what his final plans would be. Meanwhile, the grapevine filled in the blanks with what-ifs.

"Dickens, why do I keep wondering what's up with the stomach ailment? Think it's time I emailed Bev for her input?"

Before he could respond, Christie piped up. "Remind me why you not only call her the dog whisperer but also Doctor Beverly? I get that she's forever fostering unruly dogs and turning them into model canine citizens, but what's with the doctor thing?"

Somehow Christie had missed Bev's role among my group of girlfriends. Early in my career, I'd taught high school with several women who had become my long-time gal pals, as I called them. All but Bev had taught English. She'd taught Biology, Anatomy, and every once in a while Psychology. Whenever any of us or someone we knew had a health issue, Bev was our first call. Heck, we called her before we went to see our doctors.

She liked nothing better than to surf the internet and come back with explanations for whatever ailed us. Her responses ranged from "Don't worry about it. It's nothing" all the way to "Run, don't walk, to see your doctor." She'd outline what the issue was in plain English and that would be that. I was sure if I listed the symptoms Nicholas was experiencing, she'd be intrigued and find an explanation.

When I explained all that to Christie, she had a huffy response. "Dog whisperer and people doctor? Fine, as long as you don't rely on her for advice about me. Why she insisted on dragging me out from under the bed and silly things like that, I'll never understand. She doesn't know diddly about cats." I laughed as I recalled Bev's daily reports on keeping my pets while I was househunting in the Cotswolds.

"Why would she?" barked Dickens. "She's never had cats, but she sure understands dogs. She says I'm a perfect gentleman. That means she's an expert."

Dickens was fixated on Bev's dog talents and didn't exactly

answer my question. *No matter,* I thought. *I'll email her about Nicholas as soon as I have some lunch.*

He chose to stay in the garden while I ate and Christie disappeared to my office. I heard meowing from the desk while I washed my soup bowl. Her cries meant she was looking for cat treats. Sometimes, she managed to open the desk drawer where I kept them. Other times, she lay on the desktop with her head hanging over the edge and her little paws working at the left-hand drawer to no avail.

Today, she needed me. I sat down, grabbed the mouse with my right hand, and opened the treat drawer with the other. She stood and walked to the small dish to the right of my computer screen. This was her treat dish, and I sprinkled a few bits into it from a baggie. When she realized that was it, she hung her head over the drawer on the right side—the drawer she liked to curl up in. Funny how we'd fallen into this routine. *Come on*, I thought. *You know she trained you.* I was pretty sure when Henry'd built my desk, he hadn't envisioned the drawers being used for cat treats and cat naps.

I opened my email and saw both Bev and my sister Anna had sent photos of their animals. I dashed off a reply to Anna and then settled in to compose a lengthier response to Bev, one that included my questions about Nicholas.

I told her all about the drama surrounding the new Earl and his plans for Astonbury Manor and then posed my question. I listed the symptoms Ellie had shared with me. I knew Bev would check her go-to medical sites and get back to me.

Mission accomplished, I moved to the sitting room to relax in front of the fire, play Words with Friends, and read the Hercule Poirot Christmas mystery I'd purchased Thursday night. It would soon be time to get ready for the tree lighting. I planned to take Dickens but not Christie. Being outside for several hours after dark would be too chilly for her. Dickens, on the other hand, would be in heaven. The colder, the better.

I'd already been looking forward to the holiday event, but now I was also anticipating meeting the new Earl and forming my own opinion about him. I hoped the Christmas spirit would win the day and that any grumbling about the Earl's plans would be kept to a minimum. *Never a dull moment*, I thought. *Fingers crossed this festive event comes off without a hitch.*

Chapter Seven

I stood in front of my closet, trying to decide which of my several red sweaters to wear for the big night. Since red was my favorite color, I had plenty to choose from. As cold as it was predicted to be, chances were no one would see the sweater until I got to the pub afterward. Before then, I'd have my black quilted jacket zipped to my chin. They might see my red plaid scarf peeking out, but that would be about it.

It would take longer to find a parking place than to walk, so Dickens and I turned right out of the driveway and walked up Schoolhouse Lane toward the village. As we passed the entrance to Astonbury Manor on the left, I saw that the gates were outlined in white lights and the stone pillars on either side sported massive wreaths.

When we reached the end of the lane, I could see the crowd forming on the Village Green across High Street. The Village Hall was lit in white lights, but the tree in the center of the Green was still dark. The Earl would say a few words and throw the switch at seven. That would be the cue for the choir to break into song.

Dickens was straining at his leash. "Leta, I see Basil and Harry. Can we go there first?"

That seemed as good a spot as any to start, so we walked that way, dodging children dressed as elves on our way. Harry was speaking with a tall gentleman dressed in a plaid woolen waistcoat, a red velvet riding jacket, black riding breeches, and knee-high black leather boots. A top hat completed the ensemble.

"Leta," said Harry, "let me introduce you to my cousin Nick." *So this is the new Earl,* I thought.

"Very nice to meet you," I said as I studied him. He was a handsome man with dark brown hair and hazel eyes. There was a faint family resemblance between him and Harry, mostly in their coloring and height.

"Ah, the other American I've heard about," he said as he shook my hand and leaned down to pet Dickens. "Except you're clearly from the South. Whereabouts?"

"Atlanta was my home until I moved here this year, and you and Julia live in New York City, correct? I met her the other day."

"Yes, we do. I get the impression the village may be finding it difficult to adjust to their Earl having an American accent. Hopefully, they will in time."

"It's more than the accent," I heard Harry mutter.

Nicholas either didn't hear Harry or chose to let it go. I turned to Harry and inquired about the sheep. "Guess they're glad of their heavy coats in this weather, as is Basil." Basil was lying amid the flock, and children were reaching over the pen to touch the sheep. Dickens stuck his nose through the wire fencing.

"Yes, it takes cold with snow for the sheep to notice the

low temperature. Basil? He lives for the cold. Guess your Dickens is the same way, isn't he?"

I nodded as I tugged on Dickens's leash. "Dickens is just a mini version of Basil with all the same traits," I said. "Loves the cold, barks incessantly, and has a mind of his own."

"That's a Pyr for you. Ever thought of a small flock for your garden? Dickens would take to them in a heartbeat," he joked.

We were bantering back and forth when Nicholas interjected, "Could be a few available depending on what we decide to do with these."

Harry jerked his head toward his cousin and glared. "Don't need to discuss that tonight, do we?"

Nicholas shrugged. Was it possible he didn't understand how attached Harry was to his Cotswolds Lions? Regardless, this wasn't the place to discuss family business. It seemed a good time for me to check out the kegs manned by Gavin and Matthew.

Getting Dickens to leave the sheep took a bit of coaxing, but he finally barked goodbye. We encountered Gemma as we crossed the Green. I was accustomed to seeing her either in running attire or in her customary dark pantsuit for work. It was good to see her with her guard down, so to speak. Tonight, she was dressed in black leggings, brown leather boots, and a bulky green sweater with a matching knit cap. "Going to get a beer for the little Dickens?" she asked.

"Not a chance," I said. "He thinks I haven't noticed, but he's already eaten a few tidbits folks have dropped on the ground. And you know Toby, Peter, and your dad insist on feeding him scraps from the table when we're at the pub, so he'll get plenty without adding beer to the mix. Are you joining us at the pub tonight?"

Gemma said she'd stop by for a little while, but she had an

early morning shift the next day and wouldn't stay long. There was a walking path between the Ploughman and her cottage at her parents' inn, so she could enjoy a few drinks and walk home.

As I approached the beer table, Gavin waved and poured me a half-pint of Astonbury Ale. "How are sales?" I asked.

"Smashing," answered Matthew. "We should raise a good bit for the Village Hall. And the gold bags with the keychains are going over well too. Thanks for your help with those."

"Oh, it was nothing. I enjoyed spending time with your mother. Is she here somewhere?"

"Last I saw her and Julia, they were with Sarah at the soap table. I see you met my cousin."

"Yes, I did. Is that cheerful outfit the one your dad wore when he lit the tree?"

"Always. Well, at least as far back as I can remember. I can't believe what good shape it's in, but then he only wore it once or twice every December. Oh, here comes my son Sam. Let me introduce you."

Tall like his father but sporting a golden blonde beard, Sam strode up. Except for the beard, he was the spitting image of his dad. After the introductions, Sam grabbed a beer. "Want me to take over so you can make the rounds, Dad?"

"Thanks, son. Yes, I'd like to stop by the table of woolens made on the Estate and see how your mum's doing with her soap. And I can smell the sausage pasties they're selling in the Village Hall. I could do with a snack to tide me over until we get to the pub."

Dickens must have had the same idea because I caught him ducking beneath the beer table. "What are you after down there? Another scrap?"

"Yes, a crust, maybe with some meat. Can't I have it, please?" All I could do was chuckle and shake my head no.

As I stood up, I overheard Sam speaking. "Gav, when Harry picked me up at the train station this morning, he was in a state, almost incoherent with anger. Can't get a word out of Dad. He says we'll talk about everything when the tree lighting and Gran's birthday party are over. Are things as bad as Harry thinks?"

Gavin rolled his eyes and grunted. "That they are. The business about the sheep—will they stay or will they go—is messing with your brother's head. He's got to rein in his temper. Being furious won't change anything."

This was old news to me, so I wandered off and Dickens pranced along beside me. I saw Trixie handing out the red bags from the Book Nook. She was dressed in her same green vest and headband and a skirt that looked familiar.

"Isn't that Beatrix's skirt?" I asked. "Or did you find one to match?"

"Good eye, Leta. This one belongs to Aunt Beatrix, and she thought its design of book covers would be just the thing for me to wear tonight. I've gotten lots of comments about it, so I think she was right. Maybe folks will remember the book skirt and the Book Nook and stop by the shop."

I cupped my hand to her ear and whispered, "How are you managing to keep it up, given your aunt isn't as slim as you are?" We both laughed when she pulled up her vest to show me the big safety pin she'd used to gather in the waistband of the skirt.

Dickens barked and scampered off. *Where's he going now?* I thought before I realized he'd spotted Belle and Wendy. He skidded to a stop in front of the colorful display of wool sweaters, scarves, hats, and gloves where mother and daughter were admiring the goods. Everything on the table was made at Astonbury Manor by the knitting group who leased one of the cottages. Anything remaining after tonight would be taken to shops around the area for the holiday season.

"Hello, Leta," said Belle. "You're just in time to help us pick out a Christmas gift for Peter. Wendy wants to get him this light blue jumper because it's her favorite color, but I think her brother would prefer something darker."

Belle was pointing to a teal crew neck while Wendy held an arctic blue in her hands. With his greying blonde hair and blue eyes, I thought both would look good on him, but I couldn't imagine him wearing the lighter shade of blue—maybe in a shirt, but not in a sweater.

I pointed to a turtleneck in a cable knit. "Ladies, why don't I complicate matters with a third choice? Peter reminds me of my Henry in so many ways—coloring, build, love of cycling—and Henry would have gone for this cobalt blue. A bit bluer than the teal, but a more masculine shade than the soft blue. What do you think?"

"Leave it to Leta to know my brother better than I do. She's right, Mum. I prefer the arctic blue, and it would look great on Peter, but he'd never wear it. I'll get them to ring up the turtleneck."

While Wendy was paying, Belle and I wandered toward the table of sheep milk soap. Matthew's wife Sarah was doing a brisk business. Ellie was right—Astonbury Manor was well represented tonight. Julia and Ellie stood off to the side chatting.

Ellie greeted us. "Belle, I don't think you've met Julia, Nicholas's wife." The ladies exchanged greetings while I tried to get a glimpse of the soap selection. I was partial to the lavender-scented products and planned to stock up tonight.

I felt a nudge and realized Julia was leaning over my shoulder. "I can't believe Nick wants to upset this applecart by getting rid of the sheep. Astonbury Manor has made a name for itself with the soap and the woolen goods from those adorable Cotswolds Lions. I've decided my New York girlfriends are all getting soap and sweaters for Christmas, and my suitcase will be packed to the gills for the trip home."

I thought for a moment. "Maybe you could pick out a sweater for your husband as a subtle hint. Sweaters and scarves and sheep's milk soap may not turn a profit on the magnitude of a grand resort, but these products represent the Estate. Packaged as Astonbury Manor wares with an eye-catching logo, they'd make great advertising. I can see it now—a gift shop at the resort."

Julia pursed her lips. "I've already been working on him. He doesn't pick up on subtle, but it's worth a try. I think we stayed in a London hotel that had their own line of bath products—soap, lotions, shampoo, even shaving cream—and they sold them on the internet too. A reminder of their marketing might get his attention."

We both turned toward the crackling sound of a microphone. Nicholas stood near the tree with a mic in his hand and an elf by his side. When I looked closer, I realized it was my neighbor little Timmy Watson. I should have known Deborah would have him dressed as an elf.

"Greetings and Merry Christmas," Nicholas began. "First, let me say I'm honored to be here tonight to light the Astonbury Tree. Many of you know it was my grandfather, the Earl of Stow, who started this tradition almost forty years ago." He put his hand on Timmy's shoulder. "The twinkling eyes of the children and the smiling faces of the adults combined to make this my grandfather's favorite event of the season—even of the year. I know I have big shoes to fill as your new Earl, and I look forward to sharing my plans for the continued prosperity of Astonbury as I settle into my new role. For now, though, let's officially kick off the Christmas season."

When Nicholas held out his hand, Timmy placed a remote control in it. With the press of a button, the new Earl of Stow lit the tree in all its glory. Deborah and her band of pre-schoolers had done the village proud. As the crowd clapped and the words "Merry Christmas" rang out around the Village Green, the choir stationed in front of the Village Hall launched into "Hark the Herald Angels Sing."

I followed Dickens as he darted to the tree to see Timmy, who plopped on the ground to give him a belly rub. Nicholas shook hands and spoke with villagers. Most of the comments I picked up were a mix of condolences on the loss of his grandfather and congratulations on his title. There were questions about whether he'd be moving to the Manor House and whether Matthew would continue to run the Estate. It was clear from the comments that Matthew was well-respected, and I hoped Nicholas was getting the message.

Seeing Jill handing out cookies from the inn, I moved in her direction. I could do with another taste of her baking. My route took me close to the sheep pen, and I noticed Julia and Harry with their heads together. Unlike Harry's interactions with her husband, their conversation seemed congenial. *Maybe she's gathering data about the sheep to use in influencing Nicholas,* I thought.

Next, I needed a refill on my beer. A loud voice broke through the general gaiety. "No bloody way! Haven't you heard what I've been telling you? Absolutely not!" It was Gavin and he was in Nicholas's face yelling at him. Peter was holding out his hands trying to put distance between the two.

Dickens's ears perked up and he looked at me. "Leta, what's going on? Gavin never gets angry." Dickens was right. I knew Gavin was put out with Nicholas's plans, but what could have caused this eruption? Like me, Libby and Gemma had heard the commotion and were rushing that way.

Nicholas was shouting now. "They're just donkeys. Why can't they be moved?"

Peter had succeeded in separating the two men, but they were yelling at full throttle. "Moved? You think I'll move the donkeys—so you can put in a bridge? You must be out of your mind."

Nicholas retorted. "Now who's not listening? Quite a few members of the Cotswolds Planning Commission like the idea of putting in a one-lane bridge to alleviate traffic congestion in the village, and that's the perfect spot."

"Perfect or not, I'm not selling my land." By now, Gemma had grabbed her dad and Matthew had Nicholas by the arm. That was the end of the argument—for the moment. The noise of the Christmas crowd continued unabated. Not many had heard the loud voices, and only those nearest the beer table could have made out the words.

Matthew tugged Nicholas towards the Village Hall, and Peter stepped in to help pour beer. I stood in line to purchase my half-pint, and when I got to Gavin, I could tell he was still fuming. "Guess you heard that, huh, Leta? The nerve of him."

I stepped behind the table to whisper in his ear. "Gavin, I'll let you explain it to me at the pub. For now, let's focus on Christmas cheer, okay?" He nodded and gave me a quick hug.

I made a beeline for the table of sweaters. The crowd was dying down as families wandered to the shops and their cars, and I wanted to see about a sweater for Dave before the wares were packed away. With his dark good looks, he wore lots of chocolate browns and black. And goodness, the man took my breath away when he wore a tux. I'd spied a black crew neck sweater in a soft fuzzy texture. It was crisscrossed with subtle white lines. Add a crisp white shirt, and it would look smashing with either grey dress slacks or jeans. It would be just the thing to put under the tree for Dave.

I was in luck. The sweater was still there and they had it in large. Naturally, I *had* to look at everything they had in red just in case there was something I couldn't live without. Fortunately or unfortunately, I didn't see a sweater in the right shade of cherry red. Heaven forbid I wear a tomato red.

I chuckled to myself as I imagined the different reactions my sisters would have to my pickiness. Anna would roll her eyes as she did whenever I persuaded her to shop with me. I could hear her now saying, "Oh for goodness' sake, just get it!" Sophia and I, on the other hand, would be completely in sync, and we'd go from store to store until we found the one item we deemed perfect. Sophia and I were fashionistas. Anna? She'd wear tee shirts and jeans every day if she could.

As I turned to leave with my package, I bumped into the Morgans, my neighbors who lived across the street from me. "I haven't seen you guys in ages," I exclaimed. "Have you been traveling?"

They explained they'd been visiting their daughter and new grandchild in France but were happy to be home again. "I'm especially glad I'm back," said Mr. Morgan, "so I'll be here when the planning commission votes on all these plans for Astonbury Manor."

"Oh! I didn't realize you were on the planning commission. Has Nicholas filed everything already?"

Mr. Morgan cleared his throat. "Not a thing. He's busy schmoozing the commissioners individually to get us to see things his way. Since we're just back, he hasn't taken me to dinner yet. I suspect I'll get an earful at Lady Stow's birthday party tomorrow night, though."

Dickens chose that moment to bark and take off, so I waved goodbye and followed him. *Politics!* I thought. *Things are the same the world over.*

By the time Dickens and I walked to the cottage and drove to the Ploughman, I was hard-pressed to find a parking place. The place was packed with locals and tourists. I grabbed a pint of cider at the bar and made my way to the table where Peter, Rhiannon, and Toby were seated with Gavin, Libby, and Gemma. Dickens chose to wriggle his way beneath the table.

I shared a chair with Rhiannon and tried to pick up the thread of the conversation. "Let me get this straight," Toby said. "Nicholas claims he's convinced the planning commission that a new entrance to the Estate will prevent traffic conges-tion on High Street, and he sees the new entrance as a single-lane bridge across the River Elfe smack dab through the donkey pasture. Have I got that right?"

"Yes! Doesn't seem to matter to him that I *own* the proper-ty," grumbled Gavin. "If enough members of the commission see it his way, he knows they can bring pressure to bear."

Gemma put her hand on her dad's arm. "But Dad, they can't make you sell. So what can they do?"

"Sweetheart, you never want to alienate the planning commission. They could suddenly come 'round to inspect the old mill and decide all kinds of things need fixin'. They could make our lives hell. Heck, they could invoke compulsory purchase and force me to sell the pasture. They have their ways."

"But Dad, how many *really* agree with him? He says they do, but I have to wonder. I've heard you talk about the helicopter landing pad, a pool and goodness knows what else. Do the commissioners think all that's good for Astonbury? Don't they have a vision for the Cotswolds?"

Gavin blew out his breath. "There are thirty-some-odd commissioners, and there *is* a vision or a plan for the Area of Outstanding Natural Beauty, the AONB, but there's leeway in it. If enough members see the resort as a good thing, then there will be pressure to make it a reality with all its bells and whistles. I'd like to think every one of them has our best interests at heart, but you just never know."

If you grease the right palms, anything can happen, I thought.

Peter shook his head. "We've seen enough questionable development in neighboring villages to know we don't always agree with the approvals that come down. Look at what happened in Cirencester. It took years, but they eventually approved a 2,000-home development, despite what the locals thought." He slammed down his beer mug. "This could be the tip of the iceberg for Astonbury."

I was taking it all in. "Is there a way to petition the commission or the council or whatever they're called? I mean, can the village start a campaign to curtail at least some of this? A resort with a restaurant and bar is one thing, but all this other stuff? It sounds over the top."

"Over the top! I'll tell you what's over the top," interjected Harry as he pulled up a chair. He ran his fingers through his dark brown hair. "My cousin has all but decided my sheep have to go and along with 'em the weavers and knitters and Mum's soap making business. His latest idea is to turn all the cottages on the Estate into guest cottages. I don't know the exact count, but there's at least twenty of them. You'd think he could leave a few for the artisans. 'Course, if there are no sheep for wool and milk, they won't have the raw materials to ply their trade."

Libby had been quiet but now had a horrified expression on her face. "Where will you take the sheep, Harry?"

"Libby, any other time, I could lease some land and move them temporarily until I can decide what to do long-term, but it's not a good time to be doing that. Lambing could start as early as late January, and it's important my ewes are well-fed and settled. And then there's Dad and the brewery and Gran and where she'll live. It's all a bloody mess. Grandad must be rolling over in his grave."

Gavin abruptly pushed his chair back and stood up. "I can't stomach this conversation any longer. Maybe making the breakfast casserole for tomorrow morning will take my mind off all this. Got to be done, regardless."

Libby and Gemma stood up with him, and Libby grimaced. "Don't let him fool you. He'll be grumbling as he grates cheese and beats eggs, but at least he'll be doing something productive." She looked at Gemma and raised her eyebrows. "I may invite myself for a nightcap with you, dear."

The three of them leaving meant I could have a chair to myself instead of sharing with Rhiannon. I was beginning to think I was the only hungry member of the group until I suggested ordering an appetizer. The mention of food focused everyone's thoughts on the menu, at least briefly. We motioned to Barb, our favorite barmaid, and everyone but Rhiannon ordered the tree-lighting special, lamb stew with a side of Brussel sprouts. She ordered a salad.

When we saw Matthew approaching, Harry asked Barb to

add another lamb stew to the order. Matthew looked pre-occupied as he sat down. "I can see this is a happy lot," he said. "Let me guess what the topic of conversation is."

We acknowledged it was Nicholas and the plans for the Estate, and Matthew blew out his breath. "Good thing I took Mum and Sarah home. They're already worried to death over this, and more talk won't help them feel any better."

I thought back to my conversation with Ellie. "Matthew, is your mother just putting a good face on things, or is she seriously thinking about buying another country home and leaving Astonbury Manor behind?"

"Oh, she told you that idea, did she? Mum has always been the rock in this family—even more so than dad was. When he'd get exasperated over something, Mum could calm him down, and she pretty much does the same with me and Harry and Sam. Her ability to weather any storm never ceases to amaze me. Truth is it will break her heart to leave, but if staying is intolerable, she'll make a new home for herself and for *us*.

"Our family has a good life, and Mum believes we can recreate it elsewhere, as long as we stick together. Me? I'm not so sure. The problem is Nicholas doesn't know from one day to the next what he wants to do. Heck, he doesn't know from one *minute* to the next. Look at how he's got Harry all riled up over the sheep. Last night, he was leaning toward keeping them and building a nice-looking shed and barn. Tonight, he was all about getting rid of 'em."

Rhiannon gave me a sideways glance. "Isn't he a successful businessman. ? How can he be so indecisive?"

Matthew took a slug of beer. "Hell if I know. I only know we can't take much more of this. He's made our lives a living hell. Something's got to give."

Chapter Eight

Despite the tension at dinner, I'd slept well. The reality was it wasn't my fight, though I'd be gutted if the donkeys disappeared. I'd grown attached to them, as had Dickens. I'd do whatever I could to help Gavin and Libby, with a petition or such, but they'd have to steer me since I didn't know the ins and outs of village governance. I couldn't see myself carrying a picket sign, but if that's what my friends wanted, I'd be there.

Oh my goodness. Did I just use the word gutted, *at least in my head? Maybe I'm getting the hang of Brit speak after all.* I hustled to get dressed, as Peter would soon be by with Wendy and Belle to pick me up for tree shopping. My phone pinged with a text from Wendy. "Almost there."

With a travel mug of coffee in hand, I waited in the driveway and then climbed in the back seat with Wendy. I leaned over to give Belle a peck on the cheek. "Thanks for including me. I've never gone tree shopping with a crowd. Do you think they'll have wreaths? I completely forgot to look for them at the tree lighting last night."

Peter grinned and glanced in the rearview mirror. "That's why we're going to Broadway to shop. Wendy says they have the best selection of wreaths decked out in your choice of ribbons. If it were only Christmas trees we were after, we could find 'em closer."

I looked in the bed of the truck. "Why is it I picture this truck filling up pretty quickly? Trees, wreaths—I may need a dwarf spruce in a pot to put by the front door too."

Peter grinned and shook his head. "I'm all yours today, ladies, as long as you buy me lunch and keep me supplied with tea. I can see me now snoozing in the truck while you duck in the shops. Should have brought Dickens to keep me company, but I'm not sure where we'd have put him."

Belle turned to look at Wendy and me. "Don't forget we need to be home in time for me to take my nap and get ready for the party, so you girls may have to plan a shopping day for another time. Let's find our trees and maybe have lunch and call it a day."

Wendy laughed. "That's fine, Mum. I'm sure Leta and I can pick another day to shop in Broadway and Burford and who knows where else. 'Tis the season, you know."

When we reached the market, Peter made short work of selecting a tree for his flat and two wreaths for the garage. Wendy, Belle, and I took a bit longer. I remembered Henry had been much pickier about the shape of our tree than I had. As long as it was full on the side that showed, I was good. I selected a six-foot tree first and then went in search of a smaller one for my office. I had a box full of cat ornaments from my single days when I hadn't had a dog, and I planned for this smaller tree to be the cat tree.

I made short work of choosing tree number two, found a potted spruce, and moved on to wreaths. It was choosing the ribbons that took forever. The selection was endless. *Do I want plaid or white trimmed in gold or something else entirely?* It took Wendy weighing in for me to decide on red with gold sparkles for the front door and plaid for the garden gate.

Peter loaded our purchases into the bed of the truck, and we made our way to the Market Pantry. We were seated by the window and enjoyed watching the holiday shoppers stream by laden with parcels. We ladies chose the mug of soup and half sandwich option. The day's soup was tomato basil, my favorite, and I indulged in a caloric splurge—the bacon, brie, and cranberry sandwich—to accompany it. Peter, as was his habit, went for the burger and chips.

We could hear Dickens barking when we pulled into my driveway. "What's up with him?" asked Wendy.

"He knows the whole gang is out here and wants to greet us. I'll let him out while Peter starts unloading." Dickens bolted out the door and made straight for Peter. "Gee, do you think he has a favorite?"

Peter reached down to scratch Dickens's ears, and Dickens put his paws on his legs. Funny how he knew not to jump on Belle but was playful with both Peter and Timmy. He moved around to see Wendy as she stepped from the truck and Peter placed my trees and wreaths on the driveway. I could carry everything but the six-foot tree, so Peter grabbed that while I directed him to the window in the sitting room. I'd already set up the tree stand, and the two of us got the tree situated in no time. A few turns to put its best side forward, and we were done.

"Phew. I think I can get the lights on by myself, but if not,

I may ask you to come early to my tree trimming party so we can have the lights up in time for folks to hang ornaments. Thanks for all your help." I walked outside to say goodbye to Wendy and Belle. I'd see all three that night at the Manor House.

I busied myself hanging the wreaths and moving the four-foot tree to different spots in my office. I finally settled on a place in front of the floor-to-ceiling bookcase on the left side. As I looked out the picture window to the garden, I thought of getting several boxes of net lights for the bushes and the potted spruce I'd put by the front door. *I've caught the Christmas spirit,* I thought. The Christmas after Henry died, I'd barely managed to put out a few snow globes and candles, much less get a tree. I knew I'd still have some tearful moments, but I hoped today's spurt of enthusiasm was a sign I was healing.

I'd been hesitating to pull out my boxes and boxes of Christmas decorations, worried I'd have a meltdown, but since I'd made it through tree shopping without tears, I decided to chance it. *After all,* I thought, *even if I have a good cry, tonight's party will cheer me up.*

By the time I carried all the boxes from the garage to the sitting room, I was thinking I should have asked Peter or Gavin for help. *What on earth was I thinking when I shipped all this?* At least the containers were clearly labeled. In the summer, when I'd moved into my fairytale cottage and begun sorting boxes, it was apparent I'd swung back and forth from haphazard to highly organized when I was packing in Atlanta. Thank goodness the Christmas decorations were in the orga-nized category.

Dickens and Christie watched as I opened the box of teddy bears and other animals, many of which I'd acquired pre-Henry. There was my treasured Richie Bear from the now-defunct Rich's department store in Atlanta. He was a white bear with a red sweater and red knit cap. Two brown Lord & Taylor bears from different years were wearing knit scarves and hats. The Lord & Taylor locations in Atlanta had long since closed, and I still couldn't believe the flagship store on Fifth Avenue had closed after over one hundred years in business.

Christie wandered over to climb into the box. "What's with all the bears? I thought we had cats too . . . Wait, here's one." She'd found a black and white cat with a Santa hat. She sniffed everything as I pulled out several more cats, a moose, and a mouse. Each one made *me* smile and Christie purr.

Dickens was more interested in lounging in front of the fire and content to watch from afar. Next was the box holding the small red, white, and green quilted tree skirt my mother-in-law had handed down to Henry, perfect for the smaller tree. Tucked in with it were the larger green velvet tree skirt trimmed in rich burgundy and the delicate crocheted angel tree topper. I considered these items heirlooms, as Henry's mom had made them all.

"You know, Christie, I have a picture of you as a kitten, curled up with the packages beneath the tree—after you'd chewed ribbons and clawed wrapping paper. You played so hard, you conked out."

"I've learned better now. I prefer to play with the paper *after* you've unwrapped the packages. I still think the ornaments are fair game, though."

"Yes, dear. That's why I never place fragile ornaments on the lower branches where you can reach them." Thank goodness, she confined her antics to the bottom of the tree. I'd had a kitten named Moocher, another black cat, who'd climbed up the trunk of the Christmas tree one year. I was lucky I'd been there and been able to reach in and grab him without breaking a single ornament or worse, toppling the tree.

I was saving the several boxes of ornaments until last, so I turned to the box labeled *China*. I knew it wasn't china, but I hadn't known what else to call the plethora of candle holders, decorative plates, and Christmas knickknacks I'd collected. I had a handblown glass tree with tiny glass balls hanging on the branches, a wooden sleigh, and several snow globes.

Christie meowed, "I remember the big snow globe, the one on the gold base that played music. That thing scared me to death."

That got Dickens's attention. "It only scared you after you knocked it to the floor and it burst into pieces! We didn't see you for hours after the crash."

Christie turned her nose up before she replied, "Excuse me, I believe it jumped off the shelf. I had nothing to do with it."

Jumped off the shelf? That's a creative explanation. I looked around the sitting room and considered my collection. *Garland, I need garland.* I'd go out Sunday afternoon to get some, and then I could arrange candles and snowglobes in the greenery and hang the three Christmas stockings with the names Christie, Dickens, and Leta.

There, I thought. *I've made it through without tears. I'll tackle the ornaments another day. Maybe I'll just open the boxes and set them by the tree and leave it to my friends to pull them out one by one—all except the box of cat ornaments.* I moved it to the office with the idea of decorating the cat tree on my own before the tree trimming party next week.

Glancing at my watch, I realized I'd almost let the afternoon get away from me. I brewed a cup of tea and climbed the stairs to my bedroom where I pulled my burgundy velvet dress from the closet. I'd only worn it once—to the fancy dress party I'd thrown in late September. I adored the plunging neckline and the way the material draped to my ankles with a bit of swirl. Having somewhere else to wear it was a treat. The pearl necklace and cuff bracelet complemented the 1920s look. *I wonder*, I thought, as I reached to the top of the closet for the hatbox that held the fascinator I'd worn with it. I knew next to nothing about hat etiquette, so I called Ellie.

Caroline answered the phone, and I could hear pots clanging in the background. "Oh hi, Leta. Yes, Ellie's standing right here. It may be her birthday, but she can't keep herself from overseeing the preparations."

When Ellie said hello, I posed my question about wearing the fascinator. "Yes, dear, a fascinator is appropriate with either a cocktail dress or evening gown. It sounds as though you'll look smashing, and I can't wait to see your ensemble."

That settled, I called Wendy to share the news. When I'd planned my party, we'd shopped villages near and far for our outfits. If she was planning to wear the turquoise sheath she'd worn that evening, she could pull out her fascinator too.

"Funny you should call. Yes, I *am* wearing my beaded sheath, and I was searching the internet to see whether it was proper etiquette to add the fascinator. Marvelous! You and I will be the belles of the ball, even if there is a supermodel in attendance. Now, that makes me wonder what Julia will be wearing."

Wendy couldn't see me, but that didn't stop me from rolling my eyes. "I saw her in pajamas the other day, and she looked stunning. So, there's a slight chance she'll upstage us."

"Okay, then, maybe we'll be the senior belles. Mum's got her curlers in, and she's been laying out her new makeup. She's wearing her baby blue satin dress with a matching jacket. We should get someone to take a picture of the three of us—The Little Old Ladies Detective Agency in formal attire. I can see it now on our business cards."

I chuckled. "I'm good with a photo as long as we don't get called upon to do any detecting. Didn't I say after our last episode I'd had enough? Sipping champagne, nibbling canapés, and toasting Ellie will be entertainment enough for me."

Luckily, I still had time for a short nap. After that, the next step was a leisurely bath, not a shower. To me, half the fun of a black-tie affair was getting ready, and a relaxing bath—one scented with Shalimar bath oil—was a requirement. As I lay back with my head resting on a blowup pillow, I imagined myself as Audrey Hepburn or some equally glamorous movie star luxuriating in a bubble bath—one arm emerging from the strategically placed bubbles to reach for a flute of champagne.

The reality was a bit different. Instead of champagne, I had a dog on the bathroom rug and a cat on the vanity. Instead of a lady's maid handing me a silk robe, I reached for my humdrum red fleece. *Oh well.*

As I styled my greying brunette bob, I was pleased to see my sparkly strands of fairy hair had held up well since I'd acquired them at the Fall Fête, and the shiny red and silver threads were still in evidence. Carefully applied makeup, a spritz of Shalimar over the top of my head, and I was almost ready. The final touch was the fascinator—a tiny velvet head-piece adorned with crystal sequins and topped with a single black peacock feather and a short voile veil.

Twirling in front of the mirror, I pointed at Dickens and said, "Bibbidi-bobbidi-boo."

"Huh?" he barked. "What did you say?"

I shrugged. "It was worth a try. When the fairy godmother says that in Cinderella, it's magic. I was hoping you'd turn into a handsome prince—a handsome *human* prince. Maybe George Clooney—or better yet, a younger Sean Connery." *What does it say about me,* I thought, *that I can't think of a single recent movie star I find irresistible?*

Christie leaped to the top of the dresser and reached towards my head. "Dickens, you can't expect her to make sense when she's wearing a cat toy on her head. Just tell her she's pretty and let her be on her way."

"Nice try," I said as I dodged her paw. "You're not getting near my fascinator. I'm off to the ball. Just imagine, I'm going to a black-tie affair hosted by the Dowager Countess of Stow. With or without a prince, I'm looking forward to my first-ever Downton Abbey experience."

Chapter Nine

The plane trees lining the curved drive to Astonbury Manor were decorated in white lights, and the sight of the house at the end was breathtaking. Every window was alight, as were the potted plants on either side of the massive front door. Garland with red bows framed the door, and there was an honest-to-goodness red carpet leading from the gravel drive up the stairs to the front door.

As I pulled up, a young man dressed as a footman hurried to open my door and offer me his arm. I was beginning to feel like a princess—even without a prince. The Morgans were right behind me, and I heard Mrs. Morgan laugh as she was offered an arm by another footman or coachman or whatever they were. *Parking attendant* didn't quite capture it. We three approached the front door together.

"That was a new experience," said Mrs. Morgan. "You never know from year to year what special touch Ellie will add. I can't wait to see the inside of the house."

The great hall was tastefully trimmed with greenery. On my previous visits, I'd attended a meeting in the library, eaten lunch on the patio, and sat with Ellie in the kitchen. This was something else entirely. Guests mingled around the grand stairway in the hall and the drawing room to the right. Servers, all male and all dressed as footmen, were passing trays of white and red wine and canapes. *Very Downton Abbeyish*, I thought, as I looked around for Carson.

I popped a mini quiche into my mouth before accepting a glass of red wine from the next young man to pass me. Hearing my name, I turned to see Harry and Sam coming my way. "Wendy asked us to grab you as soon as you arrived. She wants a picture."

I followed them to the Christmas tree in front of a large window. There I found the Davies family. "Oh Belle," I exclaimed, "You look elegant. The softer hairstyle, the new makeup, not to mention the dress—you belong in a magazine." Belle's new look was a result of our October trip to the coast, where Wendy had treated her to a wash and set that included a makeover.

Sam and Harry arranged the three of us in front of the tree and snapped several photos with our phones. Deborah Watson joined in with her phone, so I knew we'd wind up featured online in the *Astonbury Aha!* too. Anyone could upload pictures to the community website, but Deborah could always be counted on to do so. I suggested she try to get all the male guests into a group shot at some point. I thought there was something about men in tuxedos that needed to be memorialized, especially nowadays when casual dress was the way of the world.

As Harry and Sam turned to leave, I stopped the older brother to tell him I'd like to write a column about his Cotswolds Lions and hoped he'd have some time the following week. Sam heard me and spoke before Harry could. "Are you kidding? Once you get him started, you won't be able to shut him up. And he knows plenty." Smiling, Harry elbowed his brother and told me to call him to set up a time.

Sarah hurried up and asked Deborah to snap a photo of her with her sons. She looked every bit the proud mother between her boys, Sam with his blonde beard and tousled hair and Harry with his darker coloring. Usually, she wore her long light brown hair in a single braid—a bit of an earth mother look—but tonight she'd left it loose and wavy.

"Sarah," I said, "how did sales go last night? You were doing a booming business when I was there."

Her face lit up and her eyes sparkled. "This was my best year yet at the tree lighting. The lavender you like did well, and the new balsam fir scent sold out. I don't go to many festivals because they're so much work, but it's a treat to see the people I know at this one."

"'Tis the season. That reminds me, I need some balsam fir candles. I haven't thought to stock up since I moved to Astonbury, but I always had several on hand back in Atlanta."

A cloud passed over Sarah's face. "I just hope this isn't the last year for my sheep soap. If Nicholas has his way, I may be out of business, at least for a bit. I'm sure Matthew, Harry, and I will put our heads together and come up with some kind of plan, but it's a bit disheartening right now."

I reached over and gave her a gentle hug. *He needs to make up his mind and get on with it*, I thought. *It's not fair to his family to keep them in limbo.*

As I mingled, I encountered Beatrix with George Evans. "Found me a plus-one," George boasted as he playfully put his arm around Beatrix's waist. "You know lately, I've gotten more tour bookings from the Book Nook than anywhere else? I owe this lady." I knew Beatrix carried George's flyers at the shop and talked up his business, but hadn't realized how well that was working for him.

Libby was speaking with John Watson in front of the massive fireplace. Tall, fit, and broad-shouldered, my next-door neighbor was made to wear a tux. "You know, I thought you looked smashing as Captain Hook in October, John, but you may have outdone yourself tonight. What do you think, Libby? A touch of James Bond?"

Libby grinned. "Right. At the Fall Fête, you had an Errol Flynn look, and tonight you'd give Pierce Brosnan a run for his money." We'd made John blush, and he bowed and thanked us before he wandered off.

In her chocolate brown silk dress, Libby looked elegant too. Most often she was running around the kitchen at the inn with a smudge of flour on one cheek and a dishtowel in her hand. I rarely saw her dressed up and commented on her dress.

She beamed. "Thanks. Can you believe I found it in the vintage shop in Burford—next to the chocolate shop, of all places? Perhaps next year, I'll find a fascinator too."

Across the room, Rhiannon was waving at me, so I moved in that direction. She and Toby were chatting with Nicholas and Julia. Julia was attired in a strapless form-fitting black velvet dress set off by a diamond and jet choker—she looked every inch the model. "Leta," Rhiannon greeted me, "Nicholas is telling us how he sees the new resort benefitting the village. I may be able to offer yoga classes here if the demand is great enough."

An image formed in my head and I grinned. "Why did I picture you offering goat yoga when you said that?"

"Not hardly," said Nicholas. "I'm not keen on the sheep, and we definitely don't want to add goats."

Never bashful, Toby spoke up. "What is it about the sheep

that bothers you, Nicholas? Most villagers see them as an asset. They fit the image of a country village, and the soap and jumpers are popular with the locals and tourists alike." Matthew had walked up as we were talking and appeared eager to hear his cousin's response.

"They don't fit with the image I have for the resort. You don't find sheep at upscale resorts, do you?"

I provided my two cents worth. "I don't know that I've been to a posh resort, but Highclere Castle has sheep and horses, as does Blenheim Palace, Churchill's ancestral home."

Matthew cleared his throat. "Funny you should mention Blenheim, Leta. I've just heard they're introducing white cows and a bull to the Estate. They've 12,000 acres and plan to set aside part of it for the cows. Given we have 500 acres, I don't see why you can't do the same for 100 head of sheep. Twenty-five acres is the most they need."

Julia gave her husband a stern look. "Perhaps we can discuss this further tomorrow, Nick. An upscale hotel in a rural setting could be appealing."

Fascinating dynamics. I put my glass on a passing tray and excused myself. Rhiannon did the same and followed me. We went to the spacious powder room beneath the grand stairway. "The yoga conversation was fine," said my friend, "but I'm tired of hearing about sheep." She smoothed her ivory lace dress with the asymmetrical hemline and turned to check the rear view.

"Me too. Guess it's a hot button because everyone feels so badly for Harry and Sarah and the artisans in the cottages." As we exited, I saw Gavin standing alone. He looked pensive as he stroked his goatee.

When I hugged him, he invited me to the library to see the Laguiole knife he'd told me about. "You won't believe the craftsmanship, Leta. It's a work of art." I was pretty sure I wouldn't be as excited about it as Gavin, but the library alone was worth a visit. It was straight out of a Victorian novel—floor-to-ceiling bookcases on two walls with two rolling ladders and a third wall bisected by a large fireplace with four-foot-tall display cases on either side. Like the one in the drawing room, the fireplace mantel was decked in greenery. In front of the large window on the fourth wall sat a large leather-topped desk, and scattered about the room were comfy leather chairs.

Gavin took me to a case that contained at least fifty knives. One held the place of honor. Displayed on a crystal pedestal, it sat alone on the top shelf. On the wall above it was a pastoral scene of a shepherd with his sheep.

I was surprised at my reaction. "Gosh, Gavin, the setting tells the story. That painting makes me imagine a shepherd using his knife to clean a hoof or cut a loaf of bread, just as you described."

"Exactly, that's why I've always envied Nigel. Whenever I visit, I have to make a detour to admire it. Henry would've been impressed, right?"

"Absolutely, and I suspect he'd have surfed the internet trying to figure out how to get one for his collection. This one must be quite valuable if it dates from the early 1800s."

"I have no idea what it's worth, but I've seen similar Laguioles priced anywhere from £300 to £3,000. This one is unique because of the ebony scales on the handle and detailed file work on the spine of the blade. And, of course, it has the traditional Laguiole Bee where the knife folds. I'd love to let you hold it, but the cases are kept locked."

"My, my. Well, if I can drag you away, I'd kill for another glass of wine and a bit of pate." Gavin gave an elaborate bow and offered his arm. As we moved towards the door, he stopped abruptly and gripped my hand before we could walk through. I heard two men talking in hushed tones and recognized the voices as those of Nicholas and Mr. Morgan. Glancing at Gavin, I could tell he was straining to hear the conversation just as I was.

"I can't see why you need Gavin and Libby's property. And I'm none too pleased about a bridge and a drive cutting through the pasture behind my house," Mr. Morgan said.

Nicholas's response was too low for me to make out entirely, but I heard the word "inducement." I wondered whether Gavin had picked up more than I had. His face was red and the muscles of his neck stood out. "I knew it," he spat. "He'll try to bribe his way if that's what it takes."

I turned to my friend and whispered, "Do you think you can walk by without making a scene—without getting involved?" This was neither the time nor the place.

Gavin shook himself, settled his shoulders, and managed to stride through the door with a smile.

I leaned in. "Jolly good show!" *Now I really need that glass of wine*, I thought. We were just in time for the move to the dining room for the sit-down dinner portion of the evening. I watched as Matthew offered his arm to his mother, and they led the way. In her ankle-length silver beaded skirt and matching high-necked jacket, Ellie was the picture of elegance. They were followed by Harry escorting his mother Sarah. There was a slight hiccup as Julia stood waiting for Nicholas. When he hurried up behind her, the flow to the dining room continued.

I was pleasantly surprised when Sam appeared at my side. "Would you do me the honor, Mrs. Parker?" *I could get used to this treatment*, I thought. *Complete with a young nobleman as my escort.*

When the guests were seated and the wine poured, Matthew stood to toast Ellie. "To my mother—to me, you'll always be Mum, and in settings like this, the Countess of Stow. Let it be so for one final evening before you take up the mantle of Dowager Countess. You are beloved by all in Astonbury, be they friends or family or villagers who've benefitted from your unstinting generosity through the years. I only have one wish as I raise my glass tonight. May you never, ever turn into the Dowager Countess of Grantham from Downton Abbey. We much prefer your sweet nature to her biting wit. Cheers!"

We laughed as we raised our glasses. Then it was Nicholas's turn. Tonight, he had chosen to sit at the side of the table rather than at the head as was his due as the new Earl. It was generous of him to allow Ellie a final turn in the spotlight with her son opposite her at the end of the table. "Dearest Ellie, I salute you not only as my grandmother but also as the woman who my grandfather loved and cherished. Thank you for bringing him joy in his prime and his later years." He lifted his glass and nodded towards Ellie, and we followed suit.

"I'd also like to raise a glass to the two members of our family who left us this year. First, my grandfather. You may not know Lord Stow was an RAF pilot in WWII. He fought the good fight for over nine decades, building a successful career and cherishing family above all. And second, my father, Reginald. Like his father before him, he raised a child on his own when his wife died too young. Grandfather did an outstanding job." He grinned and looked toward the ceiling. "It remains to be seen, Dad, how well you did. You left us too soon." He raised his glass a final time. "To Nigel and Reginald—we miss you."

Both Ellie and Sarah dabbed their cheeks with their

napkins, and the eyes of the male members of the family—Nicholas, Matthew, Harry, and Sam—glistened with unshed tears. As the footmen began serving the soup course, I thought what a nice job both Matthew and Nicholas had done with their heartfelt toasts.

I tried to pace myself through what turned out to be a five-course meal, if you counted the appetizers we were served in the drawing room. I was thankful it wasn't one of the nine-course extravaganzas I'd read about. We started with parsnip and leek soup, followed by roast beef and baked sole accompanied by haricots verts and parslied new potatoes. Next was an arugula salad with asparagus. I was relieved when the final course was served—coffee and birthday cake. *Thank goodness I'm cycling tomorrow,* were the words that came to mind.

Ellie put her napkin on the table, signaling dinner had come to an end. "We're much too modern to have the ladies and gentlemen adjourn to separate rooms, so please join us in the drawing room for an after-dinner drink. We have the usual selection of brandy, amaretto and such, but Caroline, our new chef, has also prepared a special treat."

When we arrived in the drawing room, the footmen who'd served dinner were now passing trays of martini glasses, but the drinks weren't like any martini I'd ever seen. "Chocolate martini, miss," was the answer I got when I asked what it was. Before I grabbed one, I moved to Wendy's side. "I'll pop if I drink one of those."

"We'll pop together, then, because I'm not passing on this. At least you're riding tomorrow with my brother." When the next tray came our way, we each grabbed a glass and headed to the couch where Belle and Libby were seated on either side of Ellie. The trio held chocolate martinis.

Belle closed her eyes and smiled. "You've outdone yourself

this year, Ellie. It will take more than a cane to get me off this couch and down the stairs. I may need a hoist."

"Dearest Belle, at our age, who cares?" She laughed as she took a miniscule sip. "Still, I'll have Caroline preparing nothing but salads for the next week." Those words had barely left her mouth when Harry spoke up to get the attention of her guests.

Sam stood by his brother's side with a large silver box tied with a gold ribbon. He held it high. "Gran, I know we don't usually do presents at the party, but Harry and I wanted to give you this tonight, especially after the toast Nicholas made to Grandad." He placed the box on the table in front of the couch where Ellie sat.

She seemed not to know what to say and looked from her grandson to the box. Finally, she untied the ribbon and lifted the lid. The crowd was so quiet, we could hear the rustle of the tissue paper as she lifted what looked like a coffee table book from the box. She gasped and whispered, "Our hero." That was the title of the book, and it had a Hawker Tempest on the front beneath the title.

"It's . . . it's the plane your grandfather flew in WWII. Oh my goodness, look at these photos." Belle put her hand on Ellie's shoulder and watched as her friend slowly turned the pages. Ellie looked up, once again with tears streaming down her cheeks. "Sam, did you interview him? You know, he never talked about his WWII experience."

"Yes, Gran. Grandad was my project for my Michaelmas and Lent terms at Cambridge. I was keen to know his story, and I'm so glad I got it out of him before he died. He shared the WWII part and the early days of his airline business too. If you're happy with it, I'll get copies for the whole family, but yours is the first."

Sarah walked up and hugged her sons. "How did you two manage to keep this secret for an entire year? Well done."

Ellie focused on her book as Belle looked on. The rest of us mixed and mingled, and before I knew it, it was nearly eleven. I was known to turn into a pumpkin as early as ten, so it was time for me to go home. Wendy, Belle, and Peter had the same idea, though quite a few guests continued to imbibe as we departed. Walking the red carpet in reverse as my car was brought around, I noticed Harry and Matthew with their heads together near the carriage house. It wouldn't do to refer to the elegant building as a garage.

I smiled as I was handed into my car and briefly imagined it as a horse-drawn carriage. It had been a memorable evening, even if I hadn't met a handsome prince nor lost a glass slipper. *Bibbidi-bobbidi-boo.*

Chapter Ten

Mid-morning After the Bicycle Ride With Peter

Back from my ride, I felt shaky as I stowed my bicycle in the garage, and it wasn't from the cold. *It's delayed shock*, I thought. How was it I'd encountered two dead bodies since I'd retired to this supposedly idyllic village? And now I'd stumbled onto an auto accident and witnessed a man dying—and not just any man, an *Earl*.

Dickens greeted me when I came in through the mudroom. "Hi, Leta, how was your ride? How's Peter?" he barked before cocking his head and studying my face. "Uh-oh, you don't look good. What's wrong?"

"Let me fix a cup of tea and I'll tell you all about it." I removed my gloves and shrugged out of my parka, and before I knew it, Dickens had run to fetch Christie from upstairs. I wasn't sure what he'd told her, but she flew down the stairs ahead of him. "What's going on? Dickens is right. You don't look good. Did you overdo it on your ride?"

Thank goodness I didn't have to deal with the morning's

shock by myself. Now wasn't the time to be alone with my thoughts. I delayed the inevitable recounting of mine and Peter's discovery by brewing a pot of tea. I knew I'd need more than a cup to get through this. Heck, a shot of brandy to steady my nerves wouldn't be half bad, but I refrained.

I blew across the cup, took a sip, and a deep breath. "I don't know where to start. Peter and I found a dead body. No, that's not right. He wasn't dead when we found him. I witnessed him dying—"

"Who was it?" my furry companions asked in unison.

I bowed my head as tears trickled down my face. "It was Nicholas, the new Earl. I spoke to him only last night at the birthday party. How can this be happening? How is it that once again someone I know—even if I didn't know him that well—has died?"

I shook my head and took another sip. When I heard my cell phone, I realized I'd left it in my parka, and I hurried to grab it before it stopped ringing. I was relieved to see it was Wendy. Who better to talk to after what had happened? "Thank goodness it's you."

"I just got off the phone with Peter. Would you like me to come over?"

"Yes," was all I could manage before my voice broke. Wendy must have gotten the message, because she hung up without a word. I trudged upstairs for a quick shower and dressed in leggings and one of Henry's faded Georgia Tech sweatshirts. *There's comfort food, and there's comfort clothing,* I thought. I was standing in the pantry staring blankly at the shelves when Wendy knocked on the door. She carried a foil-covered plate and a bottle of brandy.

"You're a sight for sore eyes. I haven't eaten anything but a banana, and suddenly I'm starving. Tell me that's one of your quiches."

"You guessed it. I made two yesterday afternoon, knowing we'd be getting in late last night. Didn't want to have to cook this morning. I left one baking for Mum and grabbed this one for us. Let me turn on the oven and we'll have breakfast in no time. Meanwhile, I believe a medicinal cup of tea is called for." Good thing I'd made a pot.

She popped the quiche in the oven, poured the brandy in the teacup, and ushered me to the sitting room. "Peter's told me the story, so there's no need for you to rehash it. What a nightmare for you and for Nicholas's family. They must be shattered. It seems like yesterday Nigel died and now this. Nicholas was so young—only in his thirties. And poor Julia."

Wendy could ramble at the best of times and didn't need any encouragement to continue. "Peter tells me Nicholas was still in his tux. So it had to have been last night he was out, not early this morning. And based on the direction of the skid-marks, he was driving toward home, so where had he been? *After* the party?"

"Good question. Peter and I told Gemma we'd left shortly before eleven, and it appeared most of the other guests were following suit. Why did Nicholas go out afterward?"

"Very mysterious. Peter also said no one had called the police station to say Nicholas was missing. Don't you think that's odd?" I nodded yes as she suggested possible explanations. "Could be Julia and Nicholas slept in separate bedrooms, but they're awfully young for that, or maybe Julia's such a sound sleeper, she didn't notice her husband never came to bed."

I sipped my brandy-laden tea and offered, "Sometimes when Henry didn't feel well, he'd sleep in one of our guest rooms so as not keep me awake. When he started coughing, he could wake the dead. And Ellie told me Nicholas hadn't been feeling well, though it was his stomach, not a cold."

Dickens and Christie wandered into the room, and I noticed the fire needed another log. When I set my cup down on the table, Christie stuck her nose in it. "Uh-uh," I said. "Cats don't drink brandy." I got a haughty look and testy meow in return.

"Don't think she liked your response!" Wendy reached over to scratch Christie's head and then went to the kitchen. I moved my teacup to the mantel as a precaution and put two logs on the fire.

When Wendy returned with the teapot in a cozy and the bottle of brandy, she explained, "I think we both need a refill, and if you change your mind about Christie, she can sip hers from a saucer. The quiche will be ready shortly. Now, back to the morning's events. If Peter's right about the tire being slashed with a knife or something, this could well be murder— or at the very least manslaughter."

"How do you get manslaughter out of someone deliberately slashing the tire?"

Wendy scrunched her lips to the side, one of her *I'm thinking* expressions. "Maybe they only wanted to cause Nicholas a bit of bother, make him have a flat—not make him run off the road. He was driving so many people bonkers with his ideas for the Estate, someone could have been intent on harassing him."

I hadn't thought of that possibility. "But it caused a blowout, much more dangerous. So, you're thinking whoever did this may be surprised and horrified at the outcome?"

Wendy stood and pretended to speak into a microphone.

"Who knows what evil lurks in the hearts of men? The Shadow *knows*." She looked at me expectantly.

"Oh my gosh, we used to listen to old broadcasts of that radio show when I was in college. It came on Sunday nights, and my roommates and I would gather in the basement of our house to listen, with the lights turned low."

My friend curtsied. "My pleasure, madam. Anything to cheer you up. But seriously, this tire thing is a puzzle."

"Well, I expect Gemma will figure it out soon enough. But oh! Gemma's leaving tomorrow for a week-long police course. Wonder if she'll have to cancel."

Dickens barked. "We could figure it out like we usually do. You know, Detectives Dickens and Christie on the case?"

I looked at my dog and shook my head no. *No way*, I thought. *No way I'm getting involved in another murder or manslaughter or whatever case.*

Wendy looked from me to Dickens. "He must be thinking what I'm thinking. Since you and Peter were first on the scene, isn't that a good reason to consider your observations and what they could mean? When we were in Dartmouth on our last case, we thought about motives and possible suspects and got pretty darned close to solving the murder."

"Ha! As I recall, we only figured it out because the killer came after *me*! This time, I'll settle for being a good neighbor and friend—doing what I can to comfort Ellie and Julia. You know, taking food and whatever else I can do to help."

"Wimp! You just need to get over the shock of finding the wreck. Then we can put our heads together. And, if Gemma takes off for a week, the police will need all the help they can get. You know, they'll send someone who doesn't know the village or the players. It's not like a knife is gonna present itself with fingerprints and say, 'Look at me, I belong to Joe Blow, and he's the killer.'"

Maybe she had a point. Wendy looked at me. Dickens looked at me. Even Christie put her little nose in my face. "Oh for goodness' sake," I said. "Let's leave it be, at least for now." I could have sworn they all three grinned. *Right, cats and dogs don't grin. Well, maybe the Cheshire Cat . . .*

After breakfast, I tidied up while Wendy called Libby. We thought Belle and Libby, as Ellie's closest friends, were the two best folks to go to the Manor House. Separately, Wendy and I would cook food to take today or tomorrow. Ellie might have a cook, but she still needed the kindness of friends.

Gemma had already given her mother a heads-up, and Libby was preparing a basket of scones to take to Ellie. She agreed that Belle joining her was a good idea and promised to assess the situation and let us know what would help the family the most. I sent Wendy on her way so she could drop her mum at Ellie's and head on to the grocery store.

I hadn't decided what I would make but was leaning toward turkey soup. It wasn't my usual Greek fare but had been my father's annual post-Thanksgiving dish. I thought of it as Daddy's version of chicken soup and was the only one of his three daughters who'd made it part of her culinary repertoire—so much so that no matter which one of us cooked Thanksgiving dinner, I was gifted the turkey carcass when it was over. I'd have to decide whether to get a whole turkey or a turkey *crown*, as the Brits called a turkey breast.

I thought about calling Dave, but it was still too early in New York City for a phone call. Instead, I played Christmas music and worked on the column about the Astonbury Tree Lighting. I knew my readers in the States would get a kick out of the sheep and, most of all, a real live Earl lighting the tree.

It was a welcome respite to think about the festive evening instead of the auto accident.

A column about Ellie's birthday party would also be a hit. The countless Downton Abbey fans were sure to get a kick out of the modern-day version of a formal dinner at a manor house. *And I'll have to call Sophia and describe it in minute detail*, I thought. As a foodie *and* an Anglophile, my sister would want to hear every little thing. For my sister Anna, the broad strokes would be sufficient.

I was tidying up my desk when my inbox pinged with an email from Bev. She'd come back with a diagnosis for what ailed the late Earl.

Don't quote me on this, but I think the poor guy could have a peptic ulcer. Whatever it is, he should see a doctor. If it's an ulcer, the doctors can figure out which kind and what's causing it. Depending on the cause, it may be treated first with antibiotics or instead with something like Prilosec. Too technical to go into, but here are links to a couple of websites if you're interested.

Not now, but soon I'd have to email her the story of why the information was too late for the patient. Poor guy indeed. If she only knew.

I pushed back from my desk and sighed, and Christie mewed and lifted her head from the file drawer. "You look a little better, Leta. How do you feel?"

That was the problem, I thought, as I tickled Christie's chin. *I feel like I want a hug—like I want someone to put his arms around me and comfort me. And that someone is a nine-hour flight away.*

"I feel better. Enough better I can face Sainsbury's and the garden center. Might as well get garland if I'm going out. I just wish Dave were here."

Christie jumped to the top of the desk and looked at me. "Wouldn't Peter do?"

"You haven't gotten over your idea that Peter should be more than a friend, have you? I don't need two boyfriends. Some women may be able to handle that juggling act, but not me."

Dickens scooted out from beneath the desk. "Don't mind her, Leta. She's always been partial to Peter."

I knew Dickens didn't fancy himself a relationship expert, but he was right about Christie's preference for Peter. "Enough, you two. Time for me to run some errands, and if there's time before dark, maybe we can take a walk to see the donkeys."

Finding a smallish fresh turkey at Sainsbury's helped me decide that turkey soup would be my food offering for the bereaved family. Lemon, orzo, onion, garlic, celery, carrots, bay leaves, and butter, along with fresh parsley, basil, and oregano were the other essential ingredients. As was typical with my father's recipes, there were no measurements.

Back home, I preheated the oven while I readied the turkey for the roasting pan. Once it was done, I'd be able to carve it for sandwiches and use the carcass to make the soup either that night or first thing Monday morning. With the turkey in the oven and the sun still shining, I had plenty of time for a visit to the donkeys with Dickens and Christie.

As soon as Dickens saw my red headband, he pranced around my feet. It used to be the sight of my ballcap got him excited, but he'd come to take any headgear as a signal a walk was forthcoming. The carrots were another signal. There was no sign of the cat. In the mudroom, I grabbed my parka and Christie's backpack and called her. Some people think cats don't respond to commands, but Christie was living proof they do—when they want to. I heard her race down the steps and assumed she'd been napping on my bed . . . or under it . . . or in a basket . . . or some other comfy spot.

I placed her backpack on the floor, and she darted into it. "Guess you want to go with us, right?"

She stuck her head out the top and gave me a look that said, "Don't ask silly questions." I tucked a small blanket around her, and we were ready to go. Since I'd gotten a workout cycling that morning, I allowed myself to walk at a leisurely pace. The sight of the donkeys running to the fence made me realize there was no longer any danger of them being relocated. *Duh!* I thought. *Matthew is now the Earl of Stow, and things will remain as they've always been.* Since Wendy was determined The Little Old Ladies Detective Agency needed to be involved in the investigation into Nicholas's accident, I wondered whether she'd gotten as far as realizing Matthew had a motive for doing in his cousin.

I groaned. I didn't want to think about there being a killer in our midst—or at a bare minimum, someone who'd unintentionally caused an accident that led to Nicholas's death. Chances were that someone was a person I knew—like Matthew or Harry or . . . Gavin. *Not ready for this,* I thought. *Don't want to go there.*

Dickens barked and jumped up to put his paws on my thighs. "Leta, come on, get the carrots out. What are you waiting for?"

I'd stopped short of the fence with my mind a million miles away—or at least across the river at Astonbury Manor. I shook myself and pulled out the carrots. "Hi, Martha. Hi, Dylan. Here you go," I said as I handed them each a carrot.

Christie stretched her paw toward Dylan's nose and I

turned to position her closer to the fence. I stood for a few minutes while Christie patted donkey noses, my mind focused on the feeling of contentment these innocent creatures brought me. When Dickens and I turned back toward home, the donkeys followed us to the end of the fence line, where I gave them each a final carrot.

I frowned as I thought back to Wendy's playful rendition of the line from *The Shadow*. "Who knows what evil lurks in the hearts of men?" Twice before, The Little Old Ladies' Detective Agency had discovered the answer to that question. Were we destined to do it again?

Chapter Eleven

The aroma of roast turkey greeted me when I opened the door, but it would be a few hours before the bird was ready to come out of the oven. I'd bought sweet potatoes at the grocery, so tonight I'd have turkey, a baked sweet potato, and maybe some green peas—kind of a mini Thanksgiving dinner for one. *Darn, what I wouldn't give for a slice of Anna's pecan pie.*

When my phone rang, I wasn't surprised to see it was Gemma. I'd expected her to follow up to confirm when I'd left the party last night and what I'd noticed at the scene of the accident. No matter that she'd chastised me for overstepping my bounds in two previous murder inquiries, she'd admitted more than once that I was more observant than most folks.

"Hi, Leta. How are you doing after this morning?"

"I've gotten over being shaky, but I can't stop replaying the ambulance scene. I've managed to distract myself with writing and grocery shopping, but the images continue to surface. It will be days, maybe weeks before I'm totally over it. I'm glad neither Ellie nor Julia had to see that."

"Yes, a sudden death is hard enough to deal with. Witnessing it is something else entirely, as you well know. I'm at Astonbury Manor now. I spoke with Ellie and Julia earlier and met Matthew at the coroner's to identify the body. With that and a visit to Quedgeley to hear from the SOCOs, it was a few hours before I got back to speak with Harry, Sam, and Sarah. I was wondering whether you had time for me to stop by. I've something to discuss with you."

Now that was an interesting statement—"something to discuss"—not a follow-up? "Sure, are you thinking soon or a bit later?"

"Could be shortly or I could run by home first. I've still got to pack for my training class, so I could do that and then come over."

I could imagine Wendy advising me to take advantage of the situation to get all the details I could. "Would you like to have dinner with me? I've got a turkey in the oven, and if you've got time, I'd be happy for the company."

"Now, that's an offer I can't refuse. Would seven be a good time?"

We agreed on seven, and I put a bottle of sauvignon blanc in the fridge. Maybe I'd make a salad too—a Greek salad, of course. As far as my friends were concerned, me serving any other kind was unacceptable. I wasn't one to keep sweets in the house, so there'd be no dessert, but I thought Gemma would forgive me.

Glancing at the clock, I realized it was a good time to catch Dave on the phone. He liked to have a bagel and coffee out on Sunday mornings and then walk in Central Park for an hour. After that, he'd return to his apartment and spend hours with the Sunday papers spread out around him on the couch. The phone rang several times before he picked up.

"You caught me mid-bite. How are you this Sunday morning—or afternoon where you are?"

"Well, I'm fine, but I've had better days. Are you at the bagel shop?"

"Yup. An onion bagel with cream cheese and lox. Heaven. What's going on to make you say 'you've had better days?' I was expecting to hear about the party at the manor house, but it sounds like something else is up."

There was nothing for it but to dive in. "Peter and I were cycling to Stow this morning and came across an auto accident. That would have been bad enough, but it was the Earl of Stow in the car, and . . . well . . . the EMTs got him into the ambulance, but he died before they could get him to the hospital."

"Oh, Leta, how bad was it? Was it a horrific scene?"

I gulped and tried to relax my shoulders. "Well, the car was down an embankment, and things didn't look that bad. We tucked our coats around Nicholas while we waited for the EMTs. Even seeing him on the stretcher was bearable. But . . . I was standing there at the back of the ambulance when . . . he died. The monitors began beeping. The EMTs began CPR. My knees buckled, but one of the EMTs got to me before I went down."

"Oh my gosh. Where was Peter? How did you get home?"

How I wished I was telling him the story face to face. I took a deep breath and started at the beginning—before finding the car. "It was a picture-perfect day in the Cotswolds —a crisp, cold, sunny morning. I cycled to Peter's garage, and we planned to have breakfast in Stow-on-the-Wold and cycle back to Astonbury." Somehow, describing the frost on the fields and the view of the river made talking about the accident a little easier.

Dave let me tell the story without interruption. He was a good listener. That was probably why he was so good at interviewing authors for the articles he wrote for literary magazines. "For goodness' sake, Leta. I'm amazed you were steady enough on your feet to cycle home. How are you feeling now?"

Would I sound clingy if I told him the truth? I thought. *That I was okay, but I'd be better if he were here with me?* I hedged. "I'm better, but not great. Wendy came over and that helped. I've kept busy with shopping, and I'll be making soup to take to the Manor House."

I knew he'd heard the words I hadn't spoken when he said, "I'd give anything if I were flying over there now and didn't have to wait until Christmas Day. This is one of those rotten situations when words aren't enough—when being held is the only thing that will help, isn't it?"

"Yes." My voice cracked. "I've been wishing you were here, but it is what it is." In the spirit of "This too shall pass," I gulped and changed the subject to the book club meeting and the Dickens book Ellie had shared. I promised to see if Ellie would be up for us visiting her library when Dave came to Astonbury. Neither Dave nor I were collectors, but he would be in awe of her copy of *Sketches by Boz* and it might prove to be the inspiration for an article.

Not as good as a hug, but hearing Dave's voice helped. I spent the remainder of the afternoon fiddling with Christmas decorations for the mantel. When I stepped back to look at the effect I'd created with the garland, I was pleased, but I knew myself well enough to know I'd keep shifting and adding items, at least until my party Saturday night.

I turned my attention to setting the table for two and preparing the sides to go with the turkey. I'd pop the sweet potatoes in the oven around 6:30, and everything would be ready for dinner at 7:30 after appetizers at seven. The only thing left to do was change clothes. Another red sweater and a touch of red lipstick would brighten my mood.

I'd cranked up the Christmas music and was lighting candles around the cottage when Gemma knocked on the door. Seeing her dressed casually with her blonde hair down on her shoulders, I could almost forget she was a Detective Sergeant. "Look at you," I said. "You'd never guess you'd worked an accident scene and been back and forth between the family and the SOCOs all day."

Gemma hugged me, and I thought, *Wow, she's never done that before*. "Ah well, it's a wonder what a shower can do. And, look at this place," she said as she wandered to the mantel. "This carved reindeer, the miniature Christmas tree . . . Did you ship all this over from the States?"

"Everything but the tree and the garland. Check it out while I get the wine and an appetizer. Is white okay?"

She nodded yes and smiled as she picked up the Richie Bear. When I returned with two glasses of wine and some hummus and pita chips, I found her admiring the child-size black wooden rocking chair I'd placed by the Christmas tree. I had no idea who had given it to me, but I had a photo of me sitting in it dressed in footie pajamas. I still had long hair, so it must have been before Sophia was born. My mother had cut my hair short when she had Sophia—as a way to simplify her life, I supposed.

I told Gemma that story as we made ourselves comfortable on the couch. Dickens looked from me to the food on the coffee table, and I knew he was debating whether an attempt to snag a chip would be worth it. "Don't even think about it," I said as I leaned forward. He retreated to his bed near the fireplace and stretched out, but I knew he hadn't given up.

I couldn't recall Gemma and I often—if ever—chatting by ourselves about inconsequential topics. Heretofore, our one-on-one conversations had been about murder investigations. This interlude was a pleasant change.

Gemma sighed and set her glass down. "I'm not sure how to broach this topic, but . . . I need your help. With the case." She clenched and unclenched her hands and then spread them on her thighs. "You know I'm leaving in the morning, but you may not have considered what that means for this case. They're sending a DCI over to take charge."

"Oh. I guess that's good, right? I mean, you get to go on to training, and someone else will handle all this."

She picked up her glass and tossed back her wine. "Not good. I'll be completely out of the loop. May have been even without the training course. We're talking about the death of an Earl. Too important for a mere Detective Sergeant, and not only that . . . my dad is an obvious suspect."

I'd thought of Gavin as a suspect because he'd been quite vocal about his dislike of the resort plans, but, of course, I didn't believe for a minute he was guilty. Gemma being cut out? I hadn't gotten that far. Made sense, though. "Well, you and I both know your dad didn't slash anyone's tires. Is that it? Can I give a character reference or something? How can I help? It's not like your DCI is going to ask my input, is it?"

I told her to sit tight and went to get the bottle of wine. As I refilled our glasses, Gemma took a tentative sip. "Got to watch my intake if I'm going to be clearheaded for my drive tomorrow. This is a tough conversation for me. What I need is for you to be my eyes and ears, and I can't believe

I'm saying this, but I need your help—I need you to *investigate*."

My eyes widened and I sat back. "I can't believe I heard you right. You want me to do what you've reprimanded me for in the past?"

"Yup, I do. DCI Burton doesn't know the lay of the land and isn't going to get much out of the villagers, and he'll only have Constable James to help him. Granted, our young constable is learning, but he's got a long way to go. Think of yourself as a private investigator hired to clear my dad, except you can't be a PI without a license. If you could, I'd get Mum to give you a pound to make it official. Anyway, I know I'm rambling, but do you think you and your band of little old ladies can help?"

My mouth dropped open and it was me who gulped wine this time. "You know we'll do anything we can to clear your dad and anyone else we see as innocent, for that matter. Hell's bells, think of the list your DCI will start with—Ellie, Matthew, Harry, your dad. If he casts the net wide, he'll likely see all the party guests as possible suspects. The list is endless. I could be on the list, since I was upset when I thought the donkeys might be moved. Not upset enough to slash Nicholas's tires, by any means. I'm not sure I even have a knife that could do the trick. By the way, will Constable James be in on this plan too? It would help if I could get information about what kind of knife and that kind of thing."

"Yes, he's ready to help. I haven't quite figured out when you share info with him versus me, but I think that will work itself out. And I'll give you his cell number so it's easy for you to find him. We just need to keep all this on the QT so DCI Burton doesn't get wind of it. You may have to help Jonas, I mean Constable James, with how to couch ideas such that our

DCI thinks he's brilliant—not that someone's feeding him clues."

Wendy's not going to believe this, I thought. *Here she's been trying to convince me to get involved, and now we've been invited in.*

I left Gemma staring into the fire as I tossed a salad and carved the turkey. When I called her to the kitchen, I refilled our glasses before we dug in. Dickens was a few steps behind her. "Dickens, is that hummus on your chin? You were just biding your time, right?"

He barked and licked his chin. "Who, me?" he said as he settled beneath the table. *Probably hoping we'll drop some turkey,* I thought.

Gemma spread her napkin in her lap. "So is this what you had for Thanksgiving when you went home?"

"Close but not quite. I didn't make the dressing, which may be my favorite part. Funny, whether I'm preparing the whole meal or celebrating elsewhere with family or friends, my making the dressing is a must." I explained that I'd only roasted a turkey so I could make turkey soup for Ellie and her family and hadn't felt compelled to prepare a full-fledged feast. Not to mention, I was trying to shed a few pounds before holiday treats became a daily indulgence.

"So, no dessert? That's good by me. Why is it men don't seem to worry about holiday weight gain like we women do? I think Dad takes the month of December as a license to overindulge his sweet tooth, much to Mum's dismay."

In an unspoken agreement, we avoided any talk of murder while we ate. When Gemma pushed back from the table with a sigh, I cleared dishes and asked whether she preferred coffee or tea. She commented that the splash of Amaretto I offered with coffee made the decision easy. Mugs in hand, we returned to the sitting room, Dickens close on our heels. Christie hadn't moved since we'd left. Funny, I never knew where she'd choose to spend an hour or two or three. Tonight, she was curled in a ball in one of the baskets.

"I'm eager to hear what you learned today, Gemma. Did you interview everyone at the Manor House? The whole family, even those who don't live in the house, like Matthew and his family?"

"Yes, in stages. When I arrived, Matthew answered the door. He and Ellie were eating breakfast in the kitchen, and Julia hadn't come down yet, so I asked if one of them would wake her. They looked confused, probably wondered why I hadn't asked for Nicholas too. I could tell Matthew didn't fancy waking his cousin's wife but didn't want his mum to have to go upstairs. Ellie must have picked up on his hesitation and suggested he escort me to Julia's room. I asked her to make some more tea.

"When we went upstairs, I could hear voices, so I knocked and sent Matthew back to the kitchen. When Julia opened the bedroom door, she was talking on her phone and, understandably, looked surprised to see me. I asked her to accompany me downstairs, and I glanced around the room, especially at the bed, as she grabbed a robe. The queen size bed looked as though only one person had slept in it, so I asked if she recalled Nicholas coming to bed. She told me they'd been sleeping in separate bedrooms since he'd been sick.

"By the time we arrived in the kitchen, Ellie had a pot of tea ready. When they were all at the table with a cup of tea in front of them, I broke the news—that there'd been an auto accident, *not* what had caused it, just that Nicholas had run off the road and been killed."

I closed my eyes and shook my head. "Julia must have been

shocked and horrified. I know your rule of thumb about the spouse always being the prime suspect, but—"

"You're right. That's the way we think, but I'm not automatically going there in this case. I took note of how each of them reacted. All three looked stunned. Julia broke into sobs. Ellie was tearful, but not overwrought. Matthew was the one who asked the questions—where, when, how."

Gemma had laid out the scenario—the skidmarks, the direction he was driving, and that he was still dressed in his tux—facts that indicated he'd gone out last night, was returning home, *and* that this was a single-car accident. There was back and forth conversation as to why Nicholas went out and where he could have been going, all of it in shocked tones.

"I asked Julia whether she felt up to identifying the body, but Matthew volunteered before she could respond. I told him it would be a few hours, and I'd ring him when I got to the morgue in Gloucester."

She'd called Constable James, and they met in Quedgeley to see what the SOCOs had come up with. They learned Peter had been correct in thinking it was a knife that slashed the tire. The SOCOs had taken Peter's fingerprints for elimination since he'd touched the fender when he found the slash mark. Oddly, there was only the one handprint just above the tire, Peter's. That told them the fender had been wiped clean.

"Now, hold on to your hat, Nancy Drew. The surprise was a big wad of dosh on the front seat—£1,000 in a white envelope."

"Whoa! Glad you explained what dosh is. I felt like I'd heard the word before, maybe in some British police series, but I couldn't place it. Now, what was that for? A note would be too much to hope for, I guess."

"No note. Did he pick up the money somewhere or was he

delivering it? My thought is it was a payoff, but for who? Someone on the planning commission? Constable James is checking texts and phone calls to see if we can establish who Nicholas had been to see. Did he meet someone to pick up the money?"

I shrugged my shoulders. "This is where Peter would say 'crikey, what next?' If he'd been driving away from the Estate, I'd think he was taking money to someone—maybe paying off someone on the planning commission. Or paying off someone who was raising a stink and lobbying the commission *not* to approve the resort—at least not with all the bells and whistles Nicholas envisioned. There are plenty of candidates on the 'I don't want a resort' list. He'd know better than to try that on your dad, but there could be others."

"But he was headed home. Doesn't it seem as though he picked up the money? Unless he drives around all the time with wads of cash on the front seat. What if someone was bribing Nicholas? But over what?"

I shook my head no. "Him being bribed doesn't make sense to me. Nicholas greasing palms to get his way seems much more likely, except that he'd gone out late at night and appeared to be returning to the Estate *with* the money. Maybe there was a miscommunication about meeting up."

"Hard to say. Maybe Constable James will discover something telling on the phone. Anyway, the only other bit I have to share is what I got from interviewing Matthew after he identified the body. We sat outside in the sunshine, and I asked him about the party, who he'd seen Nicholas speaking with, that sort of thing.

"Said Nick, as he calls him, had been deep in conversation with Mr. Morgan, your neighbor. Makes sense, since he's the Astonbury rep on the planning commission. His cousin pretty much made the rounds at the party and spoke with all the guests, so that doesn't narrow the field. And that's it. That's all I've got."

Dickens nudged Gemma's knee and barked. "We'll help you. I'll get with Basil and Blanche and see what they know."

Gemma laughed and rubbed his head. "Funny boy. Must think it's time for me to leave. And it is. Tomorrow's drive will give me time to think, so if something pops into my head, I'll let you know."

"I found I did some of my best thinking when I drove between Atlanta and Charlotte for business. Something about a four-hour drive without a computer screen in front of me seemed to free my brain." I walked her to the door and let Dickens out for his nightly inspection of the garden. "Drive safely. And rest assured, the Little Old Ladies' Detective Agency will start work tomorrow."

Right, I thought, *Gemma irritated the heck out of me when she first referred to us as little old ladies, and now we've adopted the name.* Regardless of what we called ourselves, the three of us—Wendy, Belle, and I—plus Dickens and Christie, were officially on the case. All we needed were business cards and tee shirts!

Chapter Twelve

After Gemma left, I stayed up later than usual making turkey soup to deliver to the Manor House the next day. Before I crawled in bed, I texted Wendy about meeting for the early yoga class Monday morning followed by breakfast at Toby's Tearoom. Ending the message with "Gemma wants our help" got Wendy's attention. It wasn't fair to her when I texted back "I'll tell you more tomorrow," but I needed a good night's sleep before getting into details.

Rhiannon was surprised to see me laying out my yoga mat for the early class. Funny how eight seemed early after I grew accustomed to retired life. For years, I'd met my trainer two days a week at seven. *How did I ever do that?*

The class was buzzing with news of the accident and all the questions you'd expect—"How did it happen? What does it mean for the family? Guess this makes Matthew the new Earl, doesn't it?" I never could figure out how news traveled so fast in Astonbury.

When Wendy arrived, she greeted me with a demand. "Okay, I hereby declare you're buying breakfast since you left me hanging last night. I'm dying to know what Gemma said."

Rhiannon looked up from her notes. "I would have tagged along anyway, but I can't miss a chance to hear this. I assume the words 'what Gemma said' have to do with the accident. To think we'd only just seen the Earl Saturday night."

With my index finger to my lips, I signaled her to hush. We didn't need to start tongues wagging before class. None of us would be able to clear our minds to focus on our poses—not to mention, I didn't want to be the center of a gossipy frenzy when class ended. Today's class focused on forward bends, which, among other things, were supposed to calm the brain and help relieve stress. That seemed a propitious way to prepare for detective work.

Class over, we three trooped to Toby's. Armed with scones and coffee, we got down to business. Rhiannon wasn't a member of the LOL Detective Agency—as I was now thinking of us—but she'd been at the tree lighting and the birthday party and would be a good source of information.

I hadn't spoken with Rhiannon since Peter and I had stumbled onto the accident scene, so I had to fill her in on that before I could move to my dinner with Gemma. As I was finishing up that piece, I recalled the dosh. *What a funny word*, I thought. "The thing neither Peter nor I noticed as we were trying to keep Nicholas warm was the money in the car."

"Huh? Why would there be money in the car?" asked Wendy.

The money discussion that followed didn't vary from the

one I'd had with Gemma. Was he delivering or accepting money? We three agreed it was more likely he was bribing others than *being bribed* by someone. The discovery of money had gotten a startled reaction but nothing like my next revelation. "Gemma asked for my help." I couldn't get a word in edgewise as to the circumstances that triggered the request until Wendy and Rhiannon stopped peppering me with questions.

"Are you guys done yet? Let me explain why she asked. As we speak, she's driving to a training course, and headquarters is sending in a DCI Burton to lead the investigation in her absence. As Gemma explained, they might have done so anyway, given it's an Earl who's died in suspicious circumstances. So DCI Burton will be in charge, with Constable James reporting to him." I shared the details of our arrangement and how Constable James was in on it.

Wendy rubbed her hands together in glee. "She *actually* asked for the Little Old Ladies' Detective Agency to snoop around? I never thought I'd see the day. Course, we'll have to stay one step ahead of the DCI. He's not likely to be happy about our involvement."

"Ha! You think we irritated Gemma? Can you imagine what a DCI will say or do if he finds out what we're up to? It won't be pretty."

Rhiannon grinned. "Well then, seems all the more urgent for me to tell you what I know before this DCI comes calling. My guess is he'll be interviewing the guests from Saturday night, right?"

Wendy and I both nodded, and Rhiannon launched into her recollections from the party. "First, you two always tease me when I talk about vibes, but there were certainly tense undertones and a few scathing looks. When Toby asked

Nicholas about the sheep—well if looks could kill, Matthew would have throttled Nicholas during that conversation."

"Yes, that's the way it looked to me, but in light of the accident, I wouldn't use the words—'if looks could kill.'"

"Oh! Right, I'll be careful about that. Now, the other thing is I didn't hear what was said, but I noticed Harry corner Nicholas in the hall after dinner, and their voices were angry. Wait, I did hear Nicholas say, 'your pet sheep,' which appeared to incense Harry."

Wendy pursed her lips. "I'd be incensed too if someone referred to my sheep as pets when raising them was my business. What an insult."

Rhiannon looked thoughtful. "I also had a feeling Julia and Nicholas weren't seeing eye to eye that evening. Did either of you sense any tension?"

I laughed. "My sense is she doesn't hesitate to disagree with him—firmly and politely—and he may not take it well. I got the impression at the tree lighting she wished he'd keep the sheep and the artisans, and that maybe she'd try to influence him in that direction. Come to think of it, though, she did give him an angry look at the party, and it was when you were talking with them."

Wendy chuckled. "Not unlike wives and girlfriends the world over, calming the waters when their partners are stirring things up. I've done the same a few times in my life. How 'bout you, Leta?"

"Yup. With boyfriends and with Henry. He may have been a saint in many ways, but when he got riled at something, like someone cutting him off in traffic, I had to step in. Can't tell you how many times I said, 'you can yell, but for goodness' sake, no hand signals or we could have a road rage incident on our hands.'"

Toby had wandered up as we were chatting. "What's that about hand signals? I think they serve a good purpose."

We gals looked at each other and rolled our eyes simultaneously. "Men!" I said, causing Wendy and Rhiannon to chuckle. Toby took it in stride and sat down with his cup of coffee.

"Not sure I want to join this conversation if you're going to bash men. Has this been going on since you got here this morning?"

Rhiannon ignored that jibe and told him we were discussing our observations from Saturday night and invited his input. "Hmmm. Other than that one chat with Nicholas, I didn't see much of him. I did have an interesting conversation with Gavin, though. Seems Nicholas wasn't stopping with the idea of the one-lane bridge and buying the donkey pasture. He'd approached Gavin about buying the inn proper, all the property. Can you believe that?"

"Are you kidding me?" I exclaimed. "Libby and Gavin would never sell. That's their retirement plan—run the inn until they can no longer manage, maybe hire a manager to do the heavy lifting, so to speak, and later on leave it to Gemma. I think Libby has dreams of Gemma marrying someone who would take it over someday."

Wendy tilted her head and frowned. "Why would Nicholas think Gavin would sell the inn when he's been adamant about not selling the donkey pasture?"

Toby had an answer for that. "That's a sound bargaining ploy. Keep upping the ante until someone can't refuse. Depending on what Nicholas offered, Gavin could have been walking away from a fortune, enough money to retire early. The problem was Nicholas couldn't understand anyone doing that. Couldn't understand how much Libby and Gavin enjoy running the inn, the joy they get from it—the cooking, the guests from around the world, the Fall Fête on the grounds. All of that's priceless to them."

Wendy looked at me. "What's that saying? More money than sense? Goodness knows what Nicholas was worth even before he inherited his part of his grandfather's fortune. And he wants to throw money at Gavin? Fits with the money in the car, right?"

Toby had missed that part. "What money in what car?"

As I was explaining that to him, I had a flashback to overhearing Mr. Morgan and Nicholas talking outside the library. The one word I'd made out was *inducement*. I shared the episode with my friends. "I need to talk to Mr. Morgan and find out what Nicholas told him. Was he offering him an *inducement* or telling him who he'd already approached in that manner? Wonder if Nicholas tried to bribe the wrong person."

Wendy took her handbag from the back of the chair and set it on the table. "Time to get to work, Leta. We've got food to deliver to the Manor House, and we need to figure out a divide-and-conquer plan. If we want to stay one step ahead of DCI Burton, we need to get a move on."

My first assignment was to visit the Book Nook to see what Beatrix might have observed, but as I was stepping from the curb, Toby called me. "Leta, I didn't want to mention this in the crowd, but it worries me. I saw Gavin and Nicholas arguing in the dining room Saturday night after dessert. Everyone else was in the sitting room, and I glimpsed them as I walked to the bathroom beneath the stairs. It can't have been about anything other than the donkey pasture and wanting to buy the inn."

"How could you tell it was an argument? Were they yelling at each other?"

"More like talking in loud whispers until Gavin yelled, 'Over my dead body.' I probably shouldn't worry. It's not like it was a death threat, but I took his outburst to mean he was furious."

I shook my head. "There's so much drama surrounding all this. Nicholas has ticked off much of the village, but Gavin, Harry, and Matthew have been in his crosshairs. Thanks for telling me. I'll need to chat with Gavin before long to get the whole sordid story."

I crossed the street to the Book Nook. Tommy and Tuppence were batting at ornaments on the Christmas tree in the window and stopped to look at me as I entered. I called to Beatrix. "I see you've got the unbreakable ornaments on the lower limbs. Have those two ever attempted to climb higher?"

"Heavens no, and they'd best not if they know what's good for 'em. How are you today? Have you recovered from finding Nicholas on the side of the road? What an awful experience."

I held my hands palms-up in a "who knows" gesture. "Pretty much, except the image of him in the back of the ambulance continues to pop into my head. It's hard to believe he's gone."

"I know. Of course, I never got to know him—mostly heard the negative comments about his plans for the Manor House. For all that, though, he was charming Saturday night. The toast he made to Ellie was lovely, and I liked his sense of humor."

I smiled as I reflected on his tribute to his grandfather and father woven into his toast to Ellie. "Yes, he was eloquent. Makes me wonder all the more why he couldn't find a less condescending way to express his opinions about Harry's sheep business and why he was keeping the family on tenterhooks."

"Harrumph. That's what made me dislike him before I ever met him. You'd think a businessman would be more decisive. After all, Nigel died months ago, and Nicholas has had plenty of time to firm up his plans. I can tell you your neighbor Mrs. Morgan was none too pleased as she and her husband were leaving Saturday night."

The Morgans were on my "must talk to" list, but I wondered what Beatrix knew. "Really? What was she upset about?"

"If the planning commission approved the new bridge across the River Elfe, the drive would extend from the bridge through the pasture behind the Morgans' cottage. Can you imagine being accustomed to seeing nothing but sheep and countryside for years and suddenly being confronted with traffic, especially trucks?"

"No, I can't. Guess that means the plan wouldn't haven't gotten Mr. Morgan's vote. Wonder what the other representatives on the Planning Commission thought."

"She said Nicholas was pressuring her husband to vote in favor of the plan, but she didn't go into detail."

I'd have to speak with Mr. Morgan to get the specifics. "Interesting, Beatrix. And what does George Evans think about all this?"

"Oh! George is fit to be tied. He's been bringing tour groups to the manor house for years, and he was beginning brewery tours with Matthew's help. Occasionally, Sarah helped him put together a longer tour where the group also visited the artisans on the Estate—Sarah with her soap making, the spinner, the weaver, and whoever else had taken up residence. He had the impression Nicholas didn't see tour groups as appropriate for a posh resort."

Trixie greeted me as she emerged from the storeroom carrying an armful of books. "Hi, Leta. I'm getting to where I expect to see you on Mondays, after your yoga class and coffee at Toby's. I don't think your latest book order's arrived yet, though."

"No worries. Even though they're Christmas books, I can read them whenever they get here." I'd requested a copy of Agatha Christie's *The Adventure of the Christmas Pudding* after hearing about it from Belle, who was a huge Poirot fan. And I'd also asked for Carolyn Hart's *Sugarplum Dead*. That way I'd get one mystery set in England and another set on an island off the coast of South Carolina.

"Was Toby's Tearoom still buzzing about the accident? That's all anyone could talk about Sunday," Trixie said.

"It may have died down a bit, but I heard the occasional comment. Have you heard anything interesting?"

Trixie put the books on the counter and stretched her arms. "That lot was heavy. To answer your question, the gossip is mostly a rehash of the resort plans, plus speculation as to what Nicholas's death means for the Estate."

We agreed we didn't know any more about that than the Tearoom gossips did, and we'd find out in good time. I walked outside and down High Street to my car parked in front of the yoga studio. When my phone rang, I saw it was Gemma. "Hi there. Are you on the road?"

"Yes, making good time and just got some news from the coroner. Not sure whether it will lead anywhere, but Nicholas had a stomach ulcer. It wasn't yet a bleeding ulcer, but it was pretty advanced and needed treating. I don't get why he would have let it go so long."

His ailment made me think of Ellie's comment about Julia taking care of Nicholas. "That explains the stomach issue he's had since he arrived and why Julia was plying him with rice and broth and crackers. Probably all he could eat without exacerbating his condition. I agree, though, it's odd he didn't see a doctor and tend to it. You're going to laugh at this, I know, but I'd emailed a friend of mine in the States—before Nicholas died—to ask what might be wrong with him based on the symptoms. I can't wait to tell her she was right—an ulcer."

I could imagine Gemma rolling her eyes. "A friend in the States? A doctor?"

"Now I know you're going to laugh. No, but she taught anatomy and biology and is pretty knowledgeable on health issues, or at least how to find answers online. She thought he should see a doctor pretty quickly."

"My dad avoids doctors at all costs, as do lots of men, I think. Dad always says he can tough it out. On another note, DCI Burton arrived at the Stow police station this morning. He's gone to the Manor House to speak with the family again. He told Constable James to show up in an hour. I could tell he was disappointed he didn't get invited to accompany him right off the bat. He's grown accustomed to me involving him as a way to train him. Maybe it's down to DCI Burton not knowing him, or maybe it's because the DCI is older."

I wondered how old he was to be described that way by our fairly young Detective Sergeant. "Older, as in my age, or older as in forty-something?"

"Oh for goodness' sake, Leta, what does it matter? Did I touch another *age nerve?*"

True, I'd been furious when she'd first called Wendy, Belle, and me little old ladies, but I'd since gotten over it. Except Gemma sometimes bordered on treating us as old fuddy-duddies, and I wondered if that was what she was thinking about DCI Burton. "I merely wondered whether you were talking about his looks or his approach when you said he was older."

"I've never asked him his age, but he's got grey hair and a few wrinkles. I see him as Dad's age, possibly mid-fifties. And, according to Constable James, our DCI is adhering to the 'spouse as the primary suspect' adage at least for now. Anyway, he's left him behind to follow up on cell phone data."

"Okay, I'll put Wendy in the picture. She and Belle may already be at the Manor House with quiche and fruit for the family, and I expect they'll stay awhile to comfort Ellie." *I can't wait to hear Wendy's take on DCI Burton*, I thought.

Chapter Thirteen

"What do you mean I can't go?" screeched Christie as I loaded Dickens and the turkey soup into my London taxi. "I could crawl into laps and purr. I'm an expert at the comfort business."

"Christie, there are all kinds of reasons why you accompanying us is not a good idea. I've never seen any cats at the Manor House, so I don't know whether everyone in the household likes cats, especially Blanche. And lots of people will be coming and going with food and flowers, and I can't risk you getting out and getting lost. It's a very big place."

"I promise," barked Dickens, "I'll fill you in when we get back. And maybe we can all go see Martha and Dylan." He looked at me and I gave him a reassuring nod.

"Pffft," Christie hissed. "Just be that way." And with that, she strutted from the room, her tail switching back and forth.

No sense trying to cajole her. She'd forgive us in her own time. I locked up and fastened Dickens into the backseat for the short drive. As I arrived at the Manor House, I saw I'd been right about folks coming and going. There were two delivery vans unloading flowers, Wendy's car, and several I didn't recognize. Two women were exiting the front of the house.

The front door was partially open, and Dickens and I went straight to the kitchen. I found Wendy in there making a pot of tea and organizing food in the fridge. "You're a sight for sore eyes," she said. "Today is Caroline's day off, and I could use a hand putting all this stuff away. There's been a nonstop stream of casseroles since I got here. Let's leave your soup out for lunch and store the rest."

I looked to be sure no one else was around and quietly filled Wendy in on what I'd heard from Gemma and Beatrix. "Have you seen DCI Burton?"

Wendy grinned. "Boy, have I. Gemma may think he's old, but he's quite attractive in a fit, silver fox kind of way. I've been ferrying pots of tea to the conservatory where he's setting up to interview the family. He spent time wandering the first floor, so he's only now getting started with Ellie. Mum's been sitting with her in the library, and I expect that's where she'll return unless her conversation with DCI Burton is upsetting."

"How's Ellie bearing up?"

She closed her eyes and shook her head. "She's a wonder. Calm, dignified, in control. I had to shoo her and Mum from the kitchen so Ellie wouldn't do all the work. And I shooed Blanche to get her out from under my feet. Bet that's who Dickens is looking for, right?" Dickens had sniffed his way around the kitchen and returned to sit by my side.

"Too right. As soon as I've put the soup in a pot and finished helping you, I'll escort him to sit with Belle and Blanche. Well, *sit* with Belle—*play* with Blanche." We were about finished when a neighbor arrived with pasties, followed by another with a cake. On their heels was Constable James.

He smiled when he saw me. "Hi, Leta. I see you've got Detective Dickens with you. And hello, Wendy." He stood and shuffled his feet a moment before whispering, "Gemma's filled you in about us working together on the sly, right?"

I grinned at his discomfort. "A bit like a game, isn't it? Except it's darned serious. We'll figure it out, and we'll do fine as long as you don't refer to me as Miss Marple. That moniker is reserved for Mrs. Davies, as the only white-haired member of our little group. Come with me to drop Dickens by the library and then I can show you to the conservatory to see your DCI."

Belle had met Constable James during our first case, so no introductions were necessary. I gave her a hug and Blanche a scratch behind her ears before proceeding to the conservatory and knocking on the glass door. "Enter," boomed a deep voice.

I introduced myself and told Ellie and the detective I'd be back shortly with another pot of tea. DCI Burton stood to shake my hand and, speaking in hushed tones, ushered Constable James from the sun-filled room. I took the opportunity to give Ellie a peck on the cheek and tell her how sorry I was for her loss. Wendy was right. Ellie was holding up like a trooper—or like a Dowager Countess, I supposed. And she was right about DCI Burton's looks.

DCI Burton and I passed each other in the doorway. In the hall, Constable James told me his instructions were to search Ellie and Julia's rooms while the DCI interviewed them. He was off to Ellie's room now.

"Have you or the DCI or maybe Gemma searched Nicholas's room?"

"Yes and no. The DCI will do a thorough search before we

leave. Gemma gave it a quick once-over, took his laptop, and put crime tape across the door before she left to go to the morgue. Between the morgue and the visit to the SOCOs, she couldn't do more than that. Going through the laptop is on my list after running down things I found on his phone."

"Okay. By the way, I'm curious. Have the police told the family about the slashed tire yet?"

"How did you . . . oh right, you were there at the accident. DCI Burton is sharing that bit today as he interviews them— to see what kind of reaction he gets. This will be when they first learn the accident wasn't an accident."

I bit my lip. "Um, you know no one told me and Peter to keep it under our hats? So, Wendy and a few others already know. I haven't told anyone in the family though."

Constable James didn't reply. *I need to get him more comfortable with my involvement*, I thought. "Listen, do you want to come by later tonight to exchange information? I can offer a snack and some wine—that is, if you can indulge while on duty."

He looked grateful and said he'd ring me later. How late would depend on what the DCI had in mind for him. The good news was he lived in Astonbury and leaving the station in Stow to visit me wouldn't be out of his way.

Now for one final request. "I'd love to look at Julia's room while you're in there. Think we can make that happen?"

He looked hesitant until I reminded him that Gemma had taken me with her to search a victim's caravan during the last murder investigation. When he agreed, I asked him to fetch me from the kitchen once he'd escorted Julia to the conservatory.

I wanted to see Julia's room, but I was also eager to visit Matthew and Sarah. In the kitchen when I saw Wendy, I had a brainstorm. "Wendy, what if I go to Matthew's cottage, and you look over Constable James's shoulder when he searches Julia's room? You'll have to keep a ready excuse in mind in case the DCI wanders up there before you two are done."

Her face lit up and she laughed. "You've got it. I've watched enough police shows on the telly that I should know what to do, especially now I've gotten Mum hooked on reruns of *Morse* and *Dalziel & Pascoe*. We don't binge-watch, but we *do* watch several episodes a week of each. I wonder, does being addicted to shows from the '90s mean I'm getting old? Whatever it is, Mum and I like the curmudgeonly detectives in those shows."

I grinned. "Oh come on, all three of us enjoy *Vera*. Doesn't matter when the shows were on television. Now, what do you say to coming over late this afternoon with your mum so we can compare notes?"

Wendy agreed and offered to pick up takeout from the Ploughman so we could have an early dinner while we worked. In the library, Dickens and Blanche had taken up position on either side of Belle and the three made a touching tableau—the picture of canine loyalty, even if neither dog belonged to her. There was no sign of Ellie, so I took that to mean she was still with the DCI.

"Dickens, want to take a walk? We may even see Basil." A walk with the possibility of seeing his large friend was all the inducement my boy needed. He sprang up, barked goodbye to Blanche, and followed me. Matthew's roomy cottage was positioned far enough from the Manor House to be private but close enough that he and Sarah could have dinner with Ellie without having to drive. A copse of rowan trees offered shade at the back, and two ancient oaks stood at attention on either side of the gravel area in front.

Sarah greeted me when I knocked. "Oh, Leta, come in, and Dickens too. What a nice surprise." She ruffled his fur and invited us to the sitting room. "Would you care for a spot of tea and some biscuits? I can't seem to stop eating the ones I picked up at the church booth at the tree lighting."

So much for watching my weight, I thought. *Cookies before lunch.* "How are you doing?" I asked as she returned with the tea and cookies. I never could get accustomed to calling them biscuits.

"As well as can be expected, I guess. For me, losing Nicholas is more like losing a distant relative. I never knew him well enough to think of him as Matthew's cousin. I'm more concerned about the toll it's taking on Ellie. She doesn't show it, but another death in the family following so closely on the heels of both Reggie and Nigel dying has to be hard."

I shook my finger at Dickens as he tried to put his nose in the cookies. "You're right, she appears to be holding up well. How's Matthew handling it? And the boys?"

"Sam's fairly unfazed. With a fifteen-year age difference and Nicholas visiting infrequently, they never developed a relationship to speak of. Matthew's taking it a bit harder, but not like he took Reggie's death. He and Reggie were close despite their age difference and being only half-brothers. Ellie says Matthew followed Reggie everywhere as a toddler, and when Reggie moved to the States, they stayed in touch the old fashioned way—via letters. When Matthew was at Cambridge and then here helping his dad manage the Estate, the brothers bounced ideas off each other. They both loved their heritage—the land, the manor house, this way of life.

"He was looking forward to Reggie retiring here in a few years, and his death was a terrible shock. Don't get me wrong, losing his dad was hard, but Nigel was in his nineties, you know . . ."

"And Matthew and Nicholas were never close?"

"Not especially. Nicholas didn't always come with Reggie when he visited, and if he did, it would only be for a week at the most. He was caught up in school sports and his friends in New York City. Then he was off to college, and he was soon climbing the ladder and starting his own firm. Nicholas never seemed to have much appreciation for the Estate and our way of life."

I processed that bit of information as I signaled Dickens to lie down. "Guess that explains why he had no qualms about changing it all. These past few weeks must have been painful for Matthew."

"Yes and no. My husband has a unique ability to take things in stride. He'd about convinced himself this was only a phase for Nicholas, and he'd eventually settle down and see reason. I wasn't so sure."

I stood up. "Sarah, I'm going to put Dickens outside so we can carry on a conversation. He's dying to get into those cookies." I shooed him out the front door and told him to stay close. When I returned to the sitting room, I said, "Now what was I going to ask? Oh, right. What about Harry? How's he doing with this?"

Sarah sighed and sipped her tea. "I'm not sure I know. He's not broken up over his death. He hardly knew his uncle, and what dealings he's had with him have been contentious. One minute, Harry's furious and hellbent on persuading Nicholas the sheep are a huge asset. The next he's throwing his arms in the air and calling estate agents about finding property and moving himself and the herd. It wouldn't be a stretch to say he feels well rid of him. On the other hand, I sense he feels bad that he doesn't care more, that he ought to have some familial affection for Nicholas, no matter the havoc he was wreaking."

What a mess, I thought. "Well, I guess everything will go back to normal now, right? There'll be no question of moving the sheep or bringing in someone new to run the brewery. Oh! But what about Julia? Does she have a part in any of this?"

"You're right, things should go back to normal, except Matthew has to find out if Nicholas made any business commitments regarding the Estate. Who knows what agreements he'd made or plans he'd signed off on? As for Julia? I feel bad for her. So young to be a widow."

I should have thought of that. She was much younger than I'd been when I'd lost Henry. "Have you seen her since yesterday? Maybe her dad will come down to be with her. I think she told me he lived in Northampton."

"I've seen her only briefly, and Ellie says she's hardly left her room since Gemma told her the news. Don't know about her dad. I can't believe we were laughing just the other day about the prenup she had with Nicholas. Guess she won't have to worry about that now."

I put my teacup down and sat back. "She was laughing about their prenup? What was funny about it?"

Sarah chuckled. "I'd taken a pot of potato soup and homemade bread to the manor house for lunch, and she commented she'd love the recipe except she had to be vigilant about what she ate—Nicholas had included a weight gain clause in their prenup in addition to several others. Can you believe that? I've heard about infidelity clauses, but weight?! If he chose to divorce her citing any of the clauses, she'd get only a pittance. She knew when she married him he'd been taken to the cleaners by his first wife and was paranoid about his money."

"That doesn't sound funny to me at all. By all accounts, he

was a hugely successful businessman, and I understand he wouldn't want to give away half of what he'd made pre-Julia, but weight gain? And the word pittance makes him sound like Scrooge. I wonder what the other clauses were."

Sarah grinned. "Julia didn't say, and I didn't want to ask—though I was dying to know. When I saw her Saturday morning, she told me they'd had a row about her taking a small part in a movie, and I couldn't help but think he'd forgotten to add that bit to the prenup. Honestly, men never cease to amaze me."

Her last comment prompted me to share some of the despicable traits I'd discovered about another Astonbury murder victim. Nicholas was a prince compared to that guy. I was careful not to refer to Nicholas's death as murder, since I knew the DCI was revealing that to each of the family members individually today.

I thanked Sarah for the tea and biscuits and suggested she try the turkey soup I'd left at the Manor house. When I stepped outside, Dickens was nowhere to be seen. *Stay* was the one command he usually obeyed, but not today. I wandered in the direction of the river, calling his name, and soon he came into view. He and Basil were with Harry and the sheep.

"You little Dickens," I called as I approached, "I told you to stay!"

Harry looked up and laughed. "So, he has those traits too, huh? A mind of his own and selective hearing? Basil has those in spades. 'Course the experts say Pyrs are so often out on their own, they have to think for themselves."

"And what do the experts say about their incessant barking? I'd love to hear the rationale for that. Still, they're a lovable breed."

Harry knelt between the dogs and put an arm around each

one. "Fellas, tell us about the barking." He cocked his head back and forth between them as though they were talking to him. "Uh-huh, right. Okay, I'll tell her. Leta, they say there are some things we humans aren't smart enough to understand, and we should leave it at that."

Dickens barked, "I never said that. There are things you humans don't *see or smell*, but you're plenty smart." I was cracking up. What would Harry think if he knew Dickens and I carried on regular conversations?

I scratched Dickens's chin and turned back to Harry. "I've been chatting with your mum and eating too many Christmas cookies. She seems to be doing okay. How are you doing?"

Harry looked at the sky and pulled his cap off. "I'm okay and not okay. It's no secret Nicholas and I had our problems, but him dying like that, all of a sudden in a car accident? It's a shock." He hesitated. "And you and Peter found him? That must have been horrible."

"Yes . . . it was. I wish there was something more we could have done for him . . . I just felt so helpless."

By this time, we'd turned and were walking towards his parents' cottage. Dickens was trailing behind us. "There's a pot of soup on the stove in the Manor house. Would you like some? I highly recommend it, since it's my special turkey soup. I consider it good for what ails the soul, even better than chicken soup."

"That would hit the spot, and I can check on Gran too."

"Move it, Dickens," I called over my shoulder. "So, Harry, will everything on the Estate go back to the way it was now that your dad is the Earl?"

"Oh, I think things will return to normal pretty quickly. It's unfortunate Dad and I had some heated words over Nicholas's ideas, though. We hadn't argued like that since I was a teenager, and I hope that's behind us."

Interesting, I thought. "Did your dad agree with the resort plans?"

"No, he was opposed to all of it, but we disagreed over how to work things out, how best to approach Nicholas. Dad thought we could wait him out and he'd get bored with his plans. Like we were a shiny new toy, he'd toss us aside, go back to New York City, and leave us be."

"And you," I prompted. "What did you think?"

"I couldn't afford to wait him out. I tried to explain to him that lambing season can start as early as January. Even if he'd decided he wanted the sheep gone by this week, I'd have had a hell of a time finding a suitable place for all of us—me, the sheep, and Basil. Plus we'd need to get a lambing shed built and ready. I mean, you can shut down a brewery at the drop of a hat or stop making soap, but sheep are living, breathing creatures. They deserve better.

"We misjudged him. We thought he'd only want to grab hold of his new title and play the aristocrat at big events, nothing beyond that. When he came for Grandad's funeral, we didn't get any inkling he wanted to take an active role here. Even Julia was surprised by his plans."

I looked at him and tilted my head. Worked like a charm.

"She thought she'd get to play the Lady of the Manor a few times a year, maybe wear a tiara and leave it at that. That's why she was trying to work on him behind the scenes—to make him see he'd get bored with this new business venture. And, trust me, that's all this was to him—a business venture. He was going to spend a fortune—the fortune Grandad left him—making all these changes."

The part about Julia surprised me. I'd heard her mention

she thought the sheep should stay but hadn't realized she was actively trying to influence her husband. "What did she think he should do?"

"Take his inheritance—the title and the money—and return to New York, manage his existing business, and become active in the arts. 'Can you imagine the cachet of having the Earl of Stow on the Board of Directors for Lincoln Center or the Metropolitan Museum of Art?' she said. She understood better than her husband that my dad had the running of the Estate well in hand, and messing with a good thing was a mistake. Visiting here a few times a year and hosting grand events was enough for her."

Who knew? I thought. For all the gossip in the village and among Matthew and Sarah's friends, none of us had the full story. I hadn't seen Julia as being all that involved in how her husband chose to invest his newly acquired fortune. But why shouldn't she be? Being a wealthy power couple didn't mean they didn't discuss how to spend their money or, at a minimum, how to live their lives. Sure, they had more choices than the average Joe. Sure, they could do just about anything they wanted to do. But doing what would make them happy *together?* That required partnering on decisions—or at least that was the way I saw it. That's the way it had worked in my marriage, even if Henry and I weren't in Nicholas and Julia's league financially.

I wondered what Wendy and Belle had picked up at the Manor house. By now, Wendy had gotten a glimpse of Julia's room and possibly exchanged a few words with DCI Burton—or the silver fox, as she'd described him. I wondered what his story was and had a flash of him standing beside my petite, platinum-haired friend with his arm around her. *Now, wouldn't that be an interesting turn of events?* I thought.

Chapter Fourteen

Dickens had been pre-occupied with his four-legged friends and hadn't done much sleuthing at the Estate, or so I thought until I turned my taxi toward home. I chuckled when he barked, "*Veddy, veddy* interesting. Lots going on here today."

An image of Arte Johnson from "Laugh-in" popped into my head. My family had watched every show, and the actor's portrayal of a clueless Nazi soldier who used that catchphrase never failed to make us laugh. "Dickens, where on earth did you hear that?"

"I heard it from *you!* Don't you know you say it all the time? And Wendy too."

I grinned and glanced in the mirror at my observant friend. *Funny, the things that stick with us*, I thought, *things we aren't even aware of.* "Okay, so what was interesting? Did Basil tell you something? Or Blanche?"

"Blanche is a sweet little thing, lots of fun, but more interested in playing than listening to her humans. It was what I learned while I was hanging out with Basil and Harry. You know Harry talks to Basil like you talk to me, but Harry doesn't expect answers. I feel bad for all your friends who can't understand their pets. Don't you?"

"Believe me, I know how fortunate I am to be able to 'talk to the animals,' but I haven't spent much time feeling sorry for those who can't. So, what did Basil tell you?"

"He thinks Harry had too much to drink Saturday night 'cause he smelled like alcohol and was grumpy Sunday morning when he tended to the herd. Still, he did his usual thing, checked them over to be sure they didn't have any injuries and cleaned their hooves. He didn't finish, though, 'cause his phone rang and he hurried to the house."

I nodded. "If it was morning, that was probably a call from Matthew telling him about the accident. Besides Harry nursing a hangover, did Basil see anything else?"

"Oh! Almost forgot. Basil said when Harry removed his glove to answer the phone, his hand looked red and bruised."

An injured hand doesn't seem like a big deal for a man who works with farm animals, I thought. "Is that it? Anything else useful from Basil?"

"He said Harry looked better today and wasn't as grumpy. He mused aloud or talked to Basil, whatever. Said things would be okay, that they could all stay together at the Estate. Something about his dad being right about letting events take their course. What does that mean?"

Events taking their course? I thought. Now it was my turn to muse aloud or talk to my dog. "I'm not sure, Dickens. Could Harry have been referring to the accident? Or was it an innocent admission that his dad had been right to encourage riding things out rather than getting bent out of shape over Nicholas's plans? One thing I *do* know is I need to write all these things down—what you heard from Basil and what I learned from Sarah and Harry."

As I let Dickens out of the backseat, I spied Mrs. Morgan unloading groceries from her car. If I timed it right, I could give Christie a dab of food and knock on my neighbor's door about the time she was done putting things away.

As if I could skip feeding the princess, I thought as Christie appeared in the kitchen. She stretched her four legs one at a time as she made her way to her dish. Funny, how cats could do that without toppling over. She didn't have to speak. I knew what she wanted.

Opening a new can of food, I put a forkful in her dish and watched as she sniffed it, looked up, sniffed again, and finally deigned to eat a few bites. Dickens hovered, waiting for an opportunity. He'd missed out on Christmas cookies at Sarah's and was hoping to snag a snack before dinner. Christie ate almost half a can of food—one forkful at a time—before she sauntered to the office. She was destined to be disappointed because I had different plans.

I knocked on the Morgans' front door with Dickens by my side. Funny, I'd never learned their first names. When Mrs. Morgan opened the door, she reached to pet Dickens almost before she said hello. I explained we were about to visit the donkeys and I wondered whether I could stop by afterward to chat with her. As I'd hoped, she said, "Oh, let's do it now. I've just put the kettle on, and we can sit in the kitchen."

I'd never been inside before. While my kitchen was decorated in red with hints of gold and green, hers was blue and white. Over her stove was a long shelf holding Delft pottery, and her Delft blue curtains were trimmed in a white border. It was a crisp, clean look. A runner of the same material crossed the length of the table where she placed two mugs.

I sipped tea from my blue mug. "Oh! This has ginger in it. What a nice surprise. Is it a special blend?"

"Glad you like it. I found it while shopping in Chipping Camden, and I liked it so much, I'm giving the children some for Christmas. Now, tell me what you've been up to since you found the Bentley on the side of the road. I'm so sorry the young man died, and I'm sorry you had to see it happen, my dear."

I told her a little bit about Sunday morning and more about visiting the Manor house today before I brought up the party. "It's more pleasant to talk about the party. It was my first time, and I found it amazing. What did you think?"

"Ellie is a master at entertaining. She attends to every little detail, like the footmen this year. There's always a new touch, but I thought the best part was her grandsons surprising her with the book about Nigel."

"Yes, they must have put a lot of work into that. Maybe she'll bring it to our book club meeting in January." We chatted about the food and the decorations, and then I worked my way around to plans for the Estate. "Oh! I almost forgot what I wanted to ask you. Do you know much about the plan to put in a new bridge and drive in the pasture?"

Mrs. Morgan's expression changed from sweet to bitter in a flash. "Yes I do, and I can only hope it's over and done with. Oh my goodness! I don't mean to say I'm glad Nicholas died. That must have sounded awful."

She didn't pause for a response, so she must not have felt *too* bad about her comment. "What I mean is I can't imagine Matthew and Ellie will adopt any of Nicholas's ridiculous ideas now he's gone. Why would he think my Bertie would vote for a bridge that would carry traffic behind our cottage? The very idea!"

So that was Mr. Morgan's first name, I thought. "I find it hard to believe enough members of the planning commission would see a new bridge as a good idea. How did he think he'd get the votes? Did he give Mr. Morgan any idea?"

"Harrumph. He all but told Bertie he'd greased a few palms and wouldn't mind greasing his as well. Said he was meeting with the Bourton-on-the-Water representative that very night after the party. I realize that's the way of the world, but he was so blatant about it. That's what appalled Bertie. He made it sound as though all my Bertie had to do was hold his hand out, as if he would ever do that."

I had to work not to laugh as Mrs. Morgan continued her diatribe about Nicholas. She all but called him an ugly American. "I don't think he would have been a fitting Earl at all. And a fashion model as Lady Stow? Tsk, tsk. Matthew and Sarah are much better suited to those roles."

Dickens and I said our goodbyes and invited Mrs. Morgan to pop across the street to see us some time. *Gee*, I thought, *I realize she hardly knew Nicholas, but she sure didn't mince her words despite his having just died.*

Funny how I'd become friends with the Watsons next door but hadn't seen that much of my neighbors across the way. It helped that little Timmy regularly rang the school bell hanging by my front door. That meant he wanted to play with Dickens, and the clanging also served as Deborah's notice to join me for a cup of tea when she came to retrieve her son.

Dickens and I entered through the mudroom and picked up Christie's backpack. I had to search for her and found her curled in a ball upstairs on my down comforter. I stuck my nose into the tight curl and nuzzled the little puffball. "Want to see the donkeys?" I whispered.

She stretched full out and rolled onto her back. "Maybe."

I knew she wasn't going to miss a chance to join us, and as I walked downstairs, she flew past me and beat me to the bottom. She crawled into her backpack and was ready. If not for Dickens, I would once again have forgotten a vital ingredient of our walk. "Carrots, Leta, carrots," he barked.

It was sunny, but the breeze was picking up. His fur blowing in the wind, Dickens lifted his nose to take in the scents coming his way. Christie, on the other hand, buried her pink nose in her fleece blanket. She didn't much care for the wind. As for Martha and Dylan, I'd never noticed the weather changing their behavior. They came running and nudged my arm as I pulled carrots from my pockets. When I was out of carrots, I turned my back to them so Christie could sniff their noses before we walked home.

What have I discovered today? I thought. I ticked off items in my mind—Julia was working on Harry's behalf to save the sheep, Julia and Nicholas had a prenup, Harry drank too much Saturday night, Nicholas may have tried to bribe Mr. Morgan, and Nicholas's Saturday night meeting was with someone on the Planning Commission. I wondered what Wendy and Belle had come up with.

Wendy tooted the horn when she pulled up, and Dickens and I went to greet her. "So glad you two are here," I said. "Shall I take the food while you help Belle from the car?"

When Dickens saw me grab the takeaway bags, he did an about-face and followed me in the house. He'd been on his way to see Belle, but food took priority. Only when we were settled in the kitchen with the food tucked in the oven to stay warm did he greet Belle with a nudge. Wendy played second fiddle whenever Belle accompanied her to my cottage.

As Belle rubbed his ears, Dickens barked, "You'll share your dinner, right? Leta never gives me scraps."

I laughed and told Belle he was putting the touch on her. Christie wandered in and leaped into Belle's lap from the opposite side. "No need to pet the dog. I'm here now." I'd never figured out what it was about Belle that made her their favorite visitor.

I asked if it was too early for wine and got a look of disbelief from Wendy. "You must be kidding! It's been a rough day for both me and Mum, and yours couldn't have been much easier. Uncork that bottle now." That settled, I poured the wine and sat at the table with my guests.

Belle raised her glass. "As the senior member of The Little Old Ladies' Detective Agency, I declare this meeting in session."

We clinked glasses and took our first sips. "Well, ladies, where do we start? And, oh! Do you want me to get my laptop and take notes?" I asked.

Wendy grinned. "Nah, let's just talk about our day, but before we dive into what we've uncovered about the accident, I want to tell you what I've *uncovered* about our dreamy DCI."

Belle glanced at her daughter. "Is that what you've been smiling about all afternoon? Dreamy? Don't know that I've ever heard that word from you."

I laughed aloud at that exchange. "Belle, have you ever watched *Grey's Anatomy*? That description makes me think of McDreamy, the oh-so-good-looking doctor played by Patrick Dempsey in that show. Was that what you were thinking, Wendy?"

Now my friend blushed. "Now that you mention it, maybe

I was. There's no denying our visiting DCI is attractive. And he's charming in a gruff, teasing kind of way. So, do you want the scoop?"

All it took was an affirmative nod, and she was off. "He's lived in Birmingham most recently, worked there for close to twenty years. His mum's still in Coleford, though, and he wanted to move closer to her. Leta, that's a small market town near the border with Wales. He's only recently transferred to the Gloucestershire Constabulary and is working out of the Stroud Police Station. Staying with his mum in Coleford for now until he decides where to hang his hat."

Belle patted Wendy on the shoulder. "That says a lot about him to leave a big city like Birmingham to be with his mum. Wonder how he's adjusting."

"For now, he feels well out of it. He'd about had it with the gang violence and says he's ready for a more peaceful way of life. He did comment that Astonbury didn't seem particularly peaceful with three murders in as many months, but I told him our village was normally calm and quiet."

"Yes," I said, "That's what I thought when I decided to retire here. Maybe I should have done more research before I made that decision."

Wendy had a snappy retort. "Mum, tell her. Goodness knows when we last had a murder before Leta arrived. Honestly, you're my best friend, but murder and mayhem *do* seem to follow you."

My mouth dropped open and I could feel my face getting hot. "You're joking, right? You're not implying Astonbury's had two, maybe three, murders because I live here, are you?"

Maybe it was the expression on my face, or maybe it was my tone, but Wendy backtracked pretty quickly. "No, no, it was a bad joke, Leta. I didn't mean it the way it came out. Sorry."

Belle tut-tutted and gave her daughter a meaningful look, much like the ones I'd gotten from my mother when I'd stuck my foot in my mouth. "Okay, you two, enough. It's time we ate dinner and got down to business."

Wendy stood up, hugged me and repeated she was sorry. Together, we served the takeaway and refilled the wine glasses. Dickens looked at us expectantly and appeared to decide Belle was his best bet.

After enjoying the baked chicken and veggies Wendy had gotten from the Ploughman, I cleared the table and suggested coffee. "Before we rehash the day, though, I have one more question about McDreamy. Is he married?"

Wendy tilted her head to her shoulder and smiled. "He didn't actually say, but there was no mention of a wife. My intuition tells me he's not."

I repeated Dickens' line, "Veddy, veddy interesting. You could be our inside track with him."

"I'm hoping to be more than that! Okay, let's get this show on the road. Didn't you tell me Constable James was going to stop by tonight?"

Between Wendy and me, we just might have the police angle covered. Constable James was a willing source—and DCI Burton? Well, unbeknownst to the poor man, Wendy would be on the lookout for any tidbits he might inadvertently drop.

Since Belle had stayed by Ellie's side most of the day, we started with what she'd learned. "Ellie is heartbroken about Nicholas, but she's not lost sight of her role as the rock of the family. She's especially worried about poor Julia."

"I'll bet." Wendy grimaced. "Julia looked awful as she left the conservatory after speaking with our DCI—pale and disheveled with red eyes. I tried to speak with her, but she hurried upstairs. What did Ellie tell you, Mum?"

"Julia's especially distraught because she and Nicholas had argued Saturday night and also earlier that day. The first row was about her taking a role in a movie. She didn't tell Ellie what the later disagreement was about, only that she couldn't believe her final words with her husband had been hateful."

That's going to be hard for her to live with, I thought. I reflected on my final words to Henry. He'd passed me on his bicycle as we powered uphill to our lunch destination, and I'd playfully yelled out something about wanting my chicken wings and ice-cold beer waiting for me when I arrived. No regrets in that exchange.

"Wonder what they had words about. I had the impression Julia handled her husband pretty well, and in my brief encounters with her, she seemed level-headed and calm—not at all the way you sometimes hear supermodels described. No signs of diva behavior. And Ellie used the word *caring* in explaining how well Julia looked after Nicholas's stomach problem . . . Of course, for all we know, their relationship in private could have been volatile."

Wendy looked thoughtful. "Mum, why am I thinking Ellie may have been closer to Julia than to Nicholas? Am I reading that wrong?"

Christie chose that moment to return to Belle's lap, and Belle let her get settled before replying. "No, I think you're right. When he wasn't in his room sick, Nicholas was off on business, and it was Julia who made the effort to visit with the family. Except for the day or two she visited her dad, she divided her time between Sarah, Harry, and Ellie. She walked the pasture with Harry and Basil. She toured the cottages with Sarah to observe the spinner and the weaver, and she spent several hours watching Sarah make sheep milk soap."

"That explains why she leaned toward keeping the sheep and the artisans as going concerns on the Estate," I said. "She took the time to understand what they did and what an asset they could be. Harry told me today she was trying to influence Nicholas to let the sheep stay, and I'd heard something to that effect from her Friday night. Oh! I've got another question. Did Ellie happen to mention the couple having separate bedrooms?"

"She did. Said when they first arrived, they moved into the largest guestroom, but after Nicholas was up all night sick, Julia moved down the hall. Can't say that I blame her."

I filled the wine glasses as I offered to share the *intelligence* I'd gathered. "I sound like a character from a spy novel, don't I? Maybe Maggie Hope from the Susan Elia MacNeal series?"

Belle was an Agatha Christie fan and chose to disagree. "No, you will forever be Tuppence in my book. Gemma and Dave have called you that ever since you chose to dress as Tuppence at your costume party. And in *The Secret Adversary*, both Tommy and Tuppence are spies."

"That's fine. I'm short and brunette like Tuppence, so it fits. Now, on to what I've discovered." I ticked off names on my fingers. "Before I got to the Manor house, I gathered interesting info from Toby, Beatrix, and Gemma. And after that, I spoke with Sarah, Harry, and Mrs. Morgan."

Since I hadn't found time to jot it all down, I did my best to remember everything. I held up my index finger. "Number one, Toby saw Gavin and Nicholas in a heated conversation after the gift-giving Saturday night—so heated that he heard Gavin say, 'Over my dead body.' Oh, I almost forgot Rhiannon. Wendy, do you remember her story about Nicholas approaching Gavin about selling the Inn, not just the donkey pasture? Guess the two of them could have been arguing about that."

"Yes, I remember, and I still can't believe it. I can understand Gavin's outburst if that was the topic, and what else could it have been?"

I shrugged my shoulders and held up my middle finger. "Number two, Beatrix told me Mrs. Morgan was upset as the party was ending and I confirmed that this afternoon. Seems Nicholas all but offered Mr. Morgan a bribe to vote his way on the resort plans. It sounds as though our New York business tycoon was leaving no stone unturned in pursuit of his goal. And, Mrs. Morgan said . . . wait for it . . . Nicholas planned to meet with the Bourton-on-the-Water Planning Commission rep that night after the party. Guess he'd been there and was on his way back when he had the accident."

Wendy sat forward. "And you've got more? Don't stop now."

I held up my ring finger. "Number three. Don't know that this is all that important, but Gemma called to tell me Nicholas had a stomach ulcer."

The ulcer seemed anticlimactic after the news about possible bribes, and I'd already shared what I'd heard from Harry about Julia being on his side about the sheep, so that left only my conversation with Sarah.

"Alright, ladies, this next piece is all I've got left. Julia told Sarah she and Nicholas had a prenup. Not surprising in this day and age and considering our Earl was on his third marriage."

"Good grief, his third marriage?!" Wendy said. "How did you come by that fact?"

"Oh, that. Ellie told me when we were prepping the little

Christmas bags. Now that I think about it, she also said he stayed married two or three years to the first two and that was about how long he'd been married this time. But wait until you hear about one of the clauses in the prenup."

That comment was too much for Belle. "*One* of the clauses? There were clauses plural? Oh for goodness' sake." When I told them the only one Sarah knew of was the one about weight gain, I thought they were both going to choke.

Belle stifled a yawn. "Okay girls, can we get to Wendy's report so I can get home? It's been a long day for me."

"Sure, Mum. The assignment Tuppence gave me was to accompany Constable James to Julia's room. Can't say I saw anything helpful. I wanted to spend hours in her closet looking at all those clothes. Oh my goodness, does she have clothes! There were two large suitcases and two hanging bags. I guess a model has to come prepared. And the shoes—Manolo Blahnik, Jimmy Choo, Stuart Weitzman—and those were just the names I recognized."

Belle rolled her eyes at her daughter and I giggled. "I do *love* shoes, but I've never spent that kind of money. Thankfully, I haven't been tempted, since most of them are those ridiculously high heels I'd break my neck in."

Wendy stood up. "I have to agree with you these days, but I sure loved high heels when I was younger. Now, Mum, let's get you home."

I helped them to the car and assured Wendy I'd let her know what I heard from Constable James. We had ferreted out plenty of information without a lot of effort, though I wasn't clear any of it pointed to the person who'd slashed the tire. I reminded myself that Gemma had asked us to *investigate*, not *solve* the case. *It hasn't even been 48 hours since Peter and I found the wreck,* I thought, *so why do I feel like I'm falling behind?*

Chapter Fifteen

G emma called as I was uncorking a bottle of red wine. "Hi, Leta, how goes it? I'm about to have a pint with the group and wanted to check in with you first. I thought you'd be asleep by the time I was in for the night."

"You know me too well. I'm looking forward to an early night, depending on how soon your constable gets here. I invited him to drop by when his day was done, so I could share what I'd learned and vice-versa. I've gathered a random set of facts, and I have no idea whether any of them will lead anywhere. I must say whatever good opinion I had of Nicholas is fast deteriorating."

"Ooh, you've piqued my interest, but I don't have much time right now. Can you email me later? Meanwhile, the coroner called again today to report he'd missed it earlier, but there was a bruise on Nicholas's chin. There's no doubt someone punched him. Was there any sign of a bruise Saturday night?"

I paused to think. "Not that I noticed. I'm thinking aloud

here. A woman could cover up a bruise with makeup, but I can't see a man doing that. So I'll go out on a limb and say someone punched him *after* the party. He must've had a busy evening."

"So it would appear. And the bruise is on the left side of his chin, so the person who attacked him was right-handed. If only the mark had indicated a leftie, at least that would narrow down the suspect pool. So, give me one of your facts, and I'll be on my way."

I knew which one to share. "According to Mrs. Morgan, Nicholas all but offered her husband a bribe Saturday night. And he made it sound as though it wasn't the first one he'd approached."

I heard voices in the background as she said that fit with the envelope of money being in the car. Still, we both wondered why it was there and not in someone's hand. She gave me her email and said she'd try to call or email the next day. *Would wonders never cease?* I thought. *Not one jibe in that conversation.* But then, Gemma needed me as her eyes and ears in Astonbury. Well, in my opinion, she'd needed me before, but I didn't expect she'd ever admit that.

I took my glass of wine to the sitting room, stoked the fire, and made myself comfortable on the couch with my Poirot book. It wasn't long before Constable James rang to say he was on his way. When I asked if he'd eaten, he said no but not to worry about it. Still, I pulled the turkey and mayonnaise from the fridge and the bread from the pantry.

He was effusive in his thanks when he saw the spread. It didn't seem like much to me, but I guess for a young bachelor used to takeaway as his main source of sustenance, it was a feast. Naturally, Dickens tried to put the touch on him just as he had on Belle, but when I explained to the young man that

Dickens had already gotten plenty of scraps, he did his best to ignore the pleading looks he was getting. Once he'd eaten two sandwiches, I poured us both more wine and led him to the sitting room.

It was Christie's turn to check him out. "Good thing you fed him. Tall and skinny—he could stand fattening up. A little young for you, though, isn't he?"

I couldn't figure out how to answer that question in front of Constable James, so I let it go. He chose to sit on the floor in front of the fireplace where he could rub Dickens's belly. "Can't get too comfy or I'll be asleep in no time. Let me get to what DCI Burton and I found out today, and I'll be on my way and out of your hair."

"No rush," barked Dickens.

The Constable chuckled when I shared that comment. "Puts me in mind of the scrappy little dog I had as a boy. Followed me everywhere, and whenever I reached down to his side, over he'd go—ready for a belly rub.

"Okay, down to business. First thing DCI Burton asked Lady Stow or the Dowager Countess or whatever we call her was how the inheritance worked—he wanted to know about the entail and who benefited with Nicholas gone. He took lots of notes on that. I'd had no idea that Reginald, Nicholas's dad, had died only this year."

I shook my head. "Yes, it's right out of a novel, isn't it? The way I heard it, Reggie, Nigel's older son, took a job in the States when he graduated Cambridge. He did quite well for himself, married an American, had the one son, and raised him in Manhattan. Everyone thought Reggie'd be the next Earl of Stow, but he died earlier this year before his father did. That left the way open for Nicholas to inherit the title when his grandfather died. And per the will, all of the property. Only the investments were divided among the family."

"Right, which means Matthew had the most to gain from the new Earl's death. Still, DCI Burton is looking most closely at Julia."

I rolled my eyes. "Always look at the spouse first, right? Has he uncovered anything that makes it likely it was Julia who slashed the tire? And why does that seem so unlikely to me?"

"It is kind of hard to see a beautiful model kneeling beside a car and taking a knife to a tire, isn't it? He's looking into the will to see what she gets, but her husband dying means she's lost out on being Lady Stow. I can't imagine she'd want to give that up. But we've got more work ahead of us before we can settle on her."

I agreed with everything he'd said about Julia. I wondered how much money she had in her own right. So many famous people mismanaged their huge earnings or fell prey to a dishonest manager who helped him or herself—most often himself—to the money. I expressed those thoughts to Constable James.

"All that is what DCI Burton is looking into. If she's already well set or there's no windfall, I'm not sure what her motive would be," he said. "Except he has this strange idea that someone could have been slowly poisoning Nicholas."

"What?"

"Yes, after hearing about the ulcer, he had someone at the Stroud station checking into what poisons could cause ulcer-like symptoms. He's theorizing that someone may have been out to kill the Earl one way or the other."

That sounded like a stretch to me, but I kept that thought to myself. "Perhaps he should try channeling Agatha Christie.

Her fans will tell you she compiled an extensive library on poisons. Where was it I saw that bit of trivia? Oh, it was in a mystery novel. A professor in *The Truants* is a leading expert on Christie and mentions one of the author's most well-thumbed books was one on poison." I shook my head at the way my brain worked. "Anything else?"

"Yes. I almost forgot. When DCI Burton searched the Earl's room, he found several envelopes of money in a dresser drawer. You know there was one in the car, right? We're theorizing they're bribes."

I shared my vast detective knowledge with him. "You know, one of my favorite mystery writers listed four main motives for murder, and bundles of cash seem to fall into the category of lucre. If it's not lucre, that leaves lust, loathing, and love to choose from. I guess Julia could have a lucre motive, though I can't see her having anything to do with the Earl's death."

He laughed and told me he'd seen the word lucre in books but didn't think he'd ever heard anyone say it aloud. "While DCI Burton is considering motives, I'm looking for indicators of his whereabouts that night. From his GPS, I found he'd been parked in Bourton-on-the Water for thirty minutes around midnight, and he'd texted back and forth with an unidentified number. I'd say it was about a missed meeting —'where are you? I'm here. I can't wait much longer'—that kind of thing. From there, the GPS data tells me he moved to Chipping Camden after one a.m., where he stayed for several hours.

"And I've still got the emails to go through. I guess those on his phone are identical to the ones on his laptop, but I've got to cross-reference the lot. The laptop is the one thing Gemma took from Nicholas's bedroom when she was there

Sunday. And you can't believe the emails the man sent and received. Hundreds a day on his business account and close to that on the personal one. Oh! And one other thing—today when the DCI searched the Earl's bedroom, he found a man's wedding band on the dresser. His wife identified it as his."

Chipping Camden? Now that was interesting. Was there another Planning Commission rep there? "So, Constable James —goodness, that's a mouthful—I can help you out on the Bourton-on-the-Water visit. Mrs. Morgan told me today that Nicholas was meeting with the Bourton Planning Commission rep Saturday night after the party. Strange time to be conducting business, don't you think? But I don't know about Chipping Camden."

He ducked his head like a small boy. "You know, you could call me Jonas. And, no, I haven't a clue yet what he was doing so far afield. He was on the High Street, but there are so many businesses and flats close together, I can't nail down an exact location. I'm not complaining, but now I've also got Julia's iPad to go through. The DCI confiscated it today as part of the inquiry."

I smiled. "No rest for the weary, right? As usual, you guys are overworked. I'm sure you need to get home and get some rest so you can start fresh tomorrow, but I've got a question. Did DCI Burton tell the family the cause of the accident? Or is he keeping that to himself for now?"

"Yes, he told them today someone had deliberately damaged the tire. And he asked about knives, as the SOCOs are firm it was a knife that was used to slash it. When he interviewed Matthew, Harry, and Sam—separately, of course— he asked if they carried knives. Each one reached in his pocket and pulled one out. DCI Burton says the three knives were slightly different but were the same fancy brand. He'd brought a SOCO with him to photograph the area around the carriage house and had him also take shots of the men's knives."

"Was the brand name Laguiole?"

"Yes, that's it. How on earth did you know that? Do you have one too?"

I laughed and shook my head. "No, but I got a lesson on them at the party Saturday night. Gavin showed me the prized possession in the display cabinet, a Laguiole from the 1800s that had belonged to Nigel's grandfather. So, one last question, Jonas. What are the next steps for you and DCI Burton?"

He tugged at his collar and stretched his neck. "I hate to say this, but we've got to interview guests from the party. I expect we'll get to you, Wendy, and Belle before long, but Gemma's dad, Bertie Morgan, Peter, and George Evans are first on the list."

It didn't surprise me that Gavin was on the list, but I was surprised at the others. "All the men? Why? Because they probably own knives?"

"Oh no. Didn't I say? The coroner found a bruise on the Earl's chin. Thinks someone must have punched him. Not likely it was a woman."

Right. With all random facts coming my way, I'd lost sight of Gemma telling me that. And suddenly, I remembered Dickens saying something about Harry's hand. It was time I sat quietly and processed the clues. "I think you've got your work cut out for you, and I appreciate you bringing me up to speed. By the way, Gemma called and asked me to email her whatever I come across, and I need to get on that. You'll let me know if something comes up, right?"

He promised he would and was on his way. I was tidying up the kitchen when my phone rang. *Who can that be?* I thought.

My friends know better than to call me after nine. When I looked at the screen, I was surprised to see it was Peter.

I heard voices and clinking glasses in the background. "Leta, can you come to the pub? You've got to hear this for yourself."

I couldn't believe I'd heard him right. "Me, go to the pub? It's 9:30 at night, for goodness' sake."

Peter hesitated and I wondered if he'd had one too many pints. "Trust me, you need to speak with Barb. She's heard something you need to know. I'll be at the bar when you get here."

Before I could answer one way or another, he hung up on me. *Well hell*, I thought, *the sooner I get this over with, the sooner I'll be home in bed.*

The parking lot of the Ploughman was nearly empty as was the dining area. I scowled when I spotted Peter and Barb at the bar. "This better be good," I grumbled.

He grinned at me. "Oh, it is. Barb, tell her what you told me."

Barb rolled her eyes. "It's not like I don't hear these kinds of things all the time," she said, "but Peter thinks what I overheard this time is a big deal. Straight from the horse's mouth."

She explained that Matthew and Nicholas had come in together several times last week. Matthew drank his usual Astonbury Ale while the Earl stuck to ginger ale, and despite the rumors in the village that the two were at odds, their conversation seemed congenial. She was clearing a nearby table when she saw Nicholas rub his face. It was his next words that caught her attention. "The gist was that as soon as he had Julia out of his hair for a week or two, he'd be able to think straight and make decisions about the resort. Said there was no way he was going to fund her dream of being a bigwig donor to New

York City museums. I can tell you Matthew looked surprised. You know he'd never talk about Sarah that way. And then, Matthew like to have choked on his beer when he heard there was a girlfriend in Chipping Camden."

I gasped. "A girlfriend, here in England?"

Barb smirked and wiped the counter. "Oh, but that's not the best part. Seems she's Italian, and he flew her over from New York so she'd be close by. Can you believe that? 'Course, he swore Matthew to secrecy."

Peter looked at me expectantly. "Worth coming out late for, right? I knew it would be better coming from Barb than from me."

Glancing from one to the other, I spluttered. "Yes, it is. What else did you hear, Barb?"

She thought for a moment. "Well, not as juicy as an Italian girlfriend on the side, but when they were discussing the Estate, Nicholas said he liked the prospects for the brewery, and if Harry would take the time to draw up a business plan on the sheep business, he'd consider keeping 'em. But he wasn't going to go on the boy's word alone. That prompted Matthew to comment that he'd calm Hotspur down and get him to do that, and it would help if Nicholas would stop referring to the animals as 'pet sheep.' He pointed out if they were going to work together, they needed to stop insulting each other."

It was my turn to rub my face. "This is way too much to digest. You know, Barb, after hearing how observant you are, I need to remember not to spill any secrets when I'm in here."

Barb laughed. "Glad to be of service any time, Leta. How 'bout a shot to see you off?"

"Not on your life. I'm going home to bed. And, you, Peter —you're looking mighty pleased with yourself. Can't wait to tell your sister and your mum about your work tonight.

They're not going to believe it." With that, I got down off the barstool and was on my way.

My brain swirled on the few short miles home. Had I only an hour ago told Constable James he had his work cut out for him? *He's not the only one,* I thought. *I predict the Little Old Ladies' Detective Agency is going to be plenty busy.*

Chapter Sixteen

Surprisingly, I slept like a rock and was up early Tuesday morning with plenty of time to drink coffee, tend to my demanding four-legged companions, and fire off a few emails. Doing a brain dump for Gemma helped me recall most of what I'd heard and seen the past few days, and I printed out a copy of the email to show Belle and Wendy. Next, I cut and pasted a few highlights to send Dave, and I teased him with the fact I'd had a younger man over the night before.

For the last email—to my sisters and my friend Bev—I focused on the birthday party, with only a brief mention of the cycling adventure and the discovery of the auto accident. I left out any reference to how shaken I'd been by witnessing the Earl die in the ambulance and made it sound as though my involvement with the tragedy was confined to offering food and comfort to the grieving family.

By eight, I was on the phone to Wendy. "It was too late to call you last night with what I heard from Jonas—I mean Constable James—not to mention I had calls from Gemma and your brother. I want to see Harry first thing this morning, but how about I share it all over brunch? I'm thinking we take your mum and go to Huffkins?"

That idea was fine by Wendy and even finer by Dickens when I invited him to go with us. It wasn't fine by Christie, though. Upon hearing I was taking Dickens to breakfast, she made it clear she was miffed. "Excuse me, this is two days in a row you've taken the *dog* and left me behind! How am I supposed to help find the villain if I'm stuck at home?"

She had a good point, but she wouldn't be welcome at a restaurant. "I have an idea. Why don't you go back through everything you heard last night from Belle, Wendy, and Jonas and let me know what you think when I get back? It's always good to get a fresh perspective." She didn't have a snippy retort, so I assumed she was mollified.

I called Sarah to get Harry's phone number. She indicated he was out with the sheep but usually had good reception. He answered on the first ring, and when I told him I wanted to see him, he hesitated but invited me to meet him at his cottage. As I recalled, it was a little beyond Matthew and Sarah's—a small, single-story structure, perfect for a bachelor.

Gemma texted me before I could leave my cottage. Her message started with a thumbs-up emoji before she wrote she was dying to hear more about the girlfriend but was tied up in class. She said she'd try to call later.

On the way to the Estate, I told Dickens what Gemma had shared about the bruise on the Earl's chin and asked him to remind me what Basil had mentioned about Harry's hand. It wasn't anything more than I'd remembered—his hand was red and bruised—but I wondered if his injury could have come from using his fist on Nicholas's chin. I thought about that, the wedding band, the girlfriend, and more as I drove.

I parked at the larger family cottage and walked the short

distance to see Harry. As soon as Dickens caught sight of Basil and Harry outside the cottage, he took off. He got a treat, and I got a cup of tea.

Harry and I sat at the table in the tiny kitchen, and I wasn't surprised at his puzzled expression as he asked, "Now, what's on your mind this morning, Leta?"

I started with, "Um, we talked about me finding your cousin's car, right?" That opening got me an affirmative nod. "Well, because of that, Gemma's been keeping me up to date on the investigation, and—um—she told me last night someone had punched Nicholas in the face." Here's where I had to fudge about his hand and tell a white lie. "I noticed you nursing your hand when we talked yesterday, and I wondered if it was you who punched him."

"And, what if I did? Why would you care?"

Now I was no longer fudging. "I'd care because sooner or later the DCI will figure it out, and it would be better for you if you told him before he came calling. It's always suspicious when a suspect withholds information, and you have to know you're a suspect—along with your father, your brother, and Gavin. That's just the men. You know Julia's a suspect because the spouse always is."

He shrugged his shoulders. "Dad and I know we're obvious suspects, but we know we didn't do it, and we're counting on the police to find the real killer and be done with us soon enough. We know it isn't Sam, and we're confident it isn't Gavin either. He's a friend."

"Yes, but you've got to realize the police aren't as sure as you and your dad are. You're all under suspicion, and I don't want to see any of you hauled down to the station. It would break your grandmother's heart, not to mention your mother's. If you're the one who punched your cousin, tell the police so they don't waste time trying to figure that out. And so they don't think you're holding out on them."

I could tell he wasn't convinced. "Does this have something to do with the Little Old Ladies' Detective Agency? I thought it was a village joke that you got involved in investigations, but is it true?"

Whoa, I thought. *I didn't know our bouts of amateur sleuthing had made the village grapevine.* "Yes, it's true. Like when someone died at the Fall Fête, the police considered Trixie the prime suspect, so we searched for clues that would clear her or at least point the police in a different direction. We knew she hadn't killed anyone."

"So, you're looking out for me? And Dad, and on and on?" He paused. "And if I think of anything helpful, should I tell you or go straight to the police?"

I studied him. "The answer to your first question is yes, I'm looking out for you. I don't want to see an innocent person wrongly accused. Second, clearing up who punched your cousin will keep the police from wasting resources trying to figure that out instead of finding the person who slashed the tire. And yes, I'd like to hear anything you think of."

"Okay, I'll think about your advice, and maybe I'll discuss it with Dad. If he agrees, then when I'm done with what needs doing around here, I'll call the DCI and let him know it was me who punched my cousin and why." He was muttering by then, and I almost didn't catch his last sentence. "And if he'd called my herd of Cotswolds Lions pet sheep one more time, I'd have punched him again."

Surely he wouldn't have killed him over the darned sheep, would he? As more encouragement, I reminded him that with a nickname like Hotspur, he needed to do everything he could to show the police it was a label he'd outgrown.

Tigger was chasing something in the garden when Dickens and I arrived at Sunshine Cottage but stopped when I tooted the horn. The frisky feline had found a home with my friends when we were investigating our first case. After Belle and Wendy were settled in the car, I handed Wendy the printout of the email I'd sent Gemma and asked her to look it over. She read it aloud, instead, her eyes getting wider and wider. "Are you kidding me? A girlfriend, a bruised chin? Bloody hell."

I caught her eye in the rearview mirror. "And let me tell you about my conversation with Harry this morning."

Neither of my friends was shocked that it'd been Harry who'd punched his cousin. But when I shared my surprise at our amateur sleuthing being common knowledge, Belle laughed. "Of course our shenanigans are well known. There are no secrets in a small village like ours."

Wendy grinned. "Well, if they're talking about us, I hope they're saying we're great at digging up information. Look at what we've uncovered in only one day on the job."

Belle glanced over her shoulder at Wendy. "Yes, but it helps to have the inside scoop about bruises, GPS data, and such. I think the first angle to pursue is that Italian girlfriend. She has to be somewhere in Chipping Camden, doesn't she? Why else would the man spend several hours there in the middle of the night? The gall! Did he fly her over and stash her away?"

By now, I'd parked at Huffkins, the brunch place where Peter and I'd planned to have breakfast after our ride on Sunday morning. *Was that only two days ago?* I was looking forward to the smoked salmon with scrambled eggs and toast. Wendy and her mum chose different versions of the classic Eggs Benedict. Belle went with Eggs Florentine, and Wendy ordered Eggs Royale topped with salmon instead of bacon.

Dickens had positioned himself on the floor between Wendy and Belle, knowing he'd be more likely to get handouts from the two of them than me. "Happy to share," he barked.

"You know, ladies, I believe Dickens has become more incorrigible since we've moved to England. Must be something about being allowed in restaurants, which gives him increased opportunities for handouts."

Wendy looked down at him. "No way you're getting any of my salmon. Maybe a pinch of a muffin, but that's it, and I doubt you want any spinach from Mum."

We tucked into our meal and agreed a return visit to Huffkins was a must. Belle reminded us they had another location in Burford and suggested we try it for lunch. And that led to talk of visiting the combo hat and book shop in Burford— The Mad Hatter—one of my favorite places.

I sat back and sipped my coffee. "So, how do we locate an Italian girlfriend? How many hotels are on High Street, or could she be staying in a private flat?"

Wendy knew the area better than I did and named The Cotswolds House Hotel & Spa as the ritziest place in the heart of Chipping Camden. "I bet he put her in a hotel so she could be waited on hand and foot, as befits the paramour of an Earl. Someplace chilled champagne and caviar could be sent up whenever he visited. And I bet she's in the best room they have."

"Alright, let's say that's the place. How do we find her there? We need a good story, like maybe the Earl recommended the hotel as the most charming in the area. And we're looking for a location for what? A girls' weekend? Or maybe an anniversary? He told us to ask for the best room they had to offer, that he once had a friend stay there . . ."

Now, Belle joined in. "Yes, and we can't recall the name of the room, but it had the very best amenities. I suspect the room is in his name. And, I just had an awful thought—this woman may not know he's died. It's not as though she can call the Manor house in search of him, and we know he's not answering his phone. We could be on a mission of mercy."

Wendy had been smiling but now looked crestfallen. "That's a terrible thought. It's bound to be in the papers soon. The good news is the Cotswolds Journal is a weekly paper and won't come out until Wednesday. Can you imagine finding out your boyfriend died by reading it in the newspaper? All the more reason we need to find her."

Belle had become our secret weapon, so we decided she'd take the lead at the hotel, and the cover story would involve her wanting to give her son and daughter-in-law a silver wedding anniversary weekend. We'd learned, as she liked to remind us, that it was amazing what folks would tell a little old lady.

We arrived in Chipping Camden close to lunchtime, and the High Street was crowded with shoppers. Greenery festooned the lampposts and shop windows, and the atmosphere was festive. Parking spots were in short supply, so I let Belle and Wendy out in front of the hotel and drove on. When I found a spot around the corner, I unloaded Dickens and we hurried to catch up with our friends. I needn't have worried. Wendy was standing in the entryway looking for me, and Belle was engrossed in conversation with the concierge.

Wendy bent to pet Dickens and whispered, "This is going splendidly. Mum's already gotten the name of the best suite and is about to have a cuppa in the restaurant with the manager. He's checking to see if we might be able to tour it. Peter's going to have a marvelous anniversary weekend with his yet-to-be-identified wife."

Belle looked our way and touched the concierge's sleeve. Before we knew it, we three and Dickens were seated with cups of tea and brochures, and the manager was joining us. "Mrs. Davies," she said to Belle, "I was able to locate Miss Giovanni, and she'll be out for several hours, so she's given her permission for you to glance in her room. She echoed my sentiment about how suitable it would be for your son's anniversary weekend." We'd hit paydirt. With a name like Giovanni, this had to be the Italian girlfriend.

We didn't expect to find clues in the room, but we hoped if we spent long enough touring the property, we might be introduced to Miss Giovanni. If not, we'd know which room to ring to find her later. While the manager escorted Belle to the elevator, she suggested Wendy and I visit the patio area and spa to further inspect the amenities. The more we saw, the more I tried to come up with an excuse to spend a night myself. In the entry to the spa, we picked up a pamphlet describing the treatments. I had yet to find a regular masseuse since I'd moved to Astonbury and missed seeing one twice a month. Maybe I could return and try a Swedish massage here.

As Wendy turned back to the patio, the spa receptionist beckoned me, and I chatted with her about their hours and the possibility of a massage appointment. I was leaving just as an attractive olive-complected brunette emerged from one of the rooms. Wrapped in a fluffy white terry robe, she moved to a chair and picked up a magazine. The receptionist approached her and asked, "Miss Giovanni, would you care for a glass of sparkling water?"

She had to be the girlfriend. *Nicholas had a type*, I thought. *Striking brunettes.*

I had no idea what I was going to say to her but didn't want to miss the opportunity. Fortunately, Dickens made it easy when he wandered her way. As she laughed and said hello to him, I held out my hand in greeting. "I couldn't help but hear your name, Miss Giovanni. I'm Leta Parker and this is Dickens. I'm here with friends who're deciding whether to book a special weekend for an anniversary. That's why the manager asked if you'd be willing to let them tour your room."

She held out her hand as she smiled. "I'm Maria, and oh yes," she said in lightly accented English, "this place is incredible. I've been treated like a princess the entire time."

"Well, then, our friend Nicholas was right. This may be just the place."

It was no wonder she gave me a strange look. "Nicholas, the Earl of Stow? You know him?"

"Yes, I'm a friend of his grandmother's—but wait, you know him too?"

She laughed and said he had booked the room for her. That lighthearted response answered my question. *She had no idea Nicholas was dead. Now what do I say?*

I hopped up and asked the receptionist if there was a spot where Miss Giovanni and I could chat in private. She pointed to a door to her right that was partially open, and I quickly ushered the surprised young lady through it and sat her down. "I'm afraid there's been an accident."

It was a toss-up as to whether she would shriek and cry or be dumbstruck. I was glad it was the latter. She stared at me and shook her head no. I had no choice but to break the bad news as gently as I could. It had crossed my mind that maybe Barb had gotten it wrong—that she might be nothing more than a business friend, but her reaction dispelled that notion.

She turned white as a sheet and was speechless for several moments. "No, no, there must be some mistake. He's at a conference. *Non il mio Nick*. He cannot be dead."

I don't speak Italian, but I can piece together those words—Not my Nick. Now was not the time to interrogate her, and, as it turned out, there was no need. In halting Italian and English, she asked how he had died, and her reactions to my explanation revealed plenty. She was shocked and somehow touched that I had been present when he drew his last breath. When I revealed I'd lost my husband in similar circumstances, she grabbed my hand.

Tears streamed down her face. "*Stava lasciando Julia*. She was so angry when he told her."

This time the Italian was more than I could understand, so I asked her to repeat herself in English. "He was going to leave Julia," she said. "He told her Saturday night. Told her he'd made arrangements for her to fly back to New York this week. He wanted her gone before he got back from his conference in Geneva on Thursday."

Holy hell, I thought, *when did he manage to squeeze that in?* Was it before the party? If so, Julia had done a masterful job of holding it together. No, it had to be afterward, before he departed for Bourton-on-the-Water. What a jerk!

As I was pondering his timing with his wife, Maria painted a different picture of *her* Nick—that of the romantic lover. As she cried, she told me how he'd called her from the Manor house after the party. He'd be later than usual because he had to attend to some business emails and make a stop before he got to the hotel, but he wanted her to wear the dress he'd given her earlier in the week and to order champagne.

She smiled as she shared the memory. "*Il mio amore,* my love, he was so handsome. He was still wearing his tux when he came in, with his tie loosened and his collar undone. *Mio Dio,* he cannot be dead."

I wondered whether he'd had the same effect on Julia in the past. As Maria continued, I learned she'd met him at an international investor's conference where she was a translator. She not only spoke Italian but was also fluent in Spanish and French. And she had enough of an understanding of Nick's business to hold her own over the dinner he invited her to. *So, more than a pretty face.* Not that her intelligence was any excuse for his infidelity.

As her words slowed down and her chin tilted toward her breastbone, I asked if she'd like to return to her room. She nodded yes. I left Dickens licking her hand, and I stepped out to ask the receptionist to have a pot of tea sent up. Quickly, I texted Wendy to meet me outside Maria's room. I wasn't sure what we should do next. We couldn't leave the girl alone, and I doubted there was anyone we could call to sit with her.

When we arrived upstairs, Wendy and Belle were waiting in the hallway. Belle swung into comfort mode while Wendy whispered she'd bumped into her mother and the manager leaving the room. She'd explained the situation to both of them, and the manager left to alert the concierge. The tea arrived as Wendy and I were trying to figure out next steps. When we peeked in the door, we saw Maria settled on the upholstered chaise lounge with a blanket tucked around her legs and Belle pouring a cup of tea. Dickens was sitting beside the chaise with his head resting near Maria's hand.

I pulled Belle aside. "Belle, what should we do? I'm at a loss."

She tsk-tsked me and said she would look after Maria. "I was a nurse, after all, and I know what's best for a shock. You and Wendy do whatever you need to do, and I'll be in touch. I foresee staying here for several hours at least. She may doze off. She may want to visit St. Catherines Church—if she's Catholic, that is. She may decide she wants to fly home. I don't know."

Not a word passed between Wendy and me as we walked toward my car. When I'd fastened Dickens in the backseat and we'd both gotten in, Wendy broke the ice. "I feel so bad for that poor girl. She thought her life with him was just beginning. No matter that he seemed to be a serial heartbreaker, she was in love. And, to think, she's been sitting here for two days wondering why she hasn't heard from him, not knowing he was dead."

"I know. His death was tragic enough without this. At least she thought he was busy at a conference and wasn't expecting to see him until Thursday. Is it just me, or is it hard to get fired up about pursuing the investigation?"

"No, Leta, I feel the same way. But nothing has changed. Someone engineered Nicholas's death, and we still don't know who that someone was. And you committed to Gemma that the Little Old Ladies' Detective Agency would help. The only problem is I can't wrap my head around which lead to check out next. Any ideas?"

My brain wasn't much clearer than Wendy's, but I had a thought. "I think I need a break to clear my head, maybe bake

Christmas cookies for my Saturday night party and let these different leads simmer. Do you want to meet again tonight and put pencil to paper like we've done before? I know we didn't come up with the answer when we tried it last time, but it helped to see what we had and what we were missing."

Why did this investigation seem more complex to me? Why was I hesitant to share the girlfriend story at least with Constable James? Gemma had made it clear I should speak only with the two of them, and that meant he'd be on point to share my information with the new DCI. Maybe that was why I felt compelled to have a theory of the case before sharing a handful of clues.

I voiced my questions to Wendy, and despite not having any answers, she seemed to understand. "I wonder," she said. "Could it be that this time, we *really do* know the players better than the police do? As good as Gemma was at her job procedurally, she still left room for the human factor—for her knowledge of the village dynamics. And as much grief as she gave you, she respected your judgment, albeit grudgingly. For all we know, sharing our clues with DCI Burton could send him barreling off to arrest the wrong person. Is that what it is?"

"Maybe. Whatever it is, I think you answered the question. We're not letting the DCI in on the girlfriend info just yet. I may call or stop by to see Ellie and share this new development with her. Maybe she knows how a divorce would have impacted Julia, and I don't think she'll be surprised to hear her grandson was unfaithful to his wife. Why does the word *cad* keep popping into my head?"

"Cad? You're not only a word nerd, you're also kind of old-fashioned. Did you know that?"

At least her comment made me laugh. "I know, I know. I've

read too many Agatha Christie books. I'm sure Tommy and Tuppence would have used that word or Lord Peter Wimsey in the Dorothy Sayers books. 'He was quite the cad' sounds so high-class, don't you think? Much better than calling the Earl a jerk."

Chapter Seventeen

After dropping Wendy by Sunshine Cottage, I drove on to Sainsbury's for cookie ingredients—slivered almonds, sweet butter, flour, eggs, and powdered sugar. Dickens had been unusually quiet since the scene at the hotel. Even when I let him into the garden at home, he didn't say anything. "Dickens, are you okay? Are you tired?"

He came to me, jumped up, and put his paws above my knees. "Leta, I'm sad. I think that girl had a broken heart."

I knelt and hugged him. "Yes, she did, but Belle will take good care of her. Now, go inspect the garden. Maybe that will cheer you up. Then we'll bake cookies."

The cookies would have to wait until the butter softened, so I busied myself digging out a large mixing bowl, the cookie sheets, and the wire cooling racks. Somewhere in the pantry were my Christmas cookie tins. When I went to bring in firewood, I could tell Dickens had perked up. He was sniffing along the garden wall, wagging his tail, and intermittently lifting his nose to the sky to sniff whatever scents the breeze carried.

Christie scampered into the sitting room to flop and roll in front of the crackling fire. "I miss the fire when you're gone. It gets chilly in here." When Dickens joined her, I sat between them and rubbed their bellies.

"Let's get warmed up and have a snack. What do you think?" Why was I not surprised they beat me to the kitchen? Once I'd given Christie a dab of food and Dickens a small bone from the butcher, I made myself a cup of hot chocolate, and we returned to the sitting room. I pulled my favorite fleece throw on to my lap, prompting Christie to knead the blanket and my stomach before curling into a ball. *I wish I could relax that easily*, I thought. I tried playing Words with Friends. I tried reading *Hercule Poirot's Christmas*. I was restless, and my thoughts kept returning to Maria and Julia and how devastated they must be.

Enough, I thought. I nudged Christie from my lap and went to the kitchen. The butter wasn't quite ready, so I went to my office to decorate the small tree. Opening the box of cat ornaments dispelled some of my sad thoughts, and seeing Christie stick her head in the box took care of the rest.

She provided a running commentary on the collection of cats. "This white one is a chubby thing. Oh! I want a red scarf like this one's wearing. What do you call this blotchy one? A calico?" Her final pronouncement? "You need more black cats."

Decorating the tree had cheered me up and filled the time until the butter was soft enough. The next hour was spent baking. I chopped and toasted the almonds and then mixed them with the other ingredients. The dough was rolled into balls and placed on cookie sheets. And when the cookies came out of the oven and had cooled, they were coated in lots and lots of powdered sugar. I filled a small cookie tin to take to

Ellie. The two larger tins were for my Friday night guests. Try as I might, not all the cookies made it into the waiting cookie tins. A few took a detour along the way.

The afternoon of decorating and baking had lifted my spirits, and, as I washed up, I contemplated visiting Ellie. When the phone pinged with a text, I dried my hands and grabbed it. I'd half expected it to be Gemma since she hadn't called me, but it was Wendy, and I could almost hear her excitement in the words she'd written. I laughed aloud as I read her message.

DCI Burton went to the garage to interview Peter. No big deal. Asked Peter about interviewing me. Called and came by. Guess what? He invited me to dinner! Tonight! Guess that means I'm not a suspect, right? LOL.

This required a phone call. "So, I'm being stood up? I have to hear it all. Where are you going? What are you wearing?"

"He suggested the Old Stocks Inn in Stow-on-the-Wold, and since he's working out of the police station there, I offered to meet him. And I've got the perfect outfit all planned—dark taupe leggings, sky blue turtleneck jumper, and my taupe suede booties. I cannot *believe* I'm going on a date."

It occurred to me that he might have hoped to interview Belle too. "Did he ask after Belle? Since she was at the party too?"

"Um, yes, and when I told him she wasn't home, he said he'd reschedule her. Thank goodness I didn't have to explain where she was. Of course, I'm feeling as though I need to tell Peter. I'll call Mum soon to see what she's planning. Does she want to stay the night at the hotel with Maria? Is she ready to come home? What? I haven't heard from her."

I agreed Peter needed to be put in the picture, especially if he wound up being the one to pick his mother up while Wendy was on a date. "So, as a member of the LOL Detective Agency, are you going to subtly ask your DCI questions? And, for goodness' sake, don't tell him about Maria, not yet."

We were in sync. She was all about trying to sniff out the status of the investigation and had no intention of spilling the beans about Maria. Meanwhile, she'd get in touch with Belle and text me what was going on there. And we agreed I should visit the Manor house.

Ellie was enthusiastic in her response. "Oh, Leta, I'd welcome a visit. Things are so unsettled here, and the mood in my family swings from mournful to grumpy to grumpier still. You would be a much-needed break. And please don't bring food. The fridge is full to bursting, and you and I can choose something for dinner. Just bring Dickens, so we can watch his antics with Blanche. "

Christie was lying on her back on the hearth-rug with all four paws in the air. I got a lazy glance as I stuck my black cloche on my head but no snippy comments, a reaction I took to mean she was content to be on her own. Dickens was excited about seeing Blanche and pranced by the car as I locked the door to the cottage.

The plane trees along the drive were still lit, but the house was no longer ablaze with lights in every window. It was Ellie, with Blanche at her heels, who greeted me when I knocked. As our four-legged friends scampered off, she gave me a long, tight hug. "Now I know what people mean when they say, 'You're a sight for sore eyes.' Come, let's find something to eat."

She was right about the fridge. We opted for the comfort of shepherd's pie and decided it would taste better if it were warmed in the oven rather than nuked. While Ellie opened a bottle of wine, I threw together a salad, and it wasn't long before we were enjoying the simple meal.

In the library, we chose two comfy chairs near the fireplace and propped our feet on the oversized ottoman between them. Dickens and Blanche joined us, each with a toy from Blanche's toybox. Ellie peered at me over the rim of her wine glass. "It's good to be off duty for a bit. I love my family, but dealing with their emotions plus the arrangements for the funeral has gotten overwhelming."

Sipping my wine, I nodded. "And how are you emotionally?"

"Strangely, I'm not overwrought. Perhaps because I wasn't nearly as close to Nicholas as I was to his father. Coming on the heels of losing Reginald and Nigel, I guess this could have undone me, but it hasn't. Had it been Matthew or one of his sons in that accident, it would be a different story. No doubt I'd require sedation, much as Julia has."

"How is she?"

"Heavily sedated and not well at all. Other than speaking with DCI Burton, she's not left her room. I've managed to get her to eat small bits, and I've sat with her some as she sleeps, but she's been mostly unresponsive. The doctor says he's monitoring her, but she worries me."

I wondered about the sedation. I recalled my doctor offering me tranquilizers that I'd declined. *Everyone reacts differently*, I thought. "Do you think she's taking it especially hard because she and Nicholas argued on Saturday?"

"I can't say, but I get the impression the second row was much more heated than the first. And it must have been after the party before he went out, as there was nothing in their behavior during drinks and dinner to indicate otherwise.

Maybe she'll tell me at some point. Her dad will be here in a day or two. Could be she'll open up to him."

"That's right. I forgot she visited him last week. In Northampton, right?"

"Yes. He's called to check on her a few times, but she hasn't felt up to talking to him . . . or anyone else. When I spoke with him, he mentioned how odd it was that Nicholas had a flat tire on the Bentley when Julia had just had one on her way to see him. He was proud she knew how to change it herself. Since he owns a garage, he taught her how as soon as she started driving. Still, he wasn't happy she'd had to drive the rest of the way on one of those small spares they use nowadays. He patched the original tire and felt compelled to check over her rental car—tires and all—so she'd be sure to get back here safely. He told her to be especially careful to check her tires if she made any stops along the way."

Now, that's odd. Had someone tampered with Julia's tire too? Why? Did someone want them both out of the way?

Ellie gazed at her empty wine glass. "I don't often drink this much, but if not now, when? Would you care for a digestif? Brandy, Kahlua, Amaretto?"

That sounded appealing. I opted for Amaretto and offered to return the trays to the kitchen while Ellie poured our drinks. Loading the dishwasher and handwashing the wine glasses, I pondered how to ask Ellie about the prenup. So far, the time hadn't seemed right. As I emerged from the kitchen, I saw Julia coming downstairs, clinging to the railing. I hurriedly met her on the steps. "Should you be up? Could you use some help?"

She wobbled and sat down. Staring at me glassy-eyed, she whispered, "I'm hungry." I suggested I take her to her room and bring up a bowl of soup, and she nodded yes. Turning her around, I supported her free arm as she reversed course. When I got her into the bed, I propped her in a seated position with pillows behind her and poured a glass of water.

Downstairs, I knew Ellie must be wondering what had happened to me. She thought hunger was a good sign and agreed with my suggestion that I heat soup to take to Julia while she enjoyed her digestif in the library. That she so readily accepted my offer told me she was exhausted and running out of steam.

I pulled my turkey soup from the fridge and found crackers in the pantry. When I arrived upstairs, Julia's eyes were closed, but she opened them and gave a weak smile as I approached with the soup. She closed them again and inhaled the aroma before taking a tiny sip. "Goodness, I needed this."

She ate silently and slowly, but she finished what I gave her. "Would you like more?" I asked.

"No, thank you. I think . . . I think what I want now . . . is a shower."

She pointed me to the drawer that held fresh pajamas, and I laid those out on the vanity while I got the shower running. She was unsteady but able to walk to the bathroom on her own. She agreed it was a good idea to leave the bathroom door ajar so I could hear her if she called for assistance. This pale bedraggled creature bore little resemblance to the supermodel I'd last seen at Ellie's birthday party, and I was worried about her.

She looked better when she emerged from the bathroom wrapped in an oversized burgundy bathrobe—better, but not well. Sitting on the side of the bed, she tried to open the bottle I assumed held the pills the doctor had prescribed. Unscrewing the top was too much for her, and she thrust the bottle toward me. When I handed the open bottle back, she shook out two pills and downed them with water.

She lay back on her pillows and closed her eyes. "I thought I was a strong woman, but this has done me in. Dad raised me to handle whatever came, and I always have. He'd be so disappointed I've fallen apart."

It was easy for me to offer consoling words, having gone through a similar situation with Henry. Except Nick was so much younger. My heart ached for her. "As for your dad, Julia, he was telling Ellie today how proud he was that you remembered how to change a flat tire. Still a strong woman in comparison to many—including me. Grief is a horse of a different color, and we all handle it differently."

She had begun to drift off, and she slurred her next words. "So strange. Dad told me . . . accidents . . . tires . . . in Northampton."

It seems more than strange, I thought. *Julia has a flat tire. Nicholas has a blowout. And there's a tale about tires?* Was it an odd coincidence or something more?

Julia looked up at me. "Leta, you've been so kind. May I ask one more thing of you? Will you go to Nick's room and pull his green sweater from the basket in the closet?"

I easily found the cashmere sweater folded and lying on top of the basket. Julia had removed the robe by the time I returned, and she took the sweater from my hand and held it to her nose. Only then did she snuggle beneath the covers on her side with the sweater clutched against her chest. As she closed her eyes, she mumbled, "Nick, Nick, how could you leave me?"

I brushed a stray hair from her face and sat with her a while longer. Two grieving women in one day had stirred too many difficult memories and emotions for me. It occurred to me that Ellie had to be feeling the same way given she'd lost Nigel in the fall. Too much sadness for one family.

Dickens stirred when I entered the library, but Blanche remained on her side snoring. Ellie nodded toward the glass of Amaretto she'd poured me an hour ago, and I sank gratefully into my chair and savored it. "A sad time," I said. "Julia's fortunate to have you here to look after her. I'd never have made it through Henry's death without my sisters and girlfriends, and I can't help but wish she had some friends here too."

Ellie nodded. "I know. And it won't get any easier until the funeral is over. I can't help but think you Americans handle this better—a funeral a few days or a week afterward instead of as long as two weeks on."

"I've known people in the States who took that long, but you're right, usually it's a week or less. For Henry's funeral, both sides of the family and most of our friends lived in driving distance, so there was no reason to delay. Everything up until that day was a blur to me, so I'm glad it wasn't a two-week ordeal. When will the service for Nicholas be?"

"We worked with Father Michael to find a day next week when the funeral service wouldn't put a damper on any of the several Christmas events planned. Wednesday, a week from tomorrow, is the date."

Dickens observed that the atmosphere at the Manor house was subdued. Even Blanche, who seemed never to stop darting around, was quieter on this visit. She missed her family playing with her. Ellie or Matthew might take time to rub her head, but that was about it. *Yes*, I thought, *our animals tune into our feelings.*

At home, I made quick work of feeding Christie while Dickens checked the garden. I wondered how Belle had fared with Maria but thought it too late to check on her. It had been a long sad day, and I was ready for a book and bed. A favorite flannel gown, a cat curled against my side, and a dog lying by the nightstand—I had everything I needed. *I may not be any closer to figuring out who caused the accident*, I thought, *but as Scarlett O'Hara famously said, "Tomorrow is another day."*

Chapter Eighteen

I was in my snuggly fleece robe sipping my morning coffee when Gemma called. "Sorry I couldn't get back to you yesterday. We did team-building activities in the freezing cold —building bridges over creeks, zip lining, you name it. I was exhausted. Have you found out anything more about the girlfriend?"

She couldn't believe we'd not only found the girlfriend but had also met with her and explained that Nicholas was dead. "Are you kidding me? I can't wait to hear how you managed that, but I haven't much time. Please tell me you've told Constable James."

I told her I planned to do that today. I could tell she wasn't happy with the delay, but there wasn't much she could do about it unless she wanted to preempt me and go directly to her constable or the DCI. She huffed a bit and then switched topics.

"Dad says they interviewed him and took photos of his knives, but I haven't heard what conclusions DCI Burton drew from their meeting. Do you know?"

I didn't but offered to find out. The sudden chatter in the background told me she must have entered the classroom, and I wasn't surprised by her abrupt goodbye.

The next call was from Wendy. "I was dying to call you last night, but it was too late. Can I come over?"

"Sure, if eggs and grits will do for breakfast. Are you bringing Belle?"

"Yes to breakfast. No to Mum coming. She's still at the hotel. That's part of what I have to tell you. On my way."

Not knowing what the day would bring, I opted for comfortable stay-at-home clothes—leggings and an oversized flannel shirt—red plaid, of course. When Christie wandered into the kitchen, I recalled tasking her with thinking about the case yesterday when I left for brunch. *Was that only yesterday?* I thought. I hadn't asked and she hadn't volunteered what she'd come up with. "Christie, have you had any ah-has about the accident? We sure could use some direction."

She jumped into one of the chairs and watched as I put two placemats out. "You and Dickens seemed kind of out of sorts when you came back, so I thought it could wait. I was thinking how odd it was the Earl took off his wedding ring before he left. Do men do that before they go out?"

"Not unless they're trying to disguise the fact they're married," I said. "You mean Dickens didn't tell you about the girlfriend? I guess we *were* out of sorts."

"No, he didn't. What else have you two been keeping from me? And why are you setting two places? You never tell me anything!"

Oh my, I thought, *cattitude*. I explained that Wendy was joining us, and she'd get the scoop firsthand. That seemed to appease her. By the time Wendy knocked on the door, I had the grits going on the stove and the eggs ready for the frying pan.

Grinning from ear to ear, she hugged me and sat down with a mug of coffee. "So, can I start with my date? I know you want to hear about Mum and Maria, but I've got to tell you about my DCI."

"Your DCI? Do tell!"

"Well, first, his name is Brian. The vitals are he's my age and divorced—no children. Like me, he got married right out of university, though he divorced much sooner than I did. He says a copper's wife doesn't have it easy. Spent some time on the force in Yorkshire before transferring to Birmingham and now home to the Cotswolds. The time just flew at dinner, and it's hard to say what we talked about. He laughed at the thought of doing yoga like I do, but he belongs to a gym and plays rugby. That he's fit is pretty obvious when you get a good look."

I smiled. "And did you get a good look?"

"No! That's not what I meant. But when I saw him in a jumper and not a jacket, it was clear there wasn't an ounce of fat on him. And, um, I invited him to your tree trimming party. I knew you'd be okay with that."

"Oh, Wendy. What fun. Wouldn't it be lovely if you two were still dating when Dave gets here? We could have dinner out."

She agreed and then reluctantly switched gears to the girl-friend saga. "Now, let me bring you up to speed on Mum and Maria."

"Uh-huh, I want to hear all about it, but before that, I want to know whether your DCI—Brian—has any inkling what we've been up to?"

"Kind of. When he was being questioned, Toby let the cat

out of the bag—that we've managed to get ourselves involved in two murder investigations in the past and that the police should check to see what we know. And then Brian asked Peter if that was true. Thankfully, Peter didn't go into detail, only said that since you'd discovered the accident, the police should expect you to be in the middle of things. According to Peter, Brian grumbled when he heard that and said he'd have to set you straight."

I laughed. "So kind of your brother. I need to remind him he's the one who called me to the pub Monday night to hear the girlfriend story. And I wonder if this means I've traded bickering with Gemma for confrontations with a DCI. I hope not."

"Hard to say. He was nice enough to me. I told him we were friends with Ellie, so he should expect to see us around. He *did* ask if I had anything to report, and I dodged that bullet with the quote from *The Shadow*. Since he'd never heard of the show, I had to explain the reference, and our conversation moved on to tv shows and books.

"So, let me tell you about Mum. The concierge brought in a doctor to see to Maria, and he prescribed Valium. Mum sat with her and plied her with tea and soup, but she was off and on so distraught, that Mum asked if she would like her to stay the night. And so Mum did. She got to hear in detail how Maria and Nicholas met, the secret getaways they've had, and how much in love they were—nothing very useful. Mum was, however, quite proud of her one discovery. I don't know that it's all that useful—just touching. Carefully folded atop the dresser, Mum found Nicholas's bow tie and cumberbund."

I frowned. "Why does that strike me as so sad? I feel sorry for the girlfriend *and* the wife. And it seems odd to me that they've both required sedation. Now, on to my experience last night with Julia."

I couldn't help myself. I had tears in my eyes when I told Wendy about the green sweater—or jumper, as she would say. "It was heartbreaking to see Julia so torn up. The one thing that keeps niggling at me is this whole flat tire business. Doesn't it strike you as strange that Julia also had a flat tire? And then there's what she mumbled about Northampton and tires."

"Why don't we google Northhampton and tires and see what we can find? But first, let's eat. I'm starving."

As I crumbled feta cheese to stir into the eggs, I realized Wendy was staring at the bowl. "What?" I asked.

"You're putting feta cheese in the eggs, not cheddar? I think I've seen that on menus but I've never seen anyone do it before."

That reminded me of Henry telling me to cool it on the feta cheese. "Funny, Henry liked feta in my Greek salad, but that was his limit. It took him a while, but one day he asked me to stop putting it in his scrambled eggs. Next, it was, 'Can't we have plain ol' tomatoes without feta cheese?' We had a good laugh over that." Thankfully, Wendy wanted to give it a try.

Fortified with scrambled eggs and cheese grits, we refilled our coffee mugs and moved to my office. Naturally, Dickens crawled beneath the desk and Christie leaped on top of it. She managed to dislodge a notepad and two pens before looking at me expectantly. "Treats, please," she meowed.

Wendy looked at me as I reached in the desk drawer and brought out the bag of treats. "Honestly, you'd think you understood her meows, but I guess the look is enough, right?"

"Oh yes, it's amazing what she can say with a disdainful

twitch of her tail or an imperious look. Next, she'll want the file drawer opened so she can curl up in it." And sure enough, that's what happened.

Wendy pulled a chair over as I googled different combinations of Northampton and tires until I stumbled across a news story about two deaths in Northampton caused by tire damage. Several cars parked close together in a car park had their tires deliberately tampered with. Some of the cars developed obvious flat tires such that their drivers knew immediately not to drive off. Unfortunately, the damage to the other three cars caused slow leaks unbeknownst to the owners. Subsequently, one had a minor accident with damage only to the car, but two of the drivers were involved in fatal collisions hours later on the roadway.

"Okay, we found the story. Now, what does it tell us?" I asked. "Julia's flat tire must have reminded her dad about the story, and he told her about it as a cautionary tale. As in, be careful as you travel. That makes sense to me. But does it also have something to do with Nicholas's tire?"

Wendy reread the story. "Did it give Julia the idea to mess with her husband's tire? But why would she? Did she know about Maria? Is this a case of a vengeful wife? Or was she worried Nicholas was going to divorce her and the whole prenup business meant she'd be in the poorhouse? Well, not the poorhouse, but, you know, much less wealthy?"

"This is why we need to know about the prenup and how much money Julia has in her own right from her modeling career. But can you see her wielding a knife to slash a tire? She'd have to be either furious or coldly calculating to do that. After sitting with her last night, I can't see it."

Wendy did her funny sideways motion with her mouth. "Is it time we started writing down our list of suspects, evidence, and motives? Maybe then we can talk to Constable James. Hopefully, he's got something more. *My* DCI wasn't sharing much of anything last night."

I told her I'd started a list Monday before she'd come over with her mum but hadn't gotten far. As we'd gathered more information since then, Wendy thought we should ditch my earlier thoughts and start fresh. We decided to put each person's name on one sheet of printer paper and jot down what we knew for each one. We took our paper and magic markers to the kitchen table where we could spread out.

Christie didn't stir, but Dickens followed us. "I'm ready. Detective Dickens at your service." Next time Christie complained about not being in the know, I'd have to remind her she'd slept through a sleuthing session.

"Okay, who are our suspects?" I asked. We ticked off Julia, Harry, Matthew, Sam, and Gavin and agreed there were more who were pretty far-fetched—like Ellie—but we didn't want to waste time considering them.

If we thought about opportunity, the list would include everyone who'd been at the party, assuming they could sneak out to the Bentley sometime before, during, or immediately after the celebration. I pictured my kitchen wall covered in printer paper.

I used masking tape to hang the pages on the pantry door. "Five realistic suspects, I guess. Let's start with Gavin. What's his motive? Why would he want to kill Nicholas?"

Wendy's eyes bugged out. "Why? He was angry! The very idea that Nicholas wanted the donkey pasture and had already asked planning commission members if they'd approve a new bridge—when Gavin hadn't yet agreed to sell—he was furious with him. I wonder how the police are viewing his unabashed rage."

I shook my head. "But would he kill him over that? Yes, I suppose fury is a motive, but enough of one? I don't think so. What about Matthew?"

We agreed becoming the Earl of Stow and owning the entire Estate outright seemed a darned powerful motive. If Nicholas had lived, the estate would only have passed to Matthew if Nicholas eventually died without having children. Wendy wrote "Gets the whole shebang" on Matthew's page.

She stood staring at the piece of paper that said *Harry*. "His gain isn't as lucrative in the here and now, but he gets to keep his sheep and the livelihood he treasures. And after Matthew dies, he'll gain more—much more. He'll become the Earl of Stow."

"You know we're doing the P.D. James thing again, right? Her list of murder motives—Love, Lust, Lucre, and Loathing. So, Matthew and Harry both get lots of lucre. And *duh*, I just realized the adjective *lucrative* must come from the noun lucre!"

Wendy laughed. "There you go again with your word nerd thing! Now let's look at Sam. His motive is more distant. The title has to pass to Harry, no way around that. Unless Matthew breaks the entail and carves up the acreage between his two sons, the estate would pass to Harry too. So, for Sam, there's the potential for lucre, but only way down the road."

I shook my head no. "I bet Sam lives in the here and now. If he did it, it was because he saw himself helping his father or his brother or both. And I never once saw him angry when any of this was being discussed."

Wendy grabbed the marker again. "If we're talking anger, Harry's another matter. He's made no bones as to how he feels about Nicholas's plans for the resort and what that could mean for his prized Cotswolds Lions. You and I may think sheep aren't a reason to kill someone, but for Harry, they could be. Nicholas out of the way would solve the immediate problem. I'd say a more likely motive for Harry is loathing. Lucre would be secondary."

Dickens barked, "But Harry likes dogs. He's one of the good guys."

I rubbed Dickens's head and thought of what else I knew about Harry. "He admitted he punched Nicholas Saturday night and that wild act fits with his nickname, Hotspur. Funny, in my brief encounters with him, I've noticed he can be affable one moment and cross, almost angry, the next. I think he's a strong contender—possibly stronger than his dad. Unless . . . unless Matthew would kill to protect Harry's interests."

Marker still in her hand, Wendy wrote *knife* on the pages of our male suspects. "Enough on motive. Let's look at means. It's much like our thinking on opportunity. We'd have to list every man at the party, though I don't imagine they all carried their folding knives somewhere in their tuxedos.

"And when I picture Julia's form-fitting dress, it's obvious she wasn't carrying one, but could she have picked up a different knife? If a kitchen knife would work, the answer is yes . . . for her and every *woman* at the party."

I attempted to relax my tense shoulders. "This is hard work. Whether or not Julia had the means, the Northampton story suggests she may have had an idea about how to kill her husband—if she *meant* to kill him. It's the *why* we're struggling with because we don't have enough information—we've got to find out about her finances and the prenup. And you know what? Just because Nicholas *told* Maria he was going to divorce Julia doesn't mean he was. How many men have said the same thing to their lovers, over and over again?"

"Plenty, I'm sure. Good point. We don't know for sure

what Nicholas said to Julia Saturday night. They argued, but we don't know that he mentioned divorce. There are too many unknowns about a motive for Julia. Hopefully, Constable James will give you some better info on the will and prenup soon."

I refilled both our mugs and stood by the pantry door with Wendy. "Is it unrealistic to think lots of people could have known about the tire thing? I bet it was a hot news item when it happened, and it was easy enough for us to find. And there's the big question—did the perpetrator mean to *kill* Nicholas or simply inconvenience him? I wonder what the police think?"

"That's one thing Brian *did* share. He thinks it's pretty unlikely anyone thought they'd kill Nicholas by slashing the tire. Cause him significant harm? Maybe, but it could have been nothing but a flat tire when he next went to leave the manor house or in a parking lot somewhere—a royal pain, but nothing more. If and when they find the person who did this, it will be a manslaughter charge, not murder. Unless the villain up and says he or she *meant* to kill him—which only happens on telly."

"Hell's bells," I said. "Are we letting this whole tire story get us off track?"

Wendy had the look that told me she'd run out of patience. "Aargh! Forgive me for this next line—I know it's lame—but I think we've gotten wrapped around the axle." She looked at me expectantly. "Of the car, get it?"

I rolled my eyes as we laughed together before agreeing we'd gotten as far as we could with the clues we had. If there was a clear next step, we weren't seeing it. *Sugar*, I thought. *We need sugar.* I opened the pantry door and stood on tiptoe to reach the top shelf where the cookie tins sat.

Wendy chuckled when I pried the lid off the tin and folded

back the waxed paper. "Your Christmas cookies? I get to have one now? Woo hoo!"

I bit into one, sprinkling powdered sugar down my top. "Don't we always need something sweet when our brains get stuck? But the limit on these is two at a time, so grab another one before I put them up."

Wendy simultaneously took another bite and grabbed her second cookie. "You know, you may as well print the recipe to hand out at your tree trimming party. We're all going to want it."

I laughed. "I'm happy to share the recipe, though I haven't noticed any of my friends using the Greek recipes I keep doling out. What do you guys do with them? Frame them? Tuck them away?"

"Don't know about everyone else, but Mum and I are waiting for you to start the Leta Parker Dinner Delivery Service—Greek salad, pastitsio, spanakopita, and whatever you call these things."

"Right, don't hold your breath. And the cookies are koura-biedes, but this time of year we call them Christmas cookies. To me, they taste like wedding cookies that aren't salty. Now, are you fortified? Ready to swing into action?"

The look on Wendy's face told me she didn't have any idea which direction to swing in.

"Here's the plan. I'll call Constable James and hope he knows something about Julia's financial situation, the prenup, and the will. I'll decide from there what to say to Julia. I think another conversation with her is the next step—assuming she'd not still drugged up."

"What about me? I know I need to talk to Mum and prob-ably pick her up. Is there something we need to do about Maria?"

Staring at my friend, I slowly nodded yes. "I think someone needs to tell the police about Maria, don't you?"

Wendy's mouth dropped open. "Please tell me you don't think I'm that someone. Way to nip a budding romance in the bud, don't you think? Me telling Brian what we've done and somehow explaining why I didn't tell him last night? Uh-uh."

I patted my friend on the shoulder. "I was just getting you going. If you'll call Belle for an update, then I'll share the info with Constable James. I mean, what can he do to me? Arrest me? If your DCI gets bent out of shape, you can blame it all on me."

"Phew," Wendy said as she pulled out her phone. "Let's see what Mum has to say."

Wendy put Belle on speaker, and she had good news and better news to share. First, Maria was perkier today and was making plans to fly back to New York tomorrow. The better news was that Belle had convinced her to contact the police and had volunteered to accompany her to Stow Police Station.

"Belle, let me contact Constable James before you go so he's not caught off guard. I think things will go more smoothly if I present this to him first. The more I think about it, if I alert him to the situation, he may even offer to come to the hotel. That would be less stressful for Maria, don't you think?"

We all agreed it was the best plan. The revelation that Nicholas had a girlfriend plus what he had allegedly told her about divorcing his wife would cast suspicion on Julia, but the story had to come out. I couldn't help it. I still had faith Julia wasn't guilty and that whatever the couple had argued over Saturday night, divorce hadn't come up. Maybe it was wishful thinking on my part because I'd grown to like her. It wouldn't be the first time I'd been wrong about someone—as my sister

Anna would be quick to point out. She never tired of telling me how naïve I was.

While Wendy was hanging up with Belle, I put *my* phone on speaker and rang Constable James. I was in luck. He picked up on the first ring. "Constable James—um, I mean, Jonas— Leta here. I'm hoping you have an update on the Earl's will, and I've got several bits of information for you."

He took a deep breath. "Hi, Leta. It's been a bit of a slog going through the phone and the laptop plus Julia's tablet— what a contrast. The Earl's communications are a combo of exchanges about his investment banking business, which I don't begin to understand, and back and forths on bids for a helipad and pool and other resort business. Julia's are mostly girlfriend emails about social engagements, clothes, what's going on here and in NYC and something about an acting role. The good news is DCI Burton had the connections to get a response about Nicholas and Julia's finances. It's difficult to get that kind of info quickly, but somehow he managed."

"Oh! I can't wait to hear the financial news. The only part of the prenup I've unearthed is some ridiculous clause about Julia not being able to gain weight. Can you believe that?"

I could picture him shrugging his shoulders. He sounded weary as he replied, "At this point, I can believe almost anything. These people live a different life. The prenup is fairly straightforward—a clause applying to both of them that prohibits sharing personal information with the media, the weight gain clause you know about, plus an infidelity clause, but the last two are only for the wife. So the Earl could mess around, but not his wife. Is that strange or what? Anyway, in the event the Missus violated any of the clauses, she'd get 50% less than she would otherwise."

"Is it a fifty-fifty split of everything if they divorce without any clause violations?"

"Oh no. They kept their prior assets separate—those acquired before they wed. In the event of a divorce, they'd split their subsequent gains down the middle—his and hers. She's a rich woman on her own. Tells me she's not only gorgeous but brainy. Well, I guess it's being gorgeous that got her all the dosh, but she had the brains to hold on to it."

My brain was working overtime to process the information. "As it stands now, with Nicholas dead, she gets all of his assets—the money he made before and after they married plus what he inherited from his father and grandfather. That's got to be substantial. But in a divorce, she'd be entitled only to 50% of what he made after they wed and 50% of the inherited money. Of course, either way, she doesn't get any part of the property here in Astonbury, right?"

"Right. It's that entail thing, and please don't ask me to explain that. It makes my head hurt."

I explained my brain was already on overload, so no need to rehash the entail. "But, Jonas, another question's popped into my head, though think I know the answer. You told me a Scene of Crime Officer took photos at the manor house. Was he able to establish that the knife used on the tire wasn't one of those carried by Matthew, Harry, or Sam?"

"Yes, not one of those and not one of Gavin's either. DCI Burton and the SOCO went straight to the inn after visiting the Manor house because— well, you know, because it was common knowledge how angry Gavin was with the victim. The DCI interviewed Gavin, and the SOCO photographed his collection. So, we've not found the weapon yet. Not sure what the DCI is planning to do next on that front."

I was relieved to hear the news about Gavin and glad the

DCI had gotten to him sooner rather than later. As Constable James elaborated on the interview, he made it sound as though DCI Burton no longer saw Gavin as a suspect. "Okay, if there's nothing more on your end, here's what I've found out. First, I know who punched the Earl, and he'll be in contact with the police about it. If you haven't heard from anyone by the end of the day, I'll tell you who it is, but I'd like to allow him to do it on his own first.

"Before I tell you the next bit, let me ask a question. Have you traced the Earl's whereabouts when he was in Chipping Camden?"

Constable James sighed. "I'm not superhuman, Leta. So no, not yet."

"Well then, have I got some news for you! I hope you're sitting down. He was at the Cotswolds House Hotel & Spa with a girlfriend. Had her stashed there, though I don't know how often he visited her."

Stunned silence echoed down the line until Constable James found his voice. "Are you kidding me? A drop-dead gorgeous model for a wife and he had a girlfriend too? Seriously? And how did you figure that out?"

I was tempted to respond with a quote from *The Shadow*, but I knew he'd have no idea what I was talking about. "You gave me a hint when you said his GPS put him in Chipping Camden in the middle of the night. What else could he have been up to for several hours when everything is closed? It had to be a girlfriend, so we checked around until we found her."

That story evoked a groan. "Do I even want to know how you checked? Nah, probably not. If only I were a detective on one of those American shows like *Law & Order*—this is where I'd say, 'Okay, Leta, spill it. It'll go easier on you.' And the details would come pouring out."

"Ha! Now, Jonas, you don't have to threaten me. Here's what I know." I gave him the highlights and suggested it would be best to question Maria at the hotel.

It took some persuading, but he eventually came around to my way of thinking. "Guess I should say thank you, since at least it's not a death notification. I hate those. There's no way DCI Burton will let me do this interview. He'll want to handle it, and only if I'm lucky will I get to tag along. Maybe if I suggest he meet with her in a private area in the hotel and let me search her room, I'll get to go. He seems to favor that approach . . .

"But, Leta, how am I going to explain this to him? Do I just come clean and say you called to say you found her? Well, you and Belle and Wendy? Blast! He'll have my guts for garters, no matter how I break it to him."

Gemma had put the two of us between a rock and a hard place. She'd asked me to nose around, and if she were here, I'd be sharing my information with her—well, most of it. Admittedly, I sometimes kept bits to myself. She also wanted me to keep Jonas in the know—and help him find a way to share my findings with DCI Burton, without revealing his source. No easy feat. *There's no getting around it. I've kept DCI Burton in the dark, and he's going to be furious.*

I took a deep breath. "You know what, Jonas, just blame me. I'm a big girl. If he wants to look a gift horse in the mouth, so be it. We'll just let the chips fall where they may."

Constable James hesitated. "Okay, if you say so, Leta. I'd best grab him now and get on with it. And thank you. I might have eventually sussed the girlfriend angle on my own, but not any time soon."

In for a penny, in for a pound, I thought as I hung up. I told Wendy I wanted to get to Julia before DCI Burton did, in the hopes I could find out what she and Nicholas had argued over. Who knows? I might ask her outright if she slashed the tire.

Wendy rose slowly from her chair, not looking nearly as eager as I was to spring into action. "Bloody hell, no matter that you told Constable James to blame you, it won't be long before Brian realizes I held out on him. I wonder whether he'll call me on it or never call again. The only way to prevent this would have been to tell him last night . . . I guess. Should I go to the hotel to get Mum and chance running into him or send Peter instead?"

I tried to be encouraging but didn't have a good answer to her dilemma. As she drove away, I worried she'd blame me if her new romance died an abrupt death. I hoped not. There was a reason the Walter Scott quote came to mind—'O, the tangled web we weave when first we practice to deceive.' It applied to much more than Wendy's budding romance.

Chapter Nineteen

As we turned right out of the driveway, Dickens peppered me with questions. "Oh! Are we going to the manor house or town? Are we going to see Basil or only Blanche? And what about the donkeys?"

No matter what was going on, I could count on Dickens to be in high spirits. "We'll try to do it all. How would that be? Do you think we can get your lazy sister to go with us to see Martha and Dylan?"

We bantered on the two-mile walk to the front door of the manor house. When I knocked on the door, I wasn't sure anyone had heard me until Caroline called, "Coming, I'm coming." She looked like a magazine image of a chef wearing a white apron and holding a potholder in her hand.

"Oh! Hi, Leta. Come on in. Ellie's in the kitchen with her hands in bread dough. With all the food that's been coming in the door, she doesn't need me to cook anything, so she asked for a lesson in breadmaking instead."

Dickens darted ahead of me as I chatted with Caroline. "How fun. I wish I'd been here at the beginning. Years ago, I tried my hand at breadmaking but never could produce a pretty sandwich loaf. I had to stick to round—I could manage that."

I hugged Ellie as she continued kneading dough. "You look good today. You must have gotten a good night's sleep. And how's Julia?"

"Better. She asked for breakfast in bed when I looked in on her this morning, so she's regaining her appetite. Caroline took her eggs and toast and jam."

"Good. If it's okay with you, I'll leave you to your kneading, while Dickens and I visit with her. Blanche, want to go with us?"

Ellie nodded in agreement as both dogs ran to my side. There was nothing like two frisky dogs at your heels to make you smile. And I needed to smile, given the news I was about to share and the questions I was going to ask. Did she know about the girlfriend or not? I hoped to find out.

The door wasn't tightly shut, and Dickens and Blanche busted in. I peeked around the door to see Julia grinning and patting the bed. Blanche couldn't get her short hind legs up on the bed, but Dickens didn't hesitate. I laughed and gave Blanche a boost. It was good to hear Julia laugh as the dogs licked her face. "You two are just what the doctor prescribed," she said. "Maybe if I'd had you here from the start, I could have done without the pills."

I said hello as I sat in the chair beside her bed. "You look so much better than you did when I saw you last night. How are you feeling?"

She confirmed she was some better and had been able to respond to a few condolence emails on her phone. "I'm so fortunate that Ellie has been handling everything. I guess you do what you have to do, but I'm not sure I could have handled making the arrangements like the obituary, the casket . . ."

Her voice broke, and I passed her a tissue from her bedside table. "Julia, I don't know that you're up to this, but I want to share some unpleasant news with you before the police hit you with it. Okay?" When she nodded a hesitant yes, I told her about the LOL Detective Agency and how we helped the police—admittedly, whether they wanted our help or not. And then I explained we'd discovered Nicholas had a girlfriend who was staying in Chipping Camden.

Was she faking her shock? I didn't think so. Her mouth dropped open as she gasped, "A girlfriend? Here? Not in New York?"

"I'm afraid so. You didn't know?"

She looked at me as though I had two heads. "We'd hardly been here a week. How did he come up with a girlfriend?"

Either she had no idea about the situation or she deserved an Academy Award. "Um, I'm sorry to say she's from New York and he flew her over here to stay in Chipping Camden. Does the name Maria mean anything to you?"

"Maria! He uses an interpreter sometimes for conferences. I think her name is Maria. Is it her?"

What a jerk, I thought. *How could he do this to her?* "I think so. She said she'd met him at an international investor's conference. I know this a lot to digest, but I want to ask you some questions before the police do."

Julia's face turned red. "Aargh! I could kill him!" It must have dawned on her what she'd said as her face went from red to ashen and silent tears ran down her face.

I handed her more tissue. "That's why I wanted you to hear it from me first, not the police, though you'll be hearing it again from them. Your reaction tells me you didn't know about her, much less that she was down the road in a nearby village. Now, this is a critical question—did Nicholas tell you Saturday night he wanted a divorce?"

"A divorce? Over another girlfriend? And no, she's not the first. But he usually keeps them in New York, well hidden. We rowed over the first one, and he begged me not to throw him out, swore he'd never stray again. But he did. But a divorce? It would never come to that unless I was the one who filed. He loved me in his own way, and I, for better or worse, adored him."

By now she was sobbing uncontrollably. "The git! I can't believe our last words were an argument over the estate, over the brewery and Harry's stupid sheep. Nick was leaving Sunday for an investor's conference in Geneva, and I was flying to New York to attend to final details for our annual Christmas party. I was trying to convince my stubborn husband to leave well enough alone with the estate, to set aside his elaborate plans for a resort and get on with our lives in the city."

"So, he didn't tell you he was divorcing you and wanted you to leave on Sunday?"

The sobs had given way to yelling. "No! He did *not*! He told me he was tired of my meddling in his business, which was nothing new. That's what he always said until, somehow, my *suggestions* became *his* ideas. I pointed out the stress over the resort plans had made his ulcer flare up. The idiot! The one thing he never listened to me about was his health."

I lowered my voice and spoke slowly, a technique I'd found useful in speaking with agitated co-workers during my career. When it worked, the listener calmed down. Thankfully, it worked on Julia. "Now, Julia, the police are going to ask you about the last argument and divorce. That's because Maria believes Nicholas informed you Saturday night he was divorcing you. She says that's what he told her. It's her word against yours. Do you understand why this will be so important to the police?"

She nodded yes, but I wasn't convinced it had sunk in. I asked if I could tell Ellie, since it was going to come out in a matter of hours, once DCI Burton arrived. I puzzled over how to bring the point home to her and decided to ask one more time. "Julia, do you get why the divorce question will be critical to the police? What they'll be thinking?"

She stared at me and reached for Dickens. He and Blanche had moved to the foot of the bed when the yelling started. He licked her fingers and rolled over for a belly rub. It was a moment or two before Julia responded to my question. "They'll say if I thought Nick was divorcing me, that would be a reason for me to kill him. A motive. That's ridiculous. I'd yell and scream and call him every name in the book. I'd be heartbroken. But kill him? Why would I do that?"

"You tell me. Is there any reason at all that you would kill your husband?"

Her astonished look said it all. "None. None at all."

I went to the bed and hugged her. "I believe you."

I left her to take a shower and prepare for the arrival of DCI Burton. I didn't have a crystal ball, but I felt certain he'd be here as soon as he finished with Maria. Downstairs, the aroma of baking bread was wafting through the great hall and was stronger in the kitchen. I sat at the kitchen table and put my head in my hands. I was exhausted.

Caroline offered me tea and asked if I'd like some lunch. When she placed the tea in front of me, she said, "You look knackered. You looked fine when you got here. What changed in the last hour?"

"Ah, well, it's a long story. Is Ellie around?"

Dickens and Blanche had followed me and were now barking at the door to the wine cellar. Caroline laughed, "I think those two answered you. She's fetching wine for dinner, maybe for lunch too. Who knows? Ellie told me to choose a casserole to heat up." She opened the fridge and rattled off about five options. "Anything appeal?"

I opted for the lasagna and promised myself I'd be good at dinner. I wanted to tell Ellie the latest, and I might as well do it over lunch. Maybe with a glass of wine to ease the way. Blanche and Dickens barked a greeting when Ellie came up from the cellar carrying a basket containing four bottles of wine.

She set the basket on the table and hugged me. "Now I can give you a proper hug. Oh, I smell lasagna, and I have the perfect red to go with it. As a bonus, we'll have freshly baked rolls. Now, Leta, how's our Julia?"

The kitchen was so cavernous, the table was far enough away from where Caroline was bustling around that I could whisper to Ellie without worrying about being overheard. "Much, much better. I had to share some disturbing news with her, but she's recovered . . . and I need to tell you the news too."

Ellie looked from me to Caroline and suggested we move to the library. Once we sat down, I didn't see any point in hemming and hawing. "Ellie, I'm sorry to have to tell you this, but it turns out Nicholas was having an affair, and that's where he'd been Saturday night." I proceeded with the pertinent points about what Nicholas had said to Maria, Julia's description of their argument, and my certainty that the police would soon arrive to question the widow.

Ellie looked at me with a mix of disbelief and disgust. "I can't say I'm shocked to learn he was having an affair. He was the kind of man who felt entitled. What's that old *Bonfire of the Vanities* phrase? Master of the Universe? That's how he saw himself. But the nerve! How could he bring his mistress *here*? It's . . . sordid. More than that, it's shameful. Is it any wonder he couldn't concentrate on decisions about his resort proposal? Is it any wonder his stomach was in knots? I am so glad Nigel didn't have to hear this."

I moved to the fireplace while Ellie murmured to herself. *Probably contemplating how best to handle the situation*, I thought. As I warmed my hands, my eyes wandered to the display case Gavin had shown me at the party. Something seemed off. Looking more closely, I saw that Nigel's prized knife, the one that had been handed down through the generations, wasn't in its place of honor. *Could it somehow have gotten mixed in with the others?* I thought. *No. Given the precise arrangement of the collection, a misplaced knife would stick out. So, where is it? More importantly, who has it?*

Ellie was shaking her head when Caroline knocked on the library door to let us know lunch was ready. When we stood to follow Caroline, Ellie blurted, "And to think, his outrageous behavior has made his wife—his widow—a suspect in his murder! Preposterous!"

My mind raced as I stopped by the powder room. Gavin had explained the display case with the knives was kept locked. Did that mean that only a family member could have taken the knife? Who else would know where the key was kept? I returned to the library, thinking the key was stowed somewhere in the room, and I turned in a circle looking at the bookshelves and furniture. It could be taped beneath a book-shelf or an end table, but that seemed too much like some-thing out of a mystery novel. I went to the desk and pulled out the pencil drawer. Not there. I pulled out the shallow drawer on the right. Two tiny crystal bowls sat in the front of the drawer—one with paperclips and one with rubber bands. Lying atop the paperclips was a small brass key. It turned easily when I inserted it in the lock.

Puzzling over my discovery, I stuck my head in the kitchen and offered to run upstairs to see whether Julia wanted lunch. She hesitated before saying she wasn't up for lasagna but would come downstairs shortly for turkey soup. *Had I misread her reaction this morning? Was she a better actress than I'd given her credit for? Had she taken the knife and used it on her husband's tire?*

In the kitchen, Caroline had set three places, and she quickly plated lasagna to serve Ellie and me. I sat staring at my plate unable to shake the idea that maybe Nicholas *had* told Julia he wanted a divorce—and that she had, in turn, slashed his tire. Factor in her murmurings about tires and accidents, and it made sense.

Soon, Julia joined us, and Caroline insisted the young widow make herself comfortable at the table while she fixed the soup. The conversation was muted and minimal—comments about the lasagna, the soup, and the rolls. We got expectant looks from Blanche and Dickens and succumbed by giving them each a pinch of a roll. Neither Julia nor Ellie seemed to notice how distracted I was.

The hammering of the doorknocker interrupted the quiet, and Caroline scurried from the kitchen to the front door. The three of us at the table sat up straighter and squared our shoul-ders as though expecting a confrontation.

DCI Burton strode into the kitchen, nodded his head at

Ellie, and turned to Julia. "Ma'am, would you accompany Constable James to the library, please? He's in the hall." Julia carefully folded her napkin and placed it beside her plate before doing as requested. Next, he looked at Ellie. "Please inform the Earl that I'm here and will want to meet with him before I leave, as a courtesy." When she left to call Matthew, he turned to me.

Here it comes, I thought. "Mrs. Parker, what the bloody hell do you think you've been doing? DS Taylor may have tolerated your interference in her cases, but she's not running this investigation—I am. I haven't ruled out hauling you in for obstruction of justice. I don't know how the hell you bamboozled my Constable into sharing GPS information with you, but do *not* —I repeat, do *not*—try it again. Furthermore, what the hell are you doing here now?"

I flushed and stood to my full height of 5'2". "As far as I'm aware, there's no law against making inquiries at a hotel. You should be thanking me and Wendy and Belle for furthering the investigation. You wouldn't be here now if we hadn't uncovered vital information. And —"

"Making inquiries? Is that what you call it? I have it from the hotel manager that you concocted an outlandish story to gain access to one of her guests. You ladies inserted yourselves into *my* investigation."

"And, as I was about to say—"

He spoke over me. "Is this how you Yanks do things? Run amuck, lead people like Mrs. Davies and her daughter astray? We don't do things that way here. If not for you, I'm sure Wendy would have told me the entire story last night. Now—"

I'd had it. I stepped in close and used a stern voice but not a quiet one. "Now, you listen here. Don't think you can bully me. I *found* the accident. I *watched* Nicholas die. I have every right to be curious. My friends and I have done nothing wrong. We haven't hidden anything from you. *Furthermore*"—I used air quotes—"the people in this family are *my friends*, and I intend to speak with them as often as I please."

I didn't exactly set him back on his heels, but his next words were spoken in a softer tone of voice. "I had no idea this was such an emotional issue for you. I'm sorry you saw the Earl die, but that doesn't excuse your interference—"

"How dare you imply I'm being emotional. Is that your condescending way of dismissing the fact we found a crucial clue before you could? You sexist—" Thankfully, I stopped short of calling him a sexist pig.

Dickens stood growling by my side. "My dog and I are going for a walk, and we may even speak with Harry and Basil. Please move out of my way." And he did.

Trembling with anger, I marched from the kitchen. I heard him mutter something about this not being over by a long shot. *It's over as far as I'm concerned.* I flung open the front door and almost bowled Wendy over.

"What are you doing here? Getting in line to be blessed out by your DCI? He's quite good at it, you know."

Wendy raised her hands in the surrender signal. "Tell me about it. Already had my scolding. He was a bit more polite to Mum, probably her age, but he didn't mince his words with me."

"You don't seem upset about it. Is that because he thinks I *led you astray*, as he put it? That you're innocent in all this?"

She rolled her eyes. "He doesn't listen. When he asked why I hadn't told him about Maria at dinner, I explained I'd promised you I wouldn't. That's when he went off about Yanks and busybodies. I think he even mentioned Jessica Fletcher. I tried my best to explain to him that Mum and I were in this with you—willingly, even eagerly—but he wasn't having any part of my explanation."

"How can he be good at his job if he doesn't listen? He needs us more than he knows if that's the case. So, where does that leave you two?"

Wendy tilted her head. "Who knows? I think he's trying to convince himself I'm innocent because he likes me. I suspect there could be another dinner date, but your party? I doubt he'll come to that."

I had to laugh. "Innocent? If he only knew? Why, as often as not, it's you convincing me we need to be involved. Enough about him. I'm off for a walk. Care to join me?"

"Of course I do. I wanted to check on Ellie *and* I wanted to hear how you got on with Julia. Nah. Mostly I came to talk to you, but I had a ready excuse if you weren't here. Let me get my gloves from the car. It's chillier out than I thought."

Dickens and I waited on the gravel drive as Wendy grabbed her gloves. He looked at me. "What was that guy's problem? I don't think I've ever heard anyone yell at you like that."

I scratched his chin. "He thinks I stuck my nose in his business. Thanks for growling at him. Don't think I didn't notice."

Wendy and I walked past Matthew's cottage and turned right toward Harry's smaller one and those that housed the weaver and the other artisans. Dickens wandered here and there, always in sight. I went through my conversation with Julia, and like me, Wendy leaned toward believing her—until I told her about the missing knife. We went back and forth—was Julia guilty or not?

Frowning, Wendy asked, "Who was it who wrote 'Hell hath no fury like a woman scorned?' Maybe it's been staring us in the face the entire time. Julia felt scorned and took her revenge."

No closer to an answer, we meandered past the quaint cottages, and thirty minutes into the walk, we turned toward the river. I wanted Wendy to see the waterwheel and the inn across the way further downstream. Before we got that far, we saw the flock near the water beneath the trees. Dickens barked and took off to see Basil.

Wendy shivered. "I should have dressed more warmly"

"Want to go back? You can see the waterwheel another day."

"No, I'd at least like to see the sheep and Basil. That would be a nice distraction. And isn't that Harry? Let's walk that way and then head to the Manor house."

When we joined Harry, he was tending to an ewe who'd gotten tangled in the thick vines on the riverside. "They're usually smarter than this," he said, "but there's one in every crowd." He was using his knife to carefully slice at the vines without injuring the sheep. When she was free, she moved quickly to catch up with the herd, and we followed.

Wendy hadn't met Basil before and leaned down to pet him. "Dickens and Basil are such a sight. Dickens is a Mini-Me of Basil, isn't he?"

We three laughed at her apt reference, and she walked deeper into the flock with the two dogs. I took that opportunity to ask Harry if he'd told the police yet about punching his cousin.

"Yup. Called the station this morning and left a message on the constable's voicemail. I guess it doesn't matter anymore now they've arrested Julia."

My mouth fell open. "They what?"

"Dad just called to tell me the DCI showed up, spoke to

her briefly, and arrested her. Dad convinced him to place her under house arrest for now. One of the perks of being the Earl of Stow. They took her passport, though."

Wendy walked up in time to hear the tail end of the conversation. "He's arrested her already? He only just got to the house, and I thought he was interviewing her—about the girlfriend?"

"Dad said something about a girlfriend and divorce and that being what broke the case for the police. Dad's furious. Thinks the DCI is out of line and plans to go over his head."

As we talked, he absently pulled out his knife and tossed it from hand to hand before grabbing another ewe and cleaning its hooves. "Not a good day for our family."

Wendy looked surprised at his nonchalance. "Harry, do you think Julia did it?"

"I don't like to think she did, but Gran says they rowed Saturday night. And if Nicholas had a girlfriend, Julia could've done it in a fit of jealousy, right? My cousin may have been a jerk, but he didn't deserve to die."

His willingness to believe Julia did it surprised me, and I wondered if he knew something we didn't. I had no ready reply to Harry's comments, and Wendy and I left him to his work. We wanted to get back to the Manor house and were almost to Matthew and Sarah's cottage when Wendy's phone rang. It was Belle checking in.

As she shared the sequence of events with her mother, I stopped in my tracks. *The knife.*

Wendy walked a few steps before she turned. "Are you coming?"

"I want to ask Harry something. You go on. I'll catch up with you."

Dickens barked as we turned toward the river. "More time with Basil? Cool."

Harry was working his way through the herd as they grazed on the riverbank, checking for minor injuries and cleaning hooves. He looked up and smiled as Dickens barked and ran to Basil. Harry stood and wiped his knife on his pants leg, folded it, and put it in his pocket. "Hi. Did you drop something or did Dickens insist on coming back?"

I thought it best to start with something innocuous. "Oh, Dickens is happy enough to be here. He'd stay all day if you'd have him, but it's not that. I know now's not the right time, but with all that's gone on this last week, I forgot about the column I want to write on the Cotswolds Lions and the work you've done with them. It could be a nice distraction for us both. Are you still willing? I think it will make a good story."

"Sure thing, Leta. It probably appears all I do is wander with the herd and check their hooves, but I'll give you a complete picture. I've got time this weekend, so let me know."

"Thanks. I'll ring you when I'm at home and can look at my calendar." I took a few steps in the direction of the Manor house before I stopped and turned around. I wanted it to appear I'd had a sudden thought. "You know, watching you work with that knife takes me back to Saturday night. It reminds me of the one Gavin showed me at the party, the one in the display case."

Harry squinted as he looked at me and pulled another sheep to him. "There are close to a hundred knives in those cases, Leta. Which one?"

"The one that belonged to your grandfather and his father before him. It was much fancier than the others. I'm surprised yours looks so similar. I'd have thought you'd carry a more rustic version for everyday work."

He pulled out his knife and flicked it open. "Just a simple knife, Leta. Many of them look the same. Dad and Sam have Laguiole knives too, and I hear Gavin has a new one."

"I wouldn't have thought there'd be two with the prominent scrollwork and the bee at the hinge."

Harry released the sheep he'd been holding and stood. "Why are you suddenly so interested in my knife?"

I'd run out of good answers. Answers that wouldn't put him more on his guard. I tried the direct approach. "I think it's your grandfather's, especially after noticing this morning the one in the library's gone."

He'd been moving toward my right as we spoke, causing me to turn to see him. "What's your point, Leta? What game are you playing?"

"It's not a game, Harry. When the police discover your grandfather's knife is missing, they'll want to know where it is." *They'll want to know if you used it on your cousin's tire*, I thought, *and I think you did.*

I found I was backing up as Harry moved closer to me, brandishing the knife. "And why would they want to know that? Now they've arrested Julia, what interest would they have in a missing knife?"

"Harry, they haven't found the one that's a match for the tire slash, and when they notice your grandad's knife's missing, they'll think Julia must have taken it and disposed of it. The final proof they need is the weapon—to make the match. Did you find it somewhere on the property? Maybe by the carriage house?" I didn't for a minute think that was the case. I was making things up as I went along and thankful I was talking to him in broad daylight out in the open.

A change came over him, the one I'd described to Wendy

earlier. He shifted from affable to cross. "But . . . they haven't *noticed* it's missing, have they? You're the only one who knows."

I continued backing up as I said, "Um, Wendy knows too."

"I don't think so. Otherwise, she'd be here with you, but it's only you—and me."

This was more than *cross*. This was threatening. Harry looked upward as though he were working things out. When he turned his gaze to me, his face broke out in a grin—a grin that sent a chill up my spine. "And what if it *is* Grandad's? If Gran hasn't noticed it's missing, no one else will. And that's that."

With that, he rushed me, his hands outstretched, and shoved me. I landed on my backside with my arms behind me, but my hands found only air. I was at the river's edge, tilting backward, and before I knew it, I'd tumbled in—into the river. I heard Dickens barking as I surfaced.

I knew I couldn't last long in the freezing water. As the current moved me downstream, I frantically tried to find something to grab on to and finally caught hold of a tree root jutting out from the side. I inched my way to the bank, hand over freezing hand, but that was all I could manage. I didn't have the strength to pull myself up. *You idiot*, I thought as I lost consciousness.

Chapter Twenty

When I came to, I was lying face down in the dirt with Dickens barking and someone nudging my side. *No, that's not Dickens's bark,* I thought. I looked sideways and saw it was Basil barking and trying to get his large head beneath my stomach to turn me over. I heard yelling and more barking in the distance.

Dickens arrived and licked the side of my face. "Leta, Leta, they're coming. Roll over. Sit up. Do something."

It was DCI Burton who helped Basil by grabbing my jacket and turning me onto my back. Constable James ran up behind him, followed by Wendy. The DCI unzipped my black parka and pulled it off, and soon I was covered in warm coats. I could hear someone, maybe DCI Burton, on the phone, and it wasn't long before I was loaded into a vehicle. Wendy was by my side the whole time. "What happened? Did Harry do this? Do you hurt anywhere? Oh, you've lost your hat! We're almost there." The fact I wasn't responding didn't stop her from talking.

When I heard Ellie, I knew we were at the Manor house.

She began piling blankets on top of me. "Okay, let's get her to the hospital."

That got my attention, and I struggled to sit up. "No! I'm not going to the hospital. Please, no." I heard Wendy and Ellie conferring and almost immediately, strong arms lifted me from the car and carried me up the front stairs and on to a second-floor bedroom. Wendy and Ellie together peeled my wet clothes off and covered me in warm blankets. Julia arrived with a warm cloth to wash my face and a towel to wring out my hair. Caroline appeared next with warm towels for my neck and chest and a cup of hot sweet tea. These ladies were like a portable ER. I was in good hands.

When next I stirred, it was dark outside and the lights were turned low in the room. Wendy was sitting by my side reading, and Dickens was on the bed by my feet. Dickens barked, "Leta, you're awake. Are you warm?"

Wendy came to the bed, and I could see the fire going behind her. *Ah, a room with a fireplace. I think I'll stay.* "Wendy, did they catch Harry?"

"First a cup of tea, and I'll tell you what I know." I swallowed a few sips and lay back. Dickens shifted up the bed to lie by my side and lick my hand.

Wendy shared the details of what I'd missed. "They have Harry in custody, but let's start with how Dickens and Basil saved you. I was knocking on the front door when I heard Dickens barking. When I looked over my shoulder, I saw him running at full tilt. He arrived at my side about the time Caroline opened the door. When he leaped and barked and tugged on my trousers, it was clear he wanted me to follow him. I yelled at Caroline to get Brian and took off behind Dickens.

"As I was coming up on Matthew and Sarah's cottage, a beat-up Land Rover careened past me with Harry at the wheel.

You know I'm not a runner, right? Before I knew it, Brian passed me going ninety to nothing, and Constable James was right on his heels. I did the best I could, Leta, but I couldn't keep up."

I smiled at my friend. "Does this mean I have to be nice to your DCI now?"

She chuckled. "Probably, but not until he apologizes for reading you the riot act. Anyway, he's good in an emergency. He helped Basil turn you over. Um, by the way, we're pretty sure Basil pulled you out. Do you remember that?"

"The last thing I remember before seeing Basil by my side is holding on to a root."

"Then Basil is a hero dog. We didn't think you'd pulled yourself out." She looked at Dickens. "And we thought Dickens might have tried and had to give up and go for help. Maybe dogs *do* communicate with each other. They were a hero team."

Dickens looked at Wendy and barked. "Of *course* I tried. My Leta may be short, but she's not exactly light as a feather. Basil shoved me out of the way and grabbed her, and I went for help."

I told Wendy Dickens thought I needed to lose some weight. No matter that Dickens and I constantly conversed in front of her, she never suspected we understood each other.

That got an eye roll. "Well, the dogs get top billing, but I think Brian gets a supporting actor award. He pulled your coat off, covered you in his, and called Matthew to come with his Range Rover. Do you remember being loaded in the back and not wanting to go to hospital?"

"Oh yes. Thank goodness you didn't let them insist. The last time was enough. So, did I manage to tell you it was Harry who pushed me in the river, or did you figure it out?"

"Leta, the only coherent thing you said was 'Don't take me to the hospital.' But we put two and two together. Harry speeding by plus the fact that the police had him on their suspect list was enough. We didn't know why he'd pushed you in the river, but we figured there was no way you slipped in on your own."

"I can tell I'm fading, but please tell me what Harry said while I can still keep my eyes open?"

"He tried to deny he knew anything about you being in the river. Then he said it was an accident, but he didn't have a good reason for *leaving* you there. It's like a police show on the telly. When Brian found two knives in Harry's pocket, he got suspicious. He photographed them both and texted the photos to Matthew, who identified them as Harry's and Nigel's. That sent Matthew to the library to check and sure enough, Nigel's knife was missing, just like you'd told me. Confronted with that, Harry began to open up."

I nodded. "It was the knife that caught my attention. Watching Harry use it today, I realized it looked strangely familiar. That's why I went back," I heard myself say as I dozed off, but I'd overplayed my hand.

When I woke the second time, the sun was streaming through the window, and Julia was setting a tray on the nightstand. I pushed up on my elbows, and she rushed to my side. "Good to see you awake. You didn't stir all night, and we were getting a bit worried." She threw back the covers and pulled me to my feet. "Here, let me help you." I was a little unsteady but moved slowly toward the bathroom as Julia added, "I'll run you a hot bath in a moment, with bubbles."

Surely, a bubble bath is a cure for almost anything, I thought. Julia had placed the tea tray nearby. After indulging in two cups of tea and adding hot water to the tub several times, I *forced* myself to climb out. *I may even have to go home.* Julia must have heard the tub draining because she was there in the bedroom with a tray of food when I emerged from my bath. And clean clothes were lying on the dresser. Some thoughtful person had visited my cottage and brought me leggings and a sweater.

Only after I'd eaten, dried my hair, and dressed did I feel close to my old self. Julia had left me with Dickens and Blanche, who were lying in front of the fireplace. "Dickens, are you ready to go home, ready to see—oh no, did someone feed Christie?"

Dickens barked, "Yes, all taken care of. I won't tell her you forgot about her."

I was pretty proud I was able to walk down the stairs under my own steam. I found Caroline and Julia in the kitchen and got a mug of coffee from Julia and a soapy handwave from Caroline. Julia sat and brought me up to speed. "I doubt I'll ever forgive DCI Burton for taking Maria's word over mine. I think he wanted to believe her because that would allow him to wrap up his case. Wasn't going to accept that Nick never mentioned divorce. If not for Matthew, I'd have been on my way to a cell while you were being pushed in the river."

I wrapped my hands around my mug. "And where are they with Harry? Has he confessed to more than attacking me?"

Julia hesitated. "Yes and no. He admitted using Nigel's knife to slash the tire, but he claims he only meant to ruin Nick's day, not hurt him. He tried at first to say he did it for me by saying I was unhappy. I'm no psychologist, but I think that's what the experts call projecting. Then he tried to blame me by saying I gave him the idea. Honestly! I thought we got on well. He—he not only killed my husband . . . he tried to blame me for what he did." She sniffled and dabbed at her eyes with her napkin.

"What did he mean about you giving him the idea?"

"Walking is one of the ways I stay fit when I travel, and Harry and I spent hours walking the pastures. When we walked Friday after I got back from seeing my dad, I told him about my flat tire and the story my dad told me about people who'd died after someone damaged their tires in the carpark. Turns out that's what gave him the idea. He finally admitted it was an innocent conversation, but not before he tried to drag me under the bus with him."

"How can he say he didn't *mean* to kill Nick if he knew the Northampton tire story? Two people died, didn't they?"

Julia shrugged her shoulder. "It will all be down to a good solicitor, won't it? And Matthew, the Earl of Stow, will have the very best for his son. Ten years or a life sentence will depend on whether it's seen as manslaughter or murder. He says he was drunk and not thinking straight, and he and Nick got into it outside after the party. In typical Nick fashion, he called the herd *pet sheep* again.

"On top of that, he was fiddling around with Nigel's knife —standing there opening and closing it. When Harry recognized his grandad's knife, it was the last straw, and that's when he punched him. Knowing my husband, he decided on a whim to carry the knife for a bit. Probably would have grown tired of it and put it back." Tears sprang to her eyes. "I cannot *believe* my Nick was killed because of sheep and a knife."

I shook my head in amazement. "What a convoluted story. Too much to drink, sheep, a knife, and a stupid spur-of-the-moment act. And to think the police thought it was you."

We sat staring in our coffee cups for a moment and then Julia shrugged. "In their defense, a jealous wife is much more believable than what *actually* happened, isn't it? Thank you for finding the truth, Leta."

I knocked on Ellie's door and looked in. She was sitting at her writing desk and beckoned to me. "How are you?" we said simultaneously.

I smiled and said, "I'm recovering well. The nursing staff in this fine establishment has taken good care of me. I'm more concerned about you and how you're dealing with all this." *She looks woebegone,* I thought. Not a word I'd ever used, but that's how Ellie looked.

She didn't smile or move. "It's enough to break an old woman's heart. I thought it was broken when Nigel died, but maybe it was only bruised. I got beyond that, but this, Leta? I don't know if I have the strength to carry on. It may be more than I can bear."

I hugged her. "Oh, Ellie. I'm so sorry. Would it help for Belle to come over? If I didn't think you'd seen more of me than you can take, I'd stay, but—"

"Young lady, whatever do you mean?"

I wasn't sure how to word it. "I mean I set Harry off. My bringing up the knife led to his throwing me in the river and—"

"Hogwash! My grandson brought this on himself. Perhaps both grandsons did. Nick treated Harry horribly, which was unforgivable. But, for Harry to deliberately slash Nick's tire, to do something he knew could result in serious injury or death— that's inexcusable. Harry shoving you in the river was another indefensible act. There's no getting around any of that. You simply brought it all to light sooner rather than later, and for that I'm grateful. And I know Julia is too."

Dickens and Blanche were sliding around the great hall and skidding into corners when Wendy opened the door. "Hello, we've come to collect you. Couldn't call you because your cell phone is waterlogged, possibly kaput."

"Oh hell, guess I've got to get a new one. Sounds like a shopping trip, but not today."

Peter came in behind his twin. "You're right. Not today. Today, we're taking you home and feeding you lunch. Then you can inspect your clothes from yesterday to see whether you think any of them are salvageable. I'm afraid Basil ripped a hole in your coat."

After I'd lunched on vegetable soup from Belle and shooed Peter and Wendy out the door, I was content to lie on the couch in front of the fire. I wasn't tempted to read, and I didn't miss my phone. Christie hadn't left my side and hadn't chided me for leaving her behind. My assumption was Dickens had pulled her aside and told her the story.

I dozed and contemplated the events of the past week. Nicholas had been struck down in the prime of his life. Two young women were grieving the man they loved. The Dowager Countess was reeling. I could only imagine how Sarah and Matthew must feel about their son's actions, his arrest, and his future. And Sam? How would he deal with the aftereffects of his brother's actions?

I saw an image in my mind—a single raindrop in a pond, the circle widening around it. The family was well-loved and respected in Astonbury, and their tragedy would be felt throughout the village.

And me? Should I feel guilty over what transpired between Harry and me? Had I erred by confronting him? Should I have expected he would try to kill me? I pondered my questions. Though I *did* feel guilty, I didn't think I should. And, if I was honest with myself, I hadn't just erred, I'd been *stupid* in confronting Harry. My mouth had gotten ahead of my brain. If I'd been thinking instead of talking, I might have foreseen the outcome. What was it we used to say in the project world? Proper planning prevents poor performance—or in this case, an *almost* deadly attack.

Enough soul searching, I thought. I gently removed Christie from my lap, stepped over the dog snoozing beside the couch, and went in search of my tablet. I might as well email Bev, Dave, and my sisters, and get it over with. My subject line was "So I went for a swim in the river." *At least*, I thought, *they can't call to fuss at me*. Boy, was I wrong.

When I heard the ringing sound, I couldn't figure out where it was coming from. It was my tablet, and someone was calling me using the Facebook messenger app. My sister Sophia had almost hung up by the time I realized what was going on. With Sophia, I never knew which one of her personas would greet me. Today, I got her upper-crust British accent—quintessential Sophia. "Really, Leta. You'd think socializing with the aristocracy would lead to invitations to castles and yachts, not murder."

I explained I hadn't *caused* the murder, but Sophia was

having none of it. "Admit it, Leta, you are no doubt responsible for that poor boy Harry tossing you in the river." I was too tired to argue.

The next call was from my friend Bev, who was more concerned about how I was doing. After I reassured her I was fine, she chuckled and said, "Guess I need to visit you soon, before one of your adventures leads to your early demise."

Anna didn't call because she refused to use Facebook. From her, I got a blistering email about my stupidity—she didn't use that word, but that was the essence of her message.

I placed my tablet on my lap and waited for Dave's call to come through. By now, he'd probably been to the gym and was home writing. I anticipated his response would be somewhere between Bev's and Anna's, and I wasn't far off.

"So, you went for a swim? In a river? Were you trying to give me a heart attack?"

"No, I was trying to put a humorous spin on a scary episode that ended well—at least for me. Did you like the line about my possibly booking a permanent room at the Manor house? The one with the fireplace? I could get used to that."

He chuckled. "Yes. That's one of the things I love about you—your sense of humor—no matter the circumstances. I just wish you'd take better care of yourself. What is this, the third time in as many months that you've been attacked? Some might call that a pattern."

I had to admit he had a point. I shared my soul-searching thoughts from my hours on the couch, and he helped me work through them. He pretty much agreed with my assessment. We ended the call with both of us wishing he could be here for my tree-trimming party and me promising to send pictures.

Right, I thought, *I've got a party to plan. Saturday will be here before I know it!*

Chapter Twenty-One

Dickens and Christie knew something was up. Christmas music was playing, candles were burning in every room, and two dozen wine glasses and crystal plates were arranged on the dining room table. I'd *trimmed* my four-legged friends in red plaid—a collar for Christie and a bowtie for Dickens. I was attired in black satin leggings and a red velvet top, one that draped to mid-thigh and swirled as I moved. It was one of my favorite holiday outfits.

I'd planned to serve pastitsio with salad and sides but opted instead for heavy hors d'oeuvres. Dickens was hanging around the dining room table as I set out platters of olives and cheese, hummus, prosciutto-wrapped asparagus, sausage balls, and more. I was confident no one would go hungry. In addition to the kourbiades I'd baked earlier in the week, I'd made tiny pecan tarts using my sister Anna's recipe, and I'd ordered a platter of Jill's gingerbread cookies.

"Dickens, that's it. You've put your paws on that chair one too many times." Paws on a chair meant he could lift his nose dangerously close to the food, and I wasn't taking any chances.

I let him out to the garden, where he could greet my guests without getting into any trouble. Once people like Gavin and Peter arrived, he'd get handouts without having to sneak his snout toward a platter. Those two paid no heed to my admonishments not to feed the dog.

Christie meowed, "Silly dog. What does he want with salami and cheese anyway? Now, if it were nice, soft butter or sour cream, I'd be tempted. Any chance you have salmon dip or maybe rotisserie chicken? Those are my favorites."

Chuckling at my finicky cat, I poured her a puddle of milk and placed it out of the way beneath the table. What she hadn't mentioned was the pleasure she took in sitting by bowls of nuts and pawing the contents out onto the table two or three at a time. She didn't eat them, she played with them. I'd have to enlist Wendy and Libby to keep an eye on the nut bowls.

Perry Como and I were singing "We Wish You a Merry Christmas" when Peter and Belle knocked on the door. Dickens took their arrival as his invitation to come inside, no doubt expecting a snack from his pals. Peter put a package under the tree, settled his mother in a comfortable chair, and came back for wine. "Looks lovely, Leta." He leaned over and whispered, "Look who's here. Has he apologized yet?"

I glanced up to see Wendy swirl in the door with DCI Burton in tow. Brian, as I was trying to get used to calling him, had visited me Friday to apologize for yelling at me at the Manor house. Maybe I'd read it wrong, but I'd found his apology less than sincere. I had my doubts as to whether he was the right man for Wendy, given that he'd so readily assumed I'd *led her astray*. I didn't think he realized Wendy had a mind of her own. No matter. There was no harm in a holiday romance.

I was giving a history lesson on my Woolworth's ornaments when Beatrix and Trixie arrived with Toby and Rhiannon. Toby bowed. "Toby's Taxi has arrived. Since I'm the only one who has to be up at the crack of dawn tomorrow, I volunteered to be the designated driver for the High Street contingent." That told me he was taking the early shift at Toby's Tearoom. Rhiannon had the luxury of canceling the early class at her yoga studio, and Beatrix didn't open the Book Nook until eleven on Sundays.

Mannheim Steamroller was playing "God Rest Ye Merry Gentlemen," and my friends were filling their plates and wine glasses. Belle motioned me over to the easy chair where she sat with Christie in her lap. "You've outdone yourself, Leta. Don't be surprised if the black and white cat with the Santa hat is missing when your guests leave. She may go home with me."

Christie looked at Belle before turning to me and meowing, "What does she want with a toy cat? She's got a real one at home."

I smiled as I saw George Evans arrive, followed by Jenny and Jill. For my last party, I hired the sisters to serve, but this time they were guests. George was his usual jovial self. Once he helped himself to a glass of wine, he made straight for the tree. "Good job, Leta. This old schoolhouse cottage is the perfect spot for a Christmas party. You know I point it out on my tours. People are charmed that the school bell hangs by the door to this day. Now, what are these?" He was pointing to my box of White House Christmas ornaments.

"Those are one of my favorite collections. My aunt gave one to my mother every year for close to twenty years, and I inherited the set when Mom passed away."

George knelt by the tree. "Well, expect me to be here

studying them for a bit. You know what a history buff I am. Can I be in charge of hanging these?"

I patted him on the shoulder and told him to have at it. *Time for me to get more wine*, I thought. As I turned toward the kitchen, I was surprised to see Deborah Watson come in carrying one of my Lord & Taylor bears. "Leta, when I came to feed Christie the other day, Timmy fell in love with your bear. Didn't care about the others, only this one. I knew you wouldn't mind if we borrowed him for a few days. Timmy told me this morning that it was time for *Tommy*, as he's named him, to go home. He was positive Tommy missed Christie and Dickens."

We got a good laugh out of that, and the tale prompted Belle to direct John Watson to the package beneath the tree. "We've a gift for little Timmy. Wendy, Leta, and I brought it back from the Magic Shop when we visited Totnes in October. Who knows? Perhaps he'll learn to turn the bear into a bunny." John looked confused until she explained it was a magic kit.

Looking out the kitchen window, I saw the Morgans coming up the drive. Mr. Morgan wasted no time in telling me several Planning Commission members had resigned after being accused of accepting bribes. "Good riddance," were his final words on the subject.

The last to arrive were Gavin, Libby, and Gemma. I hugged them and smiled. "Gemma, I'm so glad you made it. I thought you wouldn't be back."

She explained class had adjourned early, allowing her to get home in time. While father and daughter filled their plates, Libby whispered in my ear. "I tried to convince Ellie to change her mind and come with us but she said she wasn't up to it. I think later next week after the funeral, we should take her for a girls' lunch, maybe in Broadway—me, you, Wendy, and Belle."

Gemma took her mother's place by my side. "You and your crew of little old ladies outdid yourselves, though I wish you'd be more careful. At this rate, we may have to hire you a bodyguard. The best part for me? I hear you put our new DCI in his place. Caroline heard the whole thing and the village grapevine is on fire. Trust me, if he tries any of that rubbish on me, he won't know what hit him."

Dickens looked at me. "What does she mean about a bodyguard? I think Basil and I did a fine job." I gave him a cracker and assured him he was the best bodyguard a girl could have.

The only other no-show was Constable James. He was on duty and couldn't make it. Sipping my wine, I saw that the tree was almost fully decorated. Libby was handing Gavin the last few Woolworth's ornaments, and George was nearly finished hanging the White House collection. Off to one side, I saw DCI Burton and Gemma having what looked to be a serious conversation—until Gemma guffawed. When she grabbed Jenny and pointed toward the kitchen, I knew something was up.

Jenny politely asked me if she could take a few bottles of wine to the sitting room. She grabbed the red, and I followed with the white. As we passed through the room offering refills, Gemma got everyone's attention. "Hear ye, hear ye. Time for a few toasts." DCI Burton looked uncomfortable as Gemma invited her dad to stand by her.

Gavin kissed his daughter on the cheek. "Before we move on to more joyous topics, I liked to take a moment to acknowledge the tragic events of the past week. I know we're all thinking of our friends at Astonbury Manor and sending our condolences. I didn't want to let the evening pass without raising a glass to our much-loved Dowager Countess of Stow, Ellie. We miss her smile and hope to see it again soon."

Gemma cleared her throat. "Most of you have met DCI Burton, but I'd like to officially welcome him to the Gloucestershire Police. We hope we won't have any need for his extensive experience in dealing with gang violence, but we welcome the rest of his expertise. Hear, hear."

I detected a faint blush on DCI Burton's face as he nodded and replied. "And to you, Gemma, thanks for coaching a topnotch team at Stow."

Libby had been standing by the fireplace but stepped forward with a piece of paper in her hand. "And I have a few words from Ellie. She writes, 'I wish to thank the Little Old Ladies' Detective Agency for following their noses and solving the mystery surrounding my grandson Nicholas's death. While I would have preferred a different outcome, I thank you for pursuing the truth.'"

Despite some puzzled looks, everyone raised their glasses. Belle tapped her cane on the flagstone floor, causing Christie to jump from her lap. She fled from the room, meowing, "What was that for?"

Belle stood. "I see you've not all heard of the LOL Detective Agency. As the senior member of the team, let me introduce my partners—Leta and Wendy. And, yes, we use the nickname LOL." When the laughter died down, she looked pointedly at DCI Burton before continuing. "Contrary to popular opinion, we three are equal partners, though—*for some reason*—Leta tends to get either the bulk of the credit or the brunt of the blame for our actions—"

"Not to mention *all* of the bruises," added Wendy.

I was surprised when Gemma piped up. "I think DCI Burton and I would agree we hope to have no further need of your sleuthing services, but we'd be lying if we didn't admit how helpful you've been. Many thanks to the LOLs. Cheers."

It's time to return to the spirit of Christmas, I thought. All that remained was the tree topper. Earlier, I'd asked Gavin to lead us in a round of "Deck the Halls" as we finished the tree trimming. I'd even printed cards with the lyrics. At my signal, he launched into song.

Deck the halls with boughs of holly, Fa la la la la la la la!
'Tis the season to be jolly, Fa la la la la la la la!

As the final verse faded away, I handed Peter the starched angel and he placed it atop the tree. *What a happy ending to a harrowing week*, I thought. *How fortunate I am to have these new friends in my life.*

Once again, Toby, who had delivered the perfect toast at my costume party in the fall, found just the right words for this gathering. Quoting Tiny Tim from Charles Dickens's *A Christmas Carol*, he rose and held his glass high. "Here's to us all! God bless us every one!"

Book IV

An unexpected inheritance. Missing bequests. Can these amateur detectives pen a satisfactory solution to a literary murder?

Read *Collectors, Cats & Murder* to find out.

Have you read the earlier books featuring Leta and her friends? *Find them on Amazon!*

Receive a download of Leta's Family Recipes when you sign up for the Dickens & Christie newsletter. And be the first to know when new books are available.

Visit kathymanospenn.com for Dickens & Christie news and pics, and if you're reading a paperback version, that's where you can sign up for the newsletter.

Don't miss out on Leta's Family Recipes.

Psst... Please take a minute...

Dear Reader,

Writers put their hearts and souls into every book. Nothing makes it more worthwhile than reader reviews. Yes, authors appreciate reviews that provide helpful insights.

If you enjoyed this book, Kathy would love it if you could find the time to leave a good, honest review . . . because after everything is said and done, authors write to bring enjoyment to their readers.

Thank you,

Dickens

*Be sure to look for the recipe at the end.

**Click here to purchase and download other books in the series. Or visit <u>Amazon</u> for the paperback.

Recipe

Kourabiedes

Yield: approximately 3 dozen cookies

Ingredients

- 1 cup sweet butter
- 2 cups flour
- 1 cup blanched almonds cut in small pieces & toasted
- 1 cup powdered sugar
- 2 egg yolks
- 2 boxes powdered sugar

Preparation:

1. Preheat oven to 350°.
2. Beat butter until creamy. Add one cup powdered

sugar and beat again. Add egg yolks, one at a time, and beat after each.

3. When mixture is light in color, add flour and toasted almonds and knead well.

4. Take small pieces of dough and make balls in palm of hand. Shape into rounds and crescents.

5. Place on cookie sheet one inch apart and bake 20 min or until light brown.

6. Allow to cool slightly before removing from cookie sheet.

7. Carefully place on a flat surface that has been sprinkled with confectioners sugar (I lay wax paper on the counter).

8. Sprinkle *lots and lots* of sifted confectioners sugar over cookies.

Tip: If these cookies are purchased from a Greek bakery, they will be heavily coated in powdered sugar. I've never yet been able to coat mine as heavily and have never use two boxes of sugar.

Would you like to know when the next book is on the way? Click here to sign up for my Newsletter or visit KathyManosPenn.com to sign up there.

Acknowledgments

As I continue my writing journey, I picture a stretch limo filled with the folks who've come along for the ride. The itinerary is only loosely defined and changes along the way. We take turns driving. When a friend suggests picking up a new character, I say *why not?* When my Beta readers ask to take a detour, I don't hesitate.

On the last stretch of each trip, I gratefully turn the wheel over to my editor, Laura Ownbey. It's Laura who ensures we make it to our destination without mishap. She alerts me when I've left someone behind. She points out Dickens needs a break. She politely tells me my scribbled directions are off and gets our limo back on course. Thank you, Laura, for helping me deliver the books my readers expect and deserve.

Once again, I offer a hearty thank you to my readers. Perhaps some authors write purely for the pleasure of producing a well-crafted article or blog or book. Me? I take pleasure in the craft, but that alone wouldn't motivate me to write a third, a fourth, and who knows how many more books.

It's you, my readers, dare I say fans, who inspire me to keep on keeping on. When you write that Belle reminds you of your grandmother, that the trio of ladies makes you think of your girlfriends, or that Dickens and Christie are just like your four-legged companions—you make my heart sing.

Thank you for taking this journey with me.

Would you like to know when the next book is on the way?
Click here to sign up for my newsletter. https://bit.ly/3bEjsfi

About the Author

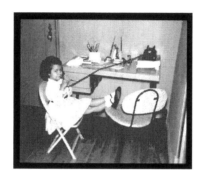

Kathy at her desk when she was four years old.

As a corporate escapee, Kathy Manos Penn went from crafting change communications to plotting page-turners. Adhering to the adage to "write what you know," she populates her mysteries with well-read, witty senior women, a sassy cat, and a loyal dog. The murders and talking pets, however, exist only in her imagination.

Years ago, when she stumbled onto a side job as a columnist for a local paper, she saw the opportunity as an entertaining diversion from the corporate grind. Little did she know that her serendipitous foray into writing "whatever struck her fancy" would lead to a cozy mystery series.

How does she describe her life? "I'm living a dream I never knew I had. Picture me sitting serenely at my desk, surrounded by the four-legged office assistants who inspire the personalities of Dickens & Christie. Why is Dickens a fiend for belly rubs? Because my real-life dog is.

The same goes for Christie's finicky eating habits and penchant for lolling on top of the desk or in the file drawer. She gets it from my calico cat who right this minute is lying on the desk swishing her tail and deciding which pen or pencil to knock to the floor next."

—Kathy

Visit www.KathyManosPenn.com to contact Kathy, read her blogs, and more.

Would you like to know when the next book is on the way? Be sure to sign up up for her newsletter here or on he website. https://bit.ly/3bEjsfi